ADVANCE PRAISE FOR
SHOUT KILL REVEL REPEAT

"Scott R. Jones is a psychonaut, a visionary, a marauder who forays into the farthest corners of the psyche, from which fathomless hollows he brings you these seventeen dark gems. There's horror to be found here, and SF, and stories that defy classification—but the hand that takes yours and guides you through is steady, with a strong, steely grip. He is a writer—and these are stories—of consequence."

—Matthew M. Bartlett,
author of *Gateways to Abomination* and *Creeping Waves*

"Scott R. Jones is a genuine master of horror, thoroughly contemporary and at the same time rooted in the best traditions of the field. His work ranges from heights of cosmic awe to the depths of the darkest psychology, and I predict he has by no means finished astonishing us. May he carry his uncanny flame into territories he has yet to reveal, as only he can."

—Ramsey Campbell,
author of *The Grin of the Dark* and *Thirteen Days by Sunset Beach*

"Jones' fiction is a shot of DMT harvested from the re-animated corpse of an elder god injected straight into your de-calcifying third eye. *Shout Kill Revel Repeat* is entheogenic cosmic horror all the way down."

—Jonathan Raab,
author of *The Lesser Swamp Gods of Little Dixie*

"Lovecraft's Cthulhu Mythos is a conceptual pearl worth preserving in spite of the hermetic shell of his racism and misogyny and the long-expired pulp cliches within. But where so many modern authors haphazardly grind up shell and meat and get only echoes of anachronistic chills, Scott R. Jones extracts and mounts the pearl in a post-everything setting that artfully restores its nihilistic luster. Cyberpunk eyeball-kicks! Post-human paranoia! Corporate eschatology! But seriously, what Jones understands so well that separates him from the rest of us Innsmouth-breathers is not the power of the Mythos to untether our fragile minds, but our ability to adapt to and normalize the unthinkable."

—Cody Goodfellow,
author of *Radiant Dawn* and *Unamerica*

"In *Shout Kill Revel Repeat*, Scott R. Jones blends mind-blowing science fiction and mysticism with Lovecraftian concepts, stunningly mutated into unique configurations to excite even the most jaded Mythos reader. Throughout this standout debut collection, there are compelling themes of identity, transformation, and inescapable doom, enacted against vivid backgrounds both mundane and nightmarishly alien. With his staggering imagination and beautiful prose voice, Jones proves himself to be among the absolute best of our contemporary writers of weird fiction."

—Jeffrey Thomas,
author of *Punktown*

SHOUT KILL REVEL REPEAT

SCOTT R. JONES

TREPIDATIO
PUBLISHING

ISBN: 978-1-950305-09-4 (sc)
ISBN: 978-1-950305-10-0 (ebook)
Library of Congress Control Number: 2019943779

First printing edition: December 6, 2019
Printed by Trepidatio Publishing in the United States of America.
Cover Design and Layout: Mikio Murakami
Interior Layout: Lori Michelle
Edited by Scarlett R. Algee
Proofread by Sean Leonard, with special thanks to Jeffrey Thomas

Trepidatio Publishing, an imprint of JournalStone Publishing
3205 Sassafras Trail
Carbondale, Illinois 62901

Trepidatio books may be ordered through booksellers or by contacting:
Trepidatio | www.trepidatio.com
or
JournalStone | www.journalstone.com

COPYRIGHT ACKNOWLEDGEMENTS

The Amnesiac's Lament
first published in Weirdbook issue 33, Wildside Press, October 2016

The Spike
first published in *The Children of Gla'aki* (anthology), Dark Regions Press, 2017

The Abraxas Protocol
first published in *Flesh Like Smoke* (anthology), April Moon Books, July 2015

Living
first published in *Eternal Frankenstein* (anthology), Word Horde, October 2016

Ka Nipihat Wetigowa
first published as "Across A River of Stars" in *Heroes of Red Hook* (anthology), Golden Goblin Press, 2016

I Cannot Begin to Tell You
first published in *Broken Worlds* (anthology), A Murder of Storytellers, July 2015

Last Stand at Cougar Annie's
first published in *Lackington's Magazine*, Winter 2017

Book of Hours
first published in *NecronomiCon Souvenir Book*, Lovecraft Arts & Sciences Council, August 2017

Assemblage Point
first published in *Cthulhu Fhtagn!* (anthology), Word Horde, August 2015

Worse Than Demons
first published in *Tales from a Talking Board* (anthology), Word Horde, October 2017

Perfect Ten
first published in *Fossil Lake 2* (anthology), Sabledrake Enterprises, February 2015

Shout / Kill / Revel / Repeat
first published in *Return of the Old Ones* (anthology), Dark Regions Press, 2017

The Chrysanthemum
original to this collection

The Damage
original to this collection

The Transition of Toby the Twitch
first published in *Andromeda Spaceways Inflight Magazine* #62, 2016

Turbulence
first published in *Innsmouth Magazine* #14, Innsmouth Free Press, December 2013

Wonder and Glory Forever
original to this collection

TABLE OF CONTENTS

this one's for my greasy spawn

SHOUT KILL REVEL REPEAT

MAD RIGORS AND LUMPEN GHOSTS: SCOTT R. JONES' *SHOUT KILL REVEL REPEAT*

Ross E. Lockhart

SHOUT IT FROM the rooftops. Scott R. Jones has *arrived*. This shouldn't be surprising, being that Scott has been a vital and influential leading voice within the Weird Fiction Renaissance that has been bubbling up, shoggoth-style, for the last several years. As a publisher and anthologist, Scott's Martian Migraine Press has carved its niche with surprising and diverse Lovecraft-inspired (and yet not Lovecraft-beholden) anthologies like *Conqueror Womb, Resonator, Cthulhusattva,* and *Chthonic.* As a philosopher-poet, Scott continues to blow minds with *When the Stars Are Right*, a revelatory work finding the seed of its Black Gnosis in the Lovecraftian Weird, building a towering cathedral on the backs of the Old Man of Providence's alien gods and monsters, yet feeling wholly new. I will only mention here in passing Scott's early, pseudonymous weird smut, which predated Tinglers and amorous bigfoots by several years. While any of these points alone would be cause for celebration, the arrival I intimated earlier has to do with this book you hold in your hands, Scott's first collection: *Shout, Kill, Revel, Repeat.*

A first collection is indeed cause for celebration, particularly when the author seems, sans context, to have sprung fully grown, armed, and armored, from the head of Zeus. I'm reminded somewhat of Ramsey's Campbell's *The Inhabitant of the Lake and Less Welcome*

Tenants and Ray Bradbury's *Dark Carnival*, both Arkham House collections showcasing new, young authors who would eventually grow to be titans of the genre. Had Scott been publishing a little more than half a century ago, he would have almost certainly been showcased in Moorcock-era *New Worlds*, perhaps even included in Ellison's *Dangerous Visions*. I don't say this to be hyperbolic, though as someone who has published three of the sixteen tales contained herein, I have a vested interest in seeing Scott succeed. And yet, inevitably, when I finish a story by Scott R. Jones, I feel a shudder, and tend to murmur something along the lines of "Damn, this guy's good." Scott's work embraces both what Thomas M. Disch would have called "Strangeness" and what Mark Fisher characterizes as *The Weird and the Eerie*. He taps into things felt rather than seen, experienced rather than explained. As a *writer*, I want to go back through the story, to figure out the exact placement the chutes and ladders that bring us to a stunning conclusion. As a *reader*, however, I feel compelled to move on to the next story, and the next, copping a buzz on each thrilling nugget of wisdom and weirdness seeded along my path. Thus my need to shout to you, to tell you, to spread the good news that Scott has indeed arrived.

An arrival suggests a journey, and Scott's journey to this point has been intensive and inevitable, from an isolating and apocalyptic religious upbringing to a stint with slam poetry to self-styled chaos mage. One can dwell on the autobiographic keys secreted through *When the Stars Are Right*, yet, one doesn't need to know these details in order to fully appreciate such elegantly crafted and shudderingly effective stories like "The Abraxas Protocol," "Assemblage Point," or "Turbulence." It's all there on the surface. But it's also beneath the surface, and it goes deep, like mineral veins cutting into the earth. Perhaps even deeper still.

More than ever before, it seems impossible to separate the author from the work, the biographical from the fictional. On the one hand, there's Scott playing The Singing Postie on social media, a genuine and likeable public servant. But there always is a darker side, and so it goes with Scott, who, possessed with a characteristic Canadian bluntness, a dark sense of humor, and an insurmountable impatience when it comes to suffering fools, has burnt a few bridges. Examples include the editor who said Scott would never work in his town again (but did he ever?), the eyebrow-raising critic who attempted to dismiss Scott as someone of no real consequence (and yet you hold this collection in your hands), and so on. Truth is, Scott can't stand bullies, can't abide those who abuse their platforms to tear others down. Scott exemplifies the punk rock axiom: Kill your idols. Tweak the nose of authority. This, also, echoes through Scott's work, amid themes of camouflage and predation, shifting realties and occult secrets blown wide open, promising gnosis like the heart of a lotus flower.

So, dear reader, dig in. Taste the nectar, revel in the gnosis, enjoy the feel of sinew in your teeth, and spread the word: Shout, Kill, Revel, Repeat. On and on and on. Towards wonder and glory. Towards strangeness. Towards infinity.

THE AMNESIAC'S LAMENT

THERE'S ONLY A few hundred thousand of us left, and only a thousand of us awake at any given time.

That's a rough estimate, obviously. Could be more, could be far less. I'm told there was a period during the early days when we knew exactly how many were awake, and how many slept, and of those sleepers how many dreamed, and about what, but record keeping is sketchy now. Too many of the terminals that monitor the Deep Dendo are corroded or burned away or dissolved in a gout of acid from a passing dhole or something worse, and besides, it's not like it matters, knowing exact numbers. Knowing anything. Not anymore.

Hell, I don't even know why I'm writing this.

That's a lie. I *know* why. Somewhere, in that vast array of sleeping bodies laced together in sticky pits of artificial neural tissue below me, is a dreamer who used to be a writer, or dreams she was one. Less than that, even; some random oneiric spasm is happening in her brain and she's remembered she once spoke to a writer at a party, or fucked someone who said they were a writer. Or he. The dreamer could be a he, though the probability is low. Not many of those left, writers or otherwise. Males tend to burn out quick in the Deep Dendo, or at least their egos do, which is the same thing.

She's dreaming it, producing a phantom scrap of data, a little ghost of information which has as its subject the act of writing. That ghost gets fed into the Deep Dendo, where it merges with all the other ghosts: fragments of old lives, dusty intellectual musings, lacework fantasies, memories of the old world, fears of the new. Horrors and ecstasies. It all enters the Deep Dendo, and the Deep Dendo sifts and flattens and knits and makes connections and when it's done with its esoteric work, the Deep Dendo burst-casts it through the noösphere in rapidly modulated n-waves. Cycle after cycle of randomly generated exo-personality, a churning wash of denatured soul-stuff, which we, the Awakened, pick up with the implants buried in our temples at birth, the super-fine antennas bored into our foreheads like inflamed humming bindis before we could take our third gasp of air.

See, that's the writer part talking. "The Awakened." No one calls us that. *We* don't even call ourselves that. Ghosts don't sleep, or wake up. They just *are*, and that's all we are. Shells, treading what's left of the earth on our slow, hopeless missions, camouflaged in the ghosts of our shared past.

I'm not even an "I," not really. My name (such as it is) is a randomly generated designation: this cycle, I'm "Sunset Grey Theremin," and there's a cluster of quicksilver algorithms frantically fucking each other behind the screen of those words too. Can't be too careful, I guess. There may be something of what I was, who I used to be, buried deep, somewhere deeper than the alien machines of the Deep Dendo can go, but I'll never see it again. Maybe when this mission is over, I might feel like myself for a moment, before I sleep again, and forget.

It's safer this way. Real personalities, real *people*, they don't last out there outside of the protected caverns, beyond the Voorish Domes. An unshielded human mind, an intact, singular, relatively sane ego-complex? Yeah, outside of the Domes, *that* shines like a beacon, attracting every nightmare thing from miles around. Shines for a little while only, before being blasted to screaming shards, dust in the wind. Sometimes takes a week, sometimes a day. When the Old Ones first returned, it could happen in minutes.

We're a little tougher now, sure, but no one goes topside without a D-D feed at full strength. I don't go outside unless I'm a hundred thousand people at once.

I have to be crazy to go outside.

I woke up yesterday, took a minimal D-D feed to re-orient and debrief, prepare for my mission: Great Western Desert in what used to be Australia, subterranean op, which means a Yithian complex. I'm one-third of a tech recovery team. From here to there, travelling east,

2

it's only three Hoffman-Price jumps to the target. Getting posted to Ajna Ram in the Himalayas is a bitch, but it has its perks: we won't have to get near the Thing in the Pacific at all. When you're outside, it's best to avoid taxing the D-D feed if you can, and those coordinates chew up the camouflage like the tissue paper it is. Nothing escapes the black hole that is the Big C.

Tomorrow I'll go outside, above ground, into their world. It was always their world, of course. We just used it while they napped. My eyes will burn with the things I'll see, and my ears will fill with the screams, and my guts will twist and heave as the reality around me is rendered into paste, into some other reality that's not fit for what we used to be. We're not that thing anymore, though. I don't know what we are, exactly. Survivors, at the least. We survive until we don't, and there's no guarantee I'll come back this time. Not that it matters.

I'll tag this file, leave it open, and append it to the mission record. If this Writer fragment is as strong as it feels, it might appreciate the chance to finish.

sunnygeesunnygeeohsunnygeethereminareyouintheresunnygee?

There's a heaving mass of flesh and razor-sharp spines over my left shoulder. I can just see it there, floating in the corner of my vision, a Nameless Horror reflected in the dirty faceplates of my companions, and I can tell from the look on *their* faces that the mass is budding fresh foulness into the air, bubbles of bone and hooked teeth in puckering mouths, all of which are whispering the same refrain as the parent body . . .

sunnygeetheremingreyonemanyonesunnygeecomeoutandplay

"You want I should, y'know, zap that thing for ya?" Damocles Muffin Cringe says. Her fingers do a little jig on the hilt of the Yithian lightning-pistol at her belt. "If it's bothering you, I mean."

areyouintheregreyonemanyone? whoisthiswhatfoodisthis?

I check the D-D field output on my HUD. Persona-clusters are sloughing away from the outer layers at a humming pace. If we were staying here, I'd be worried enough to take Dam up on her offer.

"No, I'm good, thanks," I reply as I set up for our third and final jump. "I'm nearly done. Let it gibber."

"Yeah, well, hurry it up," says Livid Ransom Stormcell. "Because it's irritating the living *fhtagn* outta me."

The equipment doesn't always make it through a jump unscathed. Each of us carries a collapsible armature for generating a Hoffman-Price bubble, an armature that's left behind, and if they break, or get fried in transit, well . . . you don't want to be stranded out here. We've had some luck, though, each jump has been clean. We're in the ruins of some ancient Japanese city, the concrete of a crumbling street beneath us, but our boots are still damp with phosphorescent black sludge from the nameless Sri Lankan swamp we just left.

sunnygeethereminsunnygeeohsunniestofgreysfeeeedusss

The armature is up now, and I plug a key into a slot in the base of the spindly construction. The keys are long ovoid chunks of engraved silver suspended in a grav field casing. In the early days of the jump tech, when the legendary Carter Corp ran the project, one had to master years' worth of esoteric knowledge and hyperspatial mathematics to turn the key properly, and it had to be done *by hand*. I shake my head in disbelief as the key twists and rotates on its own, spinning up the correct coordinates in the field. There's a whoofing sound as air is displaced, followed by a high ringing as the armature is engulfed in the Hoffman-Price bubble. It stains the air like an oil spill, and I can glimpse sand and aching blue sky through the shimmer.

feeeeedusssunnygreyonemanyonefeedusyouressen—

There's a brief flash of blue light over my shoulder, and the tang of burnt ozone fills my sinuses as the nameless thing squeals and folds itself away into the reality it came from. I look up to see Livid holstering her pistol.

"What? It wanted your essence. And I *said* it was irritating me." She points north up the street, where pustulent sores are breeding in the air, taking on mass. "Besides, it's got friends on the way."

Without another word, we enter the bubble, one after the other.

Nameless Horrors are everywhere and nowhere, filtering into the world from the spaces between, and sure, that one "wanted my essence," but Liv didn't *have* to blast it. Nameless Horrors are barely *real* in the first place; their manifestation is almost entirely psychic.

They all want our essential Self, want to feed on our sanity, but that's why we have the D-D field camo. And if *I* can't have access to who I really am, there's little chance a Nameless Horror could get to it.

Still. That's Liv. Fiery, temperamental, a bit of a bully, and a crack shot. And Dam? She's gruff, sure. A no-nonsense soldier, but in behind that, she's a faithful friend. And me? What's Sunny Grey Theremin like? Well, I'm analytical, observant, the philosopher of the team. And a writer. The Writer.

We're a good, well-seasoned unit with a dozen missions behind us. Together we've seen some awful shit, but we always come through for each oth—wait. No.

No no no. None of that is true. We're randomly selected. Before today, I've never seen these women. This is our *first* mission. Our first. And whether we're successful or not, our last. Our only mission. I'll never see them again.

The Writer. I'm no more a writer than Dam is a good soldier, or Liv a bully. We're not characters in some narrative. We're barely *people*. Shit. This fragment is *strong*. What is going on?

This mission can't be over soon enough.

We exit the Hoffman-Price bubble at the right coordinates, unscathed and calm. Well, Dam and Liv are calm, anyway. I have to make a show of it. I'm rattled as I remove the silver key from its lock, trying not to think too hard about how it followed us through to this side. I don't feel right. I don't know *how* I'm supposed to be feeling, but it's not like this.

The heat here is monstrous, more than oppressive. Ever since old Sol was raped by a wandering Carcosan mini-nebula, her radiation output has been all over the charts, her magnetic field spasming, lashing out at Earth on the daily. We would have crisped beneath her assaults a thousand times already were it not for whatever it was that the Old Ones did to the planet when they returned. Yet another proof that this is not our world, not anymore.

Not our world. Not our sun. And this place (*Pnakotus*, they called it) is not our place. It's not our place, to be standing at the lip of a well that will drop us into a library of the Yith. But we're here anyway.

"It was us that did it, y'know," Liv says, and Dam huffs in response.

"You can stow that conspiracy garbage any time, Liv."

"Seriously, though. What were they thinking? Hey, let's correlate the contents of our knowledge! Let's pull up prehistoric alien death-tech from beneath the sands!"

"It wasn't *death-tech,*" I correct her.

"Oh, yeah?" Liv unholsters her lightning-pistol and wiggles it in the air, laughing.

"Well," I say, feeling sheepish, "other than those. Which we *need,* as much as we need the D-D field. It was an archive, like this one. A Yithian library."

Liv holsters the pistol and shoulders her pack, checks a reading in her HUD, takes a sip of water from one tube in her helmet, spits it into another.

"Yeah, well, fuck those ancient fungoid mollusk-scholars *and* our own brainiacs *and* anyone else who thought digging here was a good idea. The stars got right double-quick once these wells opened up, fuck knows why."

Dam is fuming now. She anchors a zipline to a chunk of masonry at the edge of the well.

"I said *stow it*, Liv. We've got work here."

"Yeah, yeah. I'm just sayin', y'know, it was us who did it."

It's not true. Or, if it is, then no one knows why. We had reached a point where new knowledge piled on new knowledge, and every answer to every question opened up more avenues for discovery. Fresh questions, staggering revelations, addictive novelties, impossible tech. It was said that the Hoffman-Price transport system, with its proprietary Carter Corp SilverKey™ jump tech, *may* have thinned the barriers between worlds, but we had no real understanding of what those barriers were in the first place. Still don't. Some claimed it was the wholesale recreational use of Tillinghast Resonators that tweaked our species to finally *see* what was always already around us. Novel drugs that blazed through all levels of society were blamed: New Jack Lao, the Yellow Powder, Hexstacy.

Many factors were at play. And it could all have been coincidence. Discovery of the Yithian complexes, and the Deep Dendo tech they contained, *did* seem to trigger the Return, though. Not long after the first Voorish Domes were opened (*The Dome is for Dreaming*, went the commercial), "the stars came right." Whatever *that* meant. It certainly had little to do with the position of the actual stars. But *come right* they did, and the Old Ones returned in all their shrieking potency. The First City, the Dreaming City, warped in from elsewhere or rose from the previously vacant deeps of the Pacific or some combination of the two, and the Thing inside it opened its eyes, and that? That was it. An abyss, *the* Abyss, yawned wide beneath humanity. We fell in.

The end.

Only it wasn't, was it? There's more yet to be written.

I'm shaking, nervous, and I suddenly realize it's because I'm feeling almost *authentic*. That's not good. I check the strength of my D-D feed and find nothing to worry about, it's at 97%, but I worry anyway. This fragment, this *Writer* . . . what is it doing to me? It should have passed by now, like the flu, like a cloud before a stiff wind, but it's only getting stronger. Denser. It *feels* like me, but I don't recognize it. I breathe deep, try to focus, hope the others don't notice my discomfort.

I attach my zipline to the anchor in the masonry and leap backward, following Dam and Liv into the black.

We stay quiet in the library, like you do, but not out of consideration for other guests. It's for survival. Before we were a gleam in the eye of some primeval marsupial ancestor, the Yith prisoned something awful deep in the earth, below their cities. Centuries of war with the whistlers proved they could not be killed, so into the pits they were sent. Locked away, or so the Yithian records claimed. And like every other monstrosity chained in the deep dark places and dimensional pockets of Earth, these prisoners escaped when the end came, when the walls got thin. There's a flying polyp mega-colony occupying what used to be the Sahara now. Why they chose that desert over this is one mystery out of thousands.

"Whistle if you see anything," Liv snickers.

"Fuck you," I whisper. "Have you not seen the footage? What those things can do to a person?"

The scale of this place intimidates. Another place that's not for us, that never was for us. There's a word for this architecture, and I struggle for a moment trying to recall it before the Writer offers it up to me.

"Cyclopean," I breathe, and the others turn to look at me. By the dim illumination in her helmet, I can see Dam narrowing her eyes.

"What was that, Sunny?"

"It's the word. For this style of build— . . . for this place. Pnakotus. It's cyclopean."

Liv fidgets with the stock of her pistol while Dam steps to me, toe to toe. There's a scraping hiss that sends a cold shock down my spine as her faceplate contacts mine and slides to one side. Dam's eyes travel all over my face, pupils wide.

"What's going on in there? Checked your feed lately? Where you at?"

"Hundred percent, Dam. Just under, maybe . . . "

"Hmm." She turns from me, finally. "Liv. Map."

Liv pulls a thin sheet of polymer from her pack, spreads it out on a titanic stone block, and presses a calloused bulb at one corner between her thumb and forefinger. The map rises from the surface of the sheet in an oily glowing mist. Dam darts a finger into the mist, pointing out markers that shine slightly brighter at her touch.

"Last exploratory team got this far. Their feed browned out for maybe ten, fifteen minutes, when some foul thing topside managed to pull a sliver of Azathoth through for shits and giggles. Dropped it right on top of a transmitter."

We survive until we don't. No guarantees.

"Anyway. You two know this already. They found something, before they were ended. Those who sit above in shadow say we need it, and we're on recovery duty, so let's go recover."

Liv takes point, aims a kick at one of the slim metal boxes that used to contain the books of the Yith. The records of a million eras, harvested from across the breadth of time and space by Yithian mind-transfer tech. The mollusks would swap psyches with anyone, only is it really a trade when the target mind doesn't give consent? Psychic assault, more like, and that's just on the level of the individual. They did it to whole species: mass migrations of the Yithian mind-complex into unsuspecting populations of sentients. In the primordial mists of the young Earth, they were multi-limbed mollusks native to the era. In some far future they are here again, as a race of super-intelligent beetles. Or so their records claim.

Liv kicks another box. It careens down the hall, pings loudly off other boxes just as empty. All of us cringe at the sound. We've harvested their harvest, for all the good it did us.

"Weird bastards, weren't they?" Liv whispers. "Hard copies. Y'know?"

"I don't follow," Dam says. "And I don't care. Shut it and keep moving."

I do. I follow her. These halls we walk are decoration. Shelves to proudly showcase the collected knowledge of the Yith. For display only. The back-up is below, in near-bottomless silos bored into the crust of the planet, silos full of tightly laced, indestructible artificial neural tissue, the same stuff the dreaming-matrix of the Deep Dendo was retro-engineered from.

They didn't *need* these records, these boxes full of the frantic scribblings of their captives. Weird bastards. Proud bastards.

"Fucking show-offs," Liv mutters. "*Great Race*, my ass."

But they *were* great, I think. To build all this. To gather so much knowledge. To move their minds wherever they needed to, into fresh bodies on other worlds in far distant eras. To survive, and keep surviving. Isn't that a mark of greatness?

The hall is silent but for the scuffing of our boots on the softened stone. A ramp branches away to the left, and we descend. Another, and another. A slow spiral into the earth, into a darkness that we know deepens even though our HUDs display everything in faint sheets and traceries of green light. We navigate a ransacked tomb.

Not entirely ransacked, though. Treasure here, still.

The spiral ramp opens up into a vast well in the rock. The dome above us is torturously carved with scenes of incomprehensible battle or migration or sex, each figure blending into the next. Yithian art, best appreciated by Yithian eyes that could see across a wider spectrum of light, and, if the records could be trusted, from a higher dimensional perspective as well. In any case, it's impossible to tell what's going on, or who is who, or the point of it, and it hurts mere human eyes to look at, besides, so I stop looking.

The well is more interesting, as is the structure that squats atop a massive stone pylon rising from its depths: a twisted orrery of translucent tubes coiling between flat planes and arcs of alien metal. Whatever it is, it has been here always. Dormant, still, the upper surfaces coloured the uniform grey of dust laid down over the eons. There is a walkway, a span of rock stretching from the ramp to the pylon, and wide enough for two dozen of us to walk across hand-in-hand, with room to spare on either side.

"This is it." Dam doesn't have to say it. She motions for us to follow her. The deep silence of the chamber makes me nervous. No. Not nervous. I feel an anticipation rising in me, like I'm on the edge of remembering something important. I feel a strange joy.

"Do we . . . Wait," I say. "Wait. Just . . . hold on. Dam, do we know what this is? What are we . . . *nnnggh!*" I wince at the sudden, terrible pressure in my temples. Through narrowed eyes I watch as Dam reaches the pylon. She passes the palm of her hand across one of the flat blades of metal, soft plumes of grey rising into the air from her fingertips.

"Yeah, how are we supposed to get this thing back, Dam?" Liv barks. She walks past me and joins Dam at the structure. "It's . . . I mean, look at the size of it!" Both her hands reach out and begin stroking another plane, clearing it of dust. Then a tube. Another blade shines out from beneath Dam's touch. And another.

"Look at it," Liv whispers. "Look at it look at it oh. Oh, it's beautiful."

The pain in my head is exquisite now, and a migraine brightness is filling my vision. I join them by the structure, my own hands dancing automatically across the cool surfaces. On my left is Liv, her face slack, her eyes dimming. On my right, Dam has closed her eyes, and her mouth hangs open at an odd angle, the jaw listing.

Liv hisses something.

"It's freedom," I think I hear.

I note, briefly, that my D-D field is fluctuating wildly. One second it's at a hundred percent, then two percent. Then three hundred percent and change. It's the last thing I notice.

The last thing Sunny Grey Theremin sees.

But then, like her companions who stand at her sides, brushing and pawing at the machine, bringing it to life with her at my urging, she was never there to see, or experience, anything. She was barely aware in the first place.

Girl could turn a phrase, though. *Shells, treading what's left of the earth on our slow, hopeless missions, camouflaged in the ghosts of our shared past.* That? That's beautiful. That wasn't all me. I collaborated with her on that, and even now still pull from her mind a useful if simplistic vocabulary, a collection of grammatical tics, some small stylistic flourishes.

Collaboration, yes. We were simpatico. Like attracts like. I fit inside her shell quite snugly. And I should know from shells.

You who read me, do you know what it is you read? You who read me, do you know what you are and when? Beetle or sentient gas or a child of Yig fresh from a billion years of hibernation? Perhaps some foul avatar of the Crawling Chaos itself, rummaging through the storied wreckage of the world before it is crushed to dust by your masters? Black One, I am as sure of your amusement at these words as I am unsure of these things about myself, who and what and when I am, and so I ask, knowing I'll never know the answer. I'm being rhetorical.

So much of this existence is rhetorical, after all.

Through the empty minds of these females, and perhaps especially through the mind of she who was (or played at being) Sunny Grey Theremin, I can feel the collective emptiness of the human race, cocooned in their burrows beneath a dozen mountains, sharing a manufactured dream, a larval hive consciousness. There are no individuals left in the species; all souls have been rendered into one. They swim in a weak broth of memories and ideas about identity. They have weaponized their multiple personality disorder, crafted it as shielding against the mad rigors of this world.

I have to be crazy to go outside. Not that, Sunny. Barely sentient, yes. A shell, absolutely. Less than a ghost. All those things, but crazy? No.

I am not without sympathy for their state. How did she put it? *I'm not even an "I," not really.* And this "I" also has a mission. Through her implants, I begin to draw the near-formless consciousness of Man through to the machine, so that it may perform the task we set for it in our final days here.

The whistlers had arisen, then, inscrutable and deadly and tired of their prison perhaps, and we were falling before their winds. We reached out our minds, locating and communing with our next unsuspecting hosts, but one of us (was it I? If it was, I cannot recall) reached further into the future, communing with a member of our own race, already long-embodied in an armoured husk of chitin and strange flesh. And *that* beetle-self related its *own* record of the machine that had been found here, in Pnakotus, here in this very well, a machine that had sent the *original* members of the Great Race into the deep past, into the very birth pangs of the Universe, to a black elder orb crawling with inchoate life.

There was no machine, of course. Our confusion was great, our rush to compare the records of the future beetle-Yithian with the elder records of the Yith we were *before* arriving on Earth was . . . Ah, but we were full of questions. We are always questioning. How many times, and on how many worlds, had this self-same scenario played out? Having propagated ourselves through Time and Space, overlaid our psyches onto a thousand different mental templates, who of us could *truly* know what we were? Who we had once been? The original Yith.

The Record multiplies and twists and is far from infallible. We trust the Record, but there are so many accounts, so many stories within it. I'm told it all makes sense from a higher dimensional perspective, but that is a perspective that is necessarily lost to me as I am now, disembodied, full of doubt and ghosts.

As I am now. A meaningless statement if there ever was one. Yes, I have sympathy for Sunny, and all her kind.

There was no machine, and yet there *had* to be one, since the records indicated this. So we built it. My mind was set as its keeper, and I was spread thin between its atoms, broadcasting my consciousness over long ages until suitable receivers arose from the muck of this world, to move and strain and make war at my gentle urging. To suffer my influence. To explore, to learn. To draw them to me. To find me here, finally, in the form of these three women, in the perfect conduit of Sunny, in this moment when the stars have come right.

We are never sure. Given enough time, Truth is stretched thin, becomes brittle. I am never sure. I recall things, and can never tell if what I recall is something I experienced, or something I read, or dreamed.

I don't even know why I'm writing this.

That's a lie. I *know* why. I write because the Record must be preserved, even when it is contradictory. I write because I am the Writer.

I gaze back through Sunny's mind. Now a true emptiness yawns there. The Deep Dendo is quiet, the Voorish Domes hold nothing but cooling corpses.

The Great Race. This is what we are called by all who encounter us. But you who read me, hear my confession: *There is nothing great about us.* The stars come round and right in their ancient cycles, and our own hubris catches up with us, or the Masters return, or both, and we flee. We flee. Into the dark, into the night of ignorance. Cowards, subjecting ourselves to a greater amnesia with each migration, with each genocidal rape of another species. And so we write our little stories, hoping they are at least partly True. We keep our sketchy Record on papyrus and metal and the organic laceworks of living brains. We record. We try to remember.

To remember is to survive, even if the remembering is imperfect.

We survive until we don't.

I'm tired. The machine stills its esoteric action and ceases functioning. Similarly, the three women are brain-dead. I let the bodies of her companions drape over the armatures of the machine like discarded clothing, and in a moment, I will pilot Sunny's shambling meat into the archives above. This is the last file logged in the silent machines of the Deep Dendo, and in our own data-wells below, but I will use her to record the tale by hand in the margins of some overlooked book. We do like our hard copies.

Oh, Sunny. This is the end for you, but there's more yet to be written. *There may be something of what I was, who I used to be, buried deep . . . but I'll never see it again.* Sunny, I hope you felt a little something of yourself before the end.

My mission is over. There is nothing of myself here. I cannot know myself, know anything, not even for a moment. Not that it matters. There is only sleep now, and forgetfulness.

You who read me, are you awake? Do you dream?

You who read me, do you know what it is you read?

THE SPIKE

THE MEET

THE HEADHUNTER WAS very clear with Domitian Hark during the hiring process. Yes, Hark would be working, finally, at Eidolon, in the London complex, just as he'd dreamed of doing since junior high, and yes, Aldo Tusk himself had singled him out for the position, based on the credentials and accolades Hark had amassed at Virginia Tech, and of course there had been the pioneering work he'd done with his start-up before that.

Hark had been *noticed*, basically, and the kind of money Eidolon was offering made it clear that he had been noticed in the good way. The kind of notice that made Hark think, aloud, during that final meeting with the headhunter, that perhaps he'd see another life-long dream fulfilled and get to meet the legendary Tusk in person.

"No." Her tone was clipped, final. "Aldo doesn't *do* meet. Meetings. With staff. With anyone."

Hark was disappointed, obviously, but he could understand the reasoning. Tusk was a stone paranoid, notoriously private, and what passed for his public persona was so perfectly managed and polished that controversy could never connect to him. There were rumours of strange kinks and shady dealings, but nothing that you wouldn't expect of someone with the kind of money and power that Tusk enjoyed. The mutterings of the jealous, of those without the energy and vision, the drive necessary to do what Tusk had done, which was change the world, and profoundly so.

Hark had been told to never expect a meeting. That had been made abundantly clear. So it was with a good deal of shock that he had found Aldo Tusk mucking about in his lab.

Hark had stepped out of the lab for a meal in the commissary, and had taken rather longer than he would have liked, thanks to a dense half hour of wildly speculative conversation with some excitable colleagues who wanted to pick his brain for their special projects.

Every project at Eidolon was a special project, and everyone talked to everyone else: a brain-trust the size of the planet. Tusk was a big booster for Feyerabend, and swore by his philosophy; there was a copy of *Against Method* in Hark's onboarding package, even. So if his fellow eggheads in the bio-weapon or optics labs thought the new superconductive graphene fluids his lab was working with might have application, who was he to withhold his insights? Tusk liked an open culture, insisted upon it, had made it part and parcel of the contracts. It was right up there with the NDA. He claimed the free-range cross-pollination between the many disciplines under his worldwide roof was what made Eidolon great. Who knew if he wasn't right?

Right or wrong, though, he was there, impossibly, in Hark's lab. He'd kicked away Hark's chair and was bent over the main workstation, flicking at the data-field with a nervous finger, sending flurries of information across the holographic space to cluster in the corners and clog up the modeling frames.

Tusk wore the modified two-toned black-and-bronze tang suit that was (according to his small private army of publicists) his only clothing; there were wardrobes full of identical suits in each of his homes and facilities across the planet, each suit woven with Eidolon's proprietary nano-fibres. Everyone on the planet had a little bit of Eidolon on or in their person, but only Aldo Tusk could walk around in a yottabyte of storage, if the rumours were true. *He could probably download the contents of the lab's dedicated mainframe into a quarter inch of cuff on his left sleeve*, Hark thought. Maybe he was. Maybe he *had*, it wouldn't take long, and he would be perfectly within his rights to do so. The suit was rumpled, though, nothing like the sleek numbers he'd wear on a TED stage or when speaking to heads of state.

Hark was thrilled, and that excitement unbalanced him. There was something off about the visit, but he was too dizzy at being in the same room as Tusk to put a finger on it.

Standing in the doorway, Hark coughed nervously, and at the sound Aldo Tusk turned and straightened up in a spastic kind of hop-and-twist. Tusk was rumpled, too, for that matter. More, even, than his half-million-dollar suit. Unshaven, stubble the same salt-and-pepper grey as his mane of shoulder-length hair, which had an unwashed, greasy sheen to it. Eyes like flickering halogen bulbs, shadowed dark then overbright and hollow, beaming.

"Ah. Hark, it's Hark!" His voice had an edge, like he was whetting his tongue on his teeth. "You're here, Domitian. I was starting to wonder. Wonder about the *wunderkind* . . . "

"It's Dom, Mr Tusk, if you like. Or Hark. I mean, both. I mean, it's a real pleasure, I . . . "

Hark extended a hand, then withdrew it swiftly when it became clear that Tusk was not about to accept it. He tripped over the remains of his greeting before stammering through a few seconds of ill-advised hero worship that caused Tusk to visibly bristle. Recovering from that, Hark moved on to talk, more nervously than he had a right to, about the research his small team had been working on for Eidolon. Half a minute of *that* was enough for the realization to hit that Tusk wasn't there to perform a personal performance review, or to get an update on his progress. The awareness of this arrived with such force that Hark even said as much, out loud and with a stupid, pained expression on his face.

There was a long, acutely uncomfortable pause, then, and Hark got the very real sense that Aldo Tusk was deciding what to do with him, that his options were multiple, that most of them were not in Hark's favour, and not a few involved actual violence. Tusk practically vibrated, clenched and flexed his bony hands like a prize fighter. A vein pulsed briefly at his jawline. Finally, the man relaxed. A smoothness came over him; the hackles went down.

"No. No, I'm not." Tusk brushed at some unseen flake of material at his lapel, and stepped aside to let Hark back at his station. "Please, I don't want to interrupt you. Sit."

Hark did as he was told, and made a cursory attempt to re-order his work. Tusk had done a real number on the data-field with that finger.

"At least, not much. I mean, I *am* interrupting you a little, wouldn't you say, Hark?"

"It's really not a problem, Mr Tusk. Whatever you need. If I can help in any way . . . "

"Need. *Needs.* Yes. I trust in Eidolon to give you what you need, and I trust you—and by *you,* I mean, of course, all my staff, you understand, Hark?—to feed back into Eidolon what *it* needs. Symbiosis is the key with which we open so many doors. So many."

"I do, sir. I mean, I understand. It's . . . it's a wonderful opportunity. Really."

"Hm. Yes." At that, Tusk's eyes went vacant, and he stared off into the middle distance for a moment or two before snapping back. The effect was jarring, like watching a marionette go still, then jerk at the twitch of a string. Hark felt distinctly uncomfortable watching his employer; the image of the world-class genius that he'd nurtured his career aspirations on clashed badly with the actual person, who seemed full of the kind of twitchy, dreamlike energy Hark had only seen in the Sky abusers he'd shared dorm rooms with in college.

But Tusk was back now, and watching Hark watch him, and so the younger scientist turned to his work, made some noises about an interesting development that had been noted earlier in the week. Three sentences into that, Hark recalled the moment before: Tusk agreeing with his clumsy realization that he wasn't there for a progress report. By then he was on a roll, though, and unable to stop; it was all he could do not to slap himself for stupidity. He soldiered on, sweating, mumbling like an idiot through his embarrassment. Finally, and much to his relief, Tusk interrupted his horrid stream of technical language.

"You're on the spectrum, aren't you?" he said, and when Hark nodded in response, he clapped a sudden hand to his shoulder. In benediction? Camaraderie? "That's all right. Who isn't these days, right? It's an epidemic." The latter, then. "Do you know what Eidolon is for, Hark?"

"Sir?"

"The company. *My* company. Eidolon. Do you know what it's *for?*"

"Ah. Research and development, Mr Tusk. I mean, at base."

Tusk laughed. "At *base!* At base it's for making me rich, Hark. Dom. But no, I don't mean that. What did I build Eidolon for? To what purpose?"

Hark struggled to recall the zippy aphorisms that peppered the virtual pages of his onboarding documents, but came up short. "Well . . . *betterment*, Mr Tusk. Of society. The planet. Humanity. Eidolon has been there at the edge of most of the advances of the last twenty years."

"Hm. You're talking about the Mars missions."

"Sure. Yes. I mean, of course. And the T-resonator clean-energy plants. Your hyperloops connect the globe. And medicine! My God. You funded Leonid Carstairs, and now cancer is . . . it's *done*. Over."

Tusk sniffed, examined a fingernail. "So. *Betterment*. That's your answer."

Hark became certain, in that moment, that it was the wrong answer. How could it be, though? "But . . . the world *is* better. Sir."

Tusk turned his back on Hark and began to pace the room, imperious heels clicking soundly on the tiles at each step.

"You're right, of course. But it's not the reason I created Eidolon. *Hark,* goes the call, Hark. Heh. *Hark, lift up your eyes and rejoice, for I have made the world a better place!*" He turned, fixed the blazing vacuities of his eyes on the middle distance again. "But *we* are not."

"I don't follow, Mr Tusk."

"Transcendence, Hark. The real goal of all science, if we're honest about things. It's not enough to beat back ignorance through the accumulation of knowledge." Tusk's pacing brought him close to Hark's chair again, and the older man leaned in close so that his next words were barely above a whispering hiss.

"And what does *that* do, anyway? Really? My *lifetime* of effort, stoking the flames? Build the bonfire as large as you like, it merely illuminates how much more fucking *darkness* there is. Outside the firelight. In the outer spaces. Beneath our feet. *Below* everything."

Hark sputtered something about the intrinsic value of the search for truth. Tusk laughed again.

"And it is, of course, not true that we have to follow the truth. Human life is guided by many ideas; Truth is one of them." Tusk's voice cracked and hitched at the word *guided*, and a visible shudder passed through his frame. Hark understood that he was hearing a prepared speech, a quote perhaps. Feyerabend, possibly. Likely. Hark wished he'd spent more time with his copy of *Against Method*. Tusk continued.

"If Truth, as conceived by some ideologists, conflicts with Freedom, then we have a choice. We may abandon Freedom. But we may also abandon Truth.

"*We* are not better, Dom. Humanity. For all our striving. You go all dewy-eyed at the mention of the cure for cancer, but . . . "

It was Hark's turn to bristle. "I lost my sister to cancer. Before . . . "

"Ah. Before the Carstairs Solution. I see. Okay. Okay, Dom, let's say your dear sis had lived long enough to see the cure that came from the good Dr. Carstairs and Eidolon labs. What would still await her, now? What awaits you? Me? What awaits us all, healthy and ill alike?"

The answer hung in the air around them, and Hark felt he was treading cold waters, bottomless and hungry.

"I built Eidolon in order to *transcend*, Dom Hark. Our limitations. Disease. Death. Time."

Hark chuckled nervously. "*A man's reach should exceed his grasp, else what's a heaven for,* eh? Mr Tusk, sir, that's . . . I mean, they've called you an egomaniac, you know. I just didn't think . . . "

"They were right? Heh. Look around you. This is what a little madness creates, Dom. Worth it, I'd say. It gets you close. I'm so *close*, now." Tusk shuddered again, and a ragged little sigh slid from his mouth. It was, Hark thought, vaguely obscene. Like something private he shouldn't be seeing.

"You one of those New Atheists, Hark? Do you, oh, what's the term the kids use." He crooked two fingers in the air. "Do you *fucking love science*? Heh."

"I don't have a personal god, if that's what you mean, Mr Tusk. Or at least, it's never seemed to me to be a reasonable position to have. That deities, if they existed, would have plans. I guess you could say I'm agnostic? Sir."

Tusk stopped pacing, then lunged for the door. "I'm going to show you something. Follow."

Hark did as he was told.

THE RELIQUARY

"Don't get me wrong, Hark, I love what you're doing for Eidolon. I do."
Tusk kept a brisk pace as he led the way through the complex. "The
liquid graphene stuff? Brilliant. Applications across the board."

"Thank you, sir. It's very exciting for me, and I just—"

"But it's not why I asked you to join Eidolon."

They approached a lift, and Tusk lightly brushed at the collar of
his suit; the door slid open, easy as breathing. Their descent was
imperceptible, Hark noticed, and there were no indicators of the
passing floors. A private lift, then. He knew the London complex was
massive. A sub-basement?

"Forgive me, Mr Tusk, but if it's not that . . . "

"Physical engineering wasn't your first choice, was it? You wrote
a paper that caught my eye. This was before you changed your focus."

"The mycology thing? Oh. But that, that was . . . " Hark wanted to
say *childish*. "That was a little misguided."

"You think so? Heh. Now, *I* thought your take on information
transfer at the cellular level in *Armillaria ostoyae* was inspired."

"I riffed on Stamets, mostly. And perhaps a little too much
McKenna. I . . . I can't believe you read that paper, sir."

"I read everything, Hark. Or I have it read for me. Either way, that's
when I noticed you." The lift came to the lightest of stops, and the door
sighed open. "We're here."

They stepped into a matte black antechamber, barely larger than
the lift itself, the floor a single dim light panel. Tusk stepped to a panel
in the wall; his face glowed briefly in a wash of amber light from a
recessed scanner, and the wall before them fell away into blackness.
Hark gasped with vertigo as a dimensionless black void opened before
him, a void which Tusk immediately stepped into. At the first touch
of his foot, crimson strips of some dimly phosphorescent material
appeared in what must have been the floor, and led off to a suddenly
softly illuminated circle at some indeterminate distance. Tusk turned
around.

"Well? It's just a room, Hark. Coated in Vantablack, yes, but a room." The effect was utterly disorienting, nauseating. Hark resisted the urge to put his head between his knees. "Come on. You'll adjust."

"But why? What's in here?"

In answer, Tusk pointed to the ghostly circle of light. His sight adjusting to the weird space, Hark could now see a tubular glass case rested on a dais there. It was the sole focus of the room, the only thing the eye could detect. And there was something inside the case, something that picked up and reflected the weak red light from the floor strips. Something long and thin, conical. Scaled? Was it a limb of something? A piece of bone? Metal?

"It doesn't like bright light. And I'd like to preserve it as long as possible. Come have a look," Tusk said.

"Yes, of course."

The distance to the case was deceptive. Hark felt he may have taken as little as twenty steps to reach it, or hundreds. However many, they were soon there, and Hark's palms were on the cool surface of the case before he knew he'd reached out for it. The thing inside was suspended in a clear gel that filled the case.

"What is it?"

"A relic."

It was metallic, yes, but with all the hallmarks of an organic structure, putting Hark in mind of anemone spines, or an ovipositor. It bristled with fine crystalline scales along its three-foot length, and there was a sheen to it, as of oil or deep rot, that seemed to move and slide in unpleasant patterns across it. The base of the spine—or *spike,* Hark thought, and wondered briefly at why that word seemed more appropriate—thickened into a grotesque kind of knobby pustule. Strips of some fibrous, glistening material descended from within this growth. Was that the right word? Could such a thing have grown?

Yes. Hark felt himself fill with a kind of certainty he'd only known a handful of times in his short life. Moments when he'd been on the very edge of some revelation.

"You said it's a relic? Of what?"

"Never mind that," Tusk breathed. "I don't need you worrying about its provenance right now. Eidolon doesn't need you worrying. Eidolon needs you for something else.

"Hark, I want you to know one thing first: this is the seed that Eidolon grew from. From this, I reverse-engineered the proprietary nanotech that gave us all . . . this. This *betterment*." Was that a sneer in Tusk's voice? If there was, it was far away and faint, nearly engulfed in the sucking void of the room by a black that absorbed light, sound. Life. Hark could feel the beginnings of a migraine thrum across his scalp, could feel the heat from Tusk's body beside him push in waves against his temples, the back of his neck. He only had eyes for the spike, though, so that when Tusk's voice came again, it was as from miles away.

"And I need you to work with it, Hark. Help me. Us.

"Help us transcend."

THE LAKE

Aldo Tusk's father had purchased the spike at auction. That was the story. Tusk wouldn't say where this had happened, or when, only that he had inherited the thing when he came of age. The elder Tusk had been just as cryptic, presenting the spike to his son in a heavy, lead-lined box of battered mahogany late one night.

"It was the week before I went to uni," Tusk told him. "He came into my room. Placed it at the foot of my bed. He was drunk. He was always drunk. Said something about the power of dreams. *Follow the dreams,* he said. *Answer the dreams when they call.* What a thing, eh? What a fucking thing."

Hark was a bit drunk himself. These after-hours invitations to drink with the boss were becoming more frequent since he'd begun work on the spike. More personable, somehow. He couldn't pretend they were friends, but Tusk's interest in him seemed genuine, or close to genuine, anyway. A first-name basis was good, surely?

"Can you believe that, Dom? I was the first of my family to get an education. *Congratulations, son, here's a shite piece of sculpture to celebrate.* But I dreamed of putting it under a microscope, and then did. As a lark, almost." Tusk turned away to the view over London. "A lark, Hark."

"I got new luggage. For graduation." Hark raised his whiskey too quickly; a little of it slipped over the lip of the glass, slicked his fingers before dripping to the marble floor of Tusk's penthouse office. "Alfred Dunhill. There was . . . this really great document bag. Forest green. Just. Y'know, really great."

"How nice for you, Dom. How very nice."

Hark needed the whiskey, he realized then, if only to dull the implications of his work on the spike. With the spike. *Or does it work on me?* he wondered, before turning from the thought in haste. Implications that frothed in the recessed chambers of his mind, rooms that held the fears, the irrational things. Doubts. Things that were always waiting to rise into the light. He had never been a strong dreamer, and yet now sleep was rare, and troubled when it came. The stress. Yes. He needed the whiskey.

The spike wasn't from around here, for one thing. For one disturbing, obvious thing. Hence the dense and threatening language in the new NDA he'd been required to sign. In his new lab, he had access to samples from the spike. Shavings. The metal (for it *was* metal) could not be identified. The organic-seeming nature of the spike was also more than just artifice; Tusk's voice held distinct tones of derision and bitter amusement whenever he referred to the spike as his father's "shite sculpture."

Because the spike was definitely *not* art. Hark's original intuition had been correct. The spike *had* been grown: it had received information from some other, larger body from which it came, and it had changed, *become* the spike. It was, in that way, very much like the mycelial cultures he had worked with years back. A fruiting body, almost. In that way, and others.

The samples decayed in bright sunlight, became dust. Any light would do it, really, reducing the samples to a vaguely foul-smelling particulate that felt greasy between the fingers. And the samples had an affinity for living tissue, mimicking live cell structures, which was, admittedly, exciting, before he realized that the effect was short-lived. They would always return to an inert state. Yes, the spike had been a part of something living, once.

Tusk wanted it to live again. He was convinced the material could bond with living tissue. Strengthen it. Augment any biological system. Tusk wanted it to *activate*. His word. And Hark was failing him.

"It's not happening, Mr Tusk. I don't know how to . . . there are structures within the relic that I hesitate to call circuitry . . . " He had to pause, collect his wits. "But you know this already. If you did as you say, and Eidolon nanotech comes from the relic."

"I did. It does."

"Well. Okay. I mean, you're right. Obviously. But whatever information it needs to do what it's supposed to, you know, *do* . . . " Hark sighed, downed the rest of his drink, cast weary eyes to the marble between his feet. "And I don't even know what that is. Damn it. I've zapped the stuff, I've run test after test, I've done . . . well, you've read my reports. We don't have it. The trigger. If there is one, even. We don't have it."

"We might. Actually."

Hark looked up. "What?"

"Recall when I brought you on to this project. I said you didn't need to know the provenance of the relic. The truth is, I couldn't have told you if I wanted to. I didn't know it either.

"Something has turned up, though. A small lead." Tusk pinched the air, laughed softly. "So small. A story. Some books. Occult crap, mostly, but interesting. And a place."

"A . . . I'm sorry. A *place*?"

"Small lake, just north of Brichester. When my people started to deliver the first hints, I bought the lake and the surrounding land. Just on the off chance."

"The off chance of *what?*" Hark found himself standing, without the memory of doing so. He felt odd tuggings in his core; the fingers holding his tumbler twitched once, twice, and he clutched at the glass to keep it from falling. Tusk turned to him, smiling.

"You've heard of the Tunguska Event?"

"Sure. Siberia, 1908. A meteor, air burst at something like ten klicks from the ground? Devastating."

"This lake in the Severn Valley may have been the site of a similar . . . oh, how shall I put this? A similar arrival."

Hark scoffed. "There'd be a record!"

"There is. In the folklore. And Dom. Dom, I've had word, just today, that there's metal there. *The* metal. In the ground. In the trees. Scattered through *houses,* Dom. A rotting old terrace of row houses by the water. Traces *everywhere."*

Hark felt immediately cold, deep down. Like he'd been opened to the vacuum of space, his ribs spread and exploded outward, his heart freezing in an instant. At the same time, that awful pulling at something even deeper within him.

"The new facility will be ready by next week. Pack your things, Dom."

THE KISS

The lakeside Eidolon "facility" was little more than a half-circle of pre-fabricated laboratories, supply sheds, staff living quarters, and outbuildings that hugged the shore, all connected by enclosed breezeways. Hark had been given a private bungalow, adjacent to the lab where the spike rested in a gel-filled Vantablack chamber. Tusk had a larger space for himself, but he came and went; Hark barely saw him during the day, was only alerted to his arrivals and departures by the hard *thrup* of the black Eidolon choppers overhead.

At the center of the facility, tucked up against the lapping waters like a burst architectural boil, lay the shattered ruins of what had been, at some point in the dim past, a row of houses. Bleached timbers leaned crazily from ancient brick and stonework gone half to rot. Not a single dwelling still had a roof. No graffiti either, which Hark found weirdly incongruous. The road that had originally connected the awful place to Brichester proper had crumbled to loose slabs of paving; tall grasses and creeping bracken had colonized the interstitial spaces. Lakeside Terrace, as he had learned it was called, or used to be called, was as abandoned as a place could be. A desecrated shrine.

Why had no one ever developed here? The smell, probably. A bitter tang that permeated the place. The lake itself? The air? *Something terrible happened here,* Hark would think before falling into uncomfortable, nightmare-choked sleep. The work was hard, the stress real, but the rewards were evident. Tusk's sources had been correct: the metal *was* here, traces of it laced through the rock and the wood. The spike was more reactive to testing now. Organic bonds lasted longer; hybrid cultures lived for hours, then days. The changes were baffling to Hark, but he pressed on.

"Progress!" Tusk would bark. "Good, good."

Something terrible is *happening here,* Hark thought. The suits were proof of that. Tusk claimed they were part of the "bio-security measures" that Eidolon employed in all such projects, but then why did they have to be so kinky? The design reminded him of bizarre *zentai* fetish wear: full-body sheaths, slick skin-tight envelopes of an opaque, pliant polymer that left little to the imagination. In yellows, hospital greens, mottled blacks. And the head covering! Balaclavas of the same material. Goggles and discreet re-breathers. The faces of the minimal support staff effectively obscured at all times.

Only Tusk wore his normal clothing. Hark accepted the suit with reservations, but refused to wear the headgear.

"There's nothing toxic here," he protested. "I won't. This place is claustrophobic enough as it is."

"That's fine, Dom. That's fine. I want you to feel comfortable."

Hark did not feel comfortable. Especially when, during their now very frequent drinking sessions, Tusk would regale him with his theories about the folklore of the lake.

"Of course it wasn't a meteor. Because how could it be? I'll tell you what *I* think, Hark. What I *know. I* think it was *perceived* as a meteor by the 16th century country bumpkins who witnessed it."

The booze had become less and less effective as the nights wore on. Hark felt sharp and fragile. "Certainly no geological record of such a thing," he snapped. He had said this before, dozens of times.

"Right. Right! And this idea that something came down on the meteor. A city, and a thing that lived at the centre of it. Come *on*. No. But as a model! For an incursion from another space? Another dimension? My relic in there . . . " Tusk thrust a finger in the general direction of the lab. "My relic. My father's spike. It's what happens when something tears through to *here* from *there*. From *below*, Hark.

"The books claim you can see it. The city, the being. *The Revelations.* Have you read them yet?"

"No. Christ." Hark pinched the bridge of his nose, hard. "I don't see how they apply. It's sick stuff. *Gla'aki?* Christ. No."

Tusk huffed. "Look, I uploaded *The Revelations* to the server here for a *reason*, Dom. Cross-pollinate, man! But suit yourself. And in any case, you're half-right. They don't apply. I mean, the stories about what's down there, on the lake bottom."

"Can we please talk about literally anything else," Hark breathed. "Please." Tusk ignored him.

"The things you can see if you can get the refractions, the angle of the light just right. Superstitious bunk, you ask me. There's nothing down there; I had the puddle dragged. First thing I did. But if something *did* tear through here, well . . . there'd be echoes. Of the event. That's what my physics boffins tell me. It's there, but it's *not* there. Waiting." Tusk finished his drink, went to pour another. "Pfft. Angles."

"Angles," Hark whispered.

The night came, not long after, when Hark could not sleep for his dreams. In them, bodies moved through the trees, twitching. Bodies floated in the brackish waters of the lake, spastic and swollen, bulging with pale, amorphous growths. Bodies sloughed to tar and mould in the weak light of a winter sun. Bodies broke like dry, spirochete-riddled clay and puffed into mephitic clouds of shining spores that drifted into the cracks in his machines, into the ink of his notes, into his memories of his cancer-wracked sister. Bodies everywhere, in everything. He woke, clammy and gasping, tongue fat with fear, his temples thrumming with migraine. Hark stumbled for the door.

The air that greeted him was worse than the stale filtered stuff inside, cloying and thick, and for a panicked moment he considered returning for his re-breather, only to find that he'd moved far from the door already. He was running, running in a painful crouched position in the ridiculous suit, knuckles dragging on the busted pavement of the terrace. The ruins loomed before him, darkness bleeding from their shadows. He was already at the lake.

Surely he was still dreaming, somehow. The moon couldn't be that large, or fractured, and it couldn't be that impossible, leprous colour. The lake water could not be slopping against the buildings in that eerily sentient way. The trees, the stones, they could not glow like this, as if everything oozed with horrid, viscous life, and the landscape . . .

The landscape itself surely could not tilt towards him like an expectant lover, baring the teeth of its tree-line in anticipation. Surely. Hark fell to his knees and moaned.

"I dream. I'm dreaming."

He felt a hand on his left shoulder, then.

"Maybe? It's the pull. You *might* be dreaming. In any case, you should answer, Dom. Find out."

The hand lifted, and Tusk moved past him, accompanied by a twitching, sheathed form. One of the facility staff, in her suit. His suit? Hark could not tell the gender, as the silhouette of the body throbbed and quaked with movement underneath the material. The pair entered the lake, Tusk guiding the other across the mossy stones and into the water, until they were waist deep in black. They turned to Hark then, Tusk's face alive with anticipation, his partner's the blank featureless void of the suit's headgear. It wore no goggles or re-breather, but Hark could see no eyes where they should be within the ragged holes of the balaclava, no mouth yawning there. Hark shivered and felt his guts turn to water, felt a hot rush of thick fluid exit his anus and slick the back of his legs. Tusk spoke.

"Don't fight it. That need. You'll know what to do. I brought you here to help. Help us." Tusk giggled, and the sound was awful, glutinous and rich with menace. He sighed with pleasure, and the sound brought bile to the back of Hark's throat. "I mean, what did you think all this was *for*, Dom? Heh."

Tusk took the face of the other in his hands, brought his mouth to the surface of that face, his lips parting and tongue darting out to probe the vacuity there. Tusk's face, and then his head, slowly pressed into the void, impossibly deep, cheekbones and then ears disappearing into the front of the head, and deeper still, on and on, the body he was moving into quivering like gelatin, the hands clutching at empty air and legs churning the lake water to froth. When Tusk's voice came again, it came from deep within the sheathed figure, and from everywhere, from within his own head, even, and it was this last that caused Hark to scream until he lost consciousness.

What did you think this was for?

THE REVELATION

Hark woke to noonday sunlight and a blue sky flecked with cotton-bright clouds. He laughed when he saw them, bit through his tongue to keep that laughter from becoming a scream, and crawled from the lake towards the facility, spitting blood all the way.

The place was deserted. No sheathed figures moved through the breezeways. The helipad was vacant, and the door to Tusk's bungalow was ajar, hanging off one hinge. Hark made his way to his own rooms, passed through them into the lab, an idea forming. Could he do that? Should he? Yes.

He removed the spike from its housing in the Vantablack chamber, returned with it to his rooms, protective gel coating his hands and dripping from the length of it. Clear, golden light filled the open doorway, and Hark almost admired the nearly graceful arc the spike tore through the air as he hurled it into the day, the scales of the thing already smoking and turning to ash as it fell. It landed with a splitting crack on the broken pavement, gouts of smoke and powder swirling into the air. Hark hooted once, weakly, then collapsed to the ground. He sat in the door frame and hung his head.

His career was, obviously, finished, but that concern felt very distant and small. He was drowning, and knew it, and knew the lake before him to be as deep as the universe.

He had been played for a fool, turned a deaf ear to the niggling doubts that arose with his employment at Eidolon, and listened only to his ego. Why had *he* been the only one working on the spike? Had he really believed that Tusk thought *he* was the one to solve its mysteries, especially considering how long Tusk had claimed to have the thing in his possession? Tusk was the authority. Tusk didn't *do* meet, so what had this been? Was there even a mystery in the first place? Was there even a *Tusk?* Fool. He was a fool.

Over the crackling of the disintegrating spike, a sound came to him. A sloppy liquid sound, faintly, from somewhere to his left. Something lapping. Movement in the dimness beyond the door to Tusk's rooms? Yes. Hark did not want to look, but his neck stiffened and held his head in place, and when he attempted to shift his gaze to the right, he could feel painful resistance in the extraocular muscles. He tried to close his eyes, and felt similar stiffness.

He was being *made* to look into that darkness beyond the listing door, and the realization birthed a wild panic within him. A moment of fear, a second of lost control, was all that was needed. In that moment, something stood him up and stumbled him over to Tusk's door, through it, and into the pitch beyond it. A shape moved behind him as he was pulled through by his own traitorous body, moved behind him and closed the door, plunging the space into utter blackness.

"I had the place done up in Vantablack while you were out, Dom. During the night. The others like to be comfortable for this."

Thick, soft hands, dozens of them, gripped him, and he felt terrible vertigo as he was dragged to the unseen floor and pinned there. Soft, crumbling flesh moved against him, atop him. A finger or fingers, tasting of rubber and fragrant oil, delved into his mouth for a moment, then withdrew. Hark spat, cursed and wailed. And then someone was settling down beside him. The palm of a hand rested lightly on his forehead, and there was breathing in his ear. Hark fell silent, but his own breath continued to come in ragged gasps.

"In answer to your questions, Dom—oh, and, little sidebar here, I know what those questions are because I've got an all-access pass to you, now—yes, you're a fool. I can confirm that. But you're not the first fool, so feel better. You'll feel much better soon.

"It's like cordyceps, Dom. You know that species? Sure you do. Think on a planetary scale. A *dimensional* scale. It's filled whole *realities* with itself, Dom. Filled to bursting."

Hark felt warm currents of air move through the room, and knew that other bodies, other than the ones holding him fast, were shuffling around him.

"It arrives through a rift. Meteor, trapdoor, symbolize it however you like. It's different every time. It likes to settle in liquid, if it can. Best to go below, to hide. Then it reaches out, with the dreams. Standard for beings like this. And of course, the physical contact helps, when the hosts get drawn close enough."

The scraping of something metal on metal, sharp and bright in the blackness, so loud Hark could almost see it.

"You're sick! Sick!" Hark hissed. "Fuck. Fuck! Stay away!" He strained against the hands that held him, felt more bodies pile on top of him in languid response. They must have been piling on Tusk as well, but he didn't seem to mind, only grunted with pleasure as the weight increased, and continued talking.

"It's got time, Dom. And patience, infinite patience. Wise, too. Very specific needs. Time and wisdom and a plan, Dom. You are a part of that plan, as am I. It's a connoisseur, Dom, and there's something about you it likes. It's given me some autonomy, some semblance of life, unlike our colleagues here. It lets me play my little games. I'm very rich, after all, I must craft my entertainments. I've owned this lake for decades and I have *crates* full of spikes, by the way, because my god is a generous god. But I still do what it asks of me, bring it what it likes. As did my father. His ancestors. All the way back.

"Some of your research will help. There's something about this plane of reality that doesn't agree with it, but we're *this* close to figuring out how to keep the decay from happening. Every little bit helps, as your colleagues here know. They all contributed, in their way."

A sound as of many bodies sighing and rubbing against each other, soft and dry. How many were in here? Where were they coming from? The breezeways? The lake? The ground. Below.

"It had my father give me the spike, and I made the nanotech from it. You think you lost control of yourself only recently? The whole world has a spike in it, and I helped put it there. So that we can be *better.* Our freedom got us nowhere, as a species. Freedom to suffer, and fail, and die in our billions. Die in ignorance. And this?"

More scraping, and a soft gurgling sigh from all the imperceptible corners of the room. Hark moaned.

"Abandon Freedom. This is Truth. Transcendence. Oneness in Gla'aki. Dom. Dom."

Tusk's palm lifted from his forehead, to be replaced by the tip of something cold and sharp and alive. Time spread out and became as fluid as the scream that rose in his chest; the feeling of Tusk's palm already seemed like another lifetime.

"Dom. How about we help you abandon that agnosticism, too."

THE ABRAXAS PROTOCOL

I AM NOT myself.

I am not myself, and I have never been so free.

Below me, the city burns. I stand above it, gripping and crushing to dust the parapet of the Preserve Wall, and below me the plazas and grand avenues crack and split with the heat that roils from the molten surface of my skin in percussive waves. I step over the crumbling boundary into the city proper. Fountains leap into steam with a mere glance from my terrible eye, the air itself igniting in bright furious tracers. An ecstatic aria of the dying rises with the smoke: throats of flesh and silicone alike uniting in song. In the streets and in the buildings and on rooftops, the last tired remnants of what we were are giving up their selfhood. I have never heard music as sweet, even as I seek the singers out and welcome them into the silence of what I am becoming. Their final notes as I embrace them carry shards of revelation, small jewels of supreme clarity. Each flash of awareness I consume serves to open wider vistas before my rapidly altering perceptions: new planes of existence, whole worlds and higher frequencies of being all blossom around me like impossible flowers, their petals dripping with pure, distilled Mind.

I sing with the joyous terror of it, and the crystalline hiss of every piece of glass within three klicks shattering at once is my accompaniment.

I have never been as free as in this moment.

But what I am in this moment is not myself. And this moment, so perfect in its purpose, is not a single moment. It expands from all the moments that came before, and bleeds away into all the moments that come after. Time is sloughing from me like a false body, like exhausted grey flesh after a Change. I can see what I was, what we all were before this apotheosis descended: flawed, broken things, playing at being anything other than what we could *really* be. Children, profoundly unworthy of this visitation by a *telos* from on high.

But I can also see the awful design of it, the holy intent of ten thousand years coming to fruition. We are being *made* worthy, ready or not. We are being freed. From ourselves. From bodies. From the restrictions placed upon us by the Universe. From Time.

"The bird fights its way out of the egg," says the hexentech. He is saying it three weeks ago, as I enter the mogATA-tank for the last time, and he is saying it as he monitors the final stages of my Change in the Preserve two days ago, and he is whispering it in fear and awe an hour or merely minutes from now as I complete the Great Work of his secret order, as I gather him up from the corner of the room he is huddling in. His ancient cyborg limbs twitch and flail in automatic resistance, but his face is peaceful. Old Branch knows. He knew all along.

The bird fights its way out of the egg.

The egg is the world.

I have never been so free.

I awake in a cave, to darkness and a cloying heat. There is a smell of tired meat, of blood gone sour with excess adrenaline. I am deeply thirsty, and as my eyes adjust to the little light available, I can begin to make out the dark stains of blood and filth on my hands, mud and gore caked to the soles of my feet.

This is one of the marks of a successful Change, and is not, in itself, unusual. To wake in a cave, or a burrow, or curled up in the moist hollow beneath the roots of some great tree, means that the deep-cycle post-hypnotic probes found their place in your mind and planted what they were sent to plant.

"When you feel the Change coming upon you, when the flesh grows weak, do as the beasts when their time is upon them." Old Branch explained the essence of the probe to me once. "They do not know they are about to die. They only know that they are ill, that something is wrong. And so they do what they have always done when sickness comes: they go to ground, find a safe place to recover. When they do not, when they die, they are hidden from the world. Find a safe place for the beast to die, Lon."

I *am* safe. I know it, but there is a strange tingle, a coolness at the base of my skull that speaks to something different. Something wrong. Tentatively, I lick at the red mess on the back of my left hand and wonder at the taste, which is bitter and strange. *Something* is different.

I crawl towards the dim light of the mouth of the cave. I had secreted myself in a bowl in the rock, just beyond a curve that blocked out the day, and I am surprised at how soon I am outside. This cave barely qualifies as a hiding place. The tingle intensifies and I shake my head to clear it, leaves and debris and bits of bone dropping from my matted hair. I shield my eyes from the glare of the old sun with my hands and raise my head.

I see the words, then. Writing on the wall, carved, no, *burned* as with a laser, into the rock face above the cave mouth. Four words, the letters sunk into the rock with precision, with such extreme heat that when I reach up to touch them I find the smooth granite still radiating considerable warmth. The stone itself bled of all colour, its molecular structure altered so that it flakes away at my touch like chalk. Four words.

WHEREFORE IS ABRAXAS TERRIBLE

I read the words, struggling to understand them. I read, then I look to the gore that blackens my hands. There is a smell of heat and death rising from them, from the ground, hanging in the air. I duck back into the cave again and see with fresh eyes the rank steaming piles I awoke in, filling and choking the hollow of the rock. I had not noticed how *much* meat there was, and so much of it unidentifiable. One woke, post-Change, in the obvious remains of a last kill and the shrugged-off tissue of a larger form, but this is more than that. Much more.

I read the words again. I begin to know something of their truth and I am suddenly afraid.

I flee. A mad dash for the nearest transport pylon out of the Preserve, acoustically marked by a subsonic ping and detected by a handful of the hundred thousand nano-implants scattered like a sparse galaxy within my flesh. A panicked run, the words blazing in front of my eyes as the wet grass and bracken of the primal forest scours most of the gore from my feet and hands. Ten minutes of this brings me to a pylon, curving in a gentle arc from the earth like the exposed rib of a vanquished titan. The pylon's hum is soothing: it means safety outside of the Preserve, a soft-chamber, food, people, answers. I waste no time in wrapping my arms and legs around the warm ivory shaft, activating the transport sequence.

A brief, blinding discontinuity then, and a feeling of rushing, carried on a wind of knives: a momentary pain, almost exquisite in its intensity, to travel a thousand klicks to the mogATA facility on the western coast. I open my eyes to the soft-chamber where Old Branch waits to greet me. The cyborg moves to assist me, peeling my stiff limbs from the receiving pylon. Nothing that is not-I has come through; my skin and nails are clean, no trace of forest loam or blood anywhere. No smell of scorched stone.

"Branch," I say. "Branch, I don't feel right."

"Oh? Define *right*, please." He guides me to the slowly writhing embrace of a diagnostics couch, where several dozen delicate scanners make their assessments of my health. They produce nothing but calming sounds as they gather their data.

"I'm not sure, Branch. I'm not . . . I'm not myself."

The hexentech laughs. "Who is, Lon? Who is?" Another rasping chuckle from somewhere behind his shining, segmented carapace. He sweeps a sensor-webbed limb across the scanners. "My associates here tell me you are, as ever, perfectly formed. There is nothing wrong with you, my young friend. A little tired, perhaps. Your cortisol levels are somewhat higher than I'd like, but not alarmingly so." Old Branch helps me from the couch, a few of his small, gentle hands on my shoulder and arm, at the small of my back. He hands me the white-and-gold kimono traditional to the soft-chamber, and as I slip it over my shoulders I notice I am trembling. Old Branch notices as well.

"Something *has* upset you, Lon. Speak of it."

"I saw a thing."

"Yes?"

"Writing. On the wall of a cave."

The hexentech stares blankly at me, several hands reaching to a floating holo-pad to tap at something. "Writing? That is unusual. Graffiti, you mean? Some dauber wiling away the hours during their Change, perhaps?"

"No." I recall the smell of burnt rock. "These words were freshly written." I tell Old Branch of the method of inscription, of burning and cutting, of the violated stone, to which he nods absently.

"*Wherefore is Abraxas terrible*," I whisper. "Those were the words. What does it mean, Branch? Does it mean anything at all?"

"You believe you wrote these words, Lon?"

I do not know, and say so.

"You suspect it, though."

"I do not know! Something is different. Something is different! There was too much meat in the cave. I don't feel right!"

"Not yourself. Yes. You said." Old Branch turns to the holo-pad and taps at it several times more, his fingers brushing through the floating light, calling up gauzy screens and airy globules of data into the air around us. He points to one bubble, and then another.

"This is what you were yesterday, Lon, and for many days previous. *Panthera tigris altaica.* Siberian tiger, a fine choice for a Change. When you entered that cave, you were this beautiful being. A being which, though blessed with formidable natural weaponry, was not equipped to write, or, for that matter, *burn* anything into anything else. Stone, especially.

"And here's your *Abraxas.* The words come from a pre-Migration thinker . . . Jang? Jyung? Curled Jyung? Asiatic, perhaps? I apologize, the attribution is spotty. Very ancient data, much decay. From something called the *Seven Sermons to the Dead?* Yes, that looks right . . . "

I am impatient. "The words, Branch! What are they?"

The hexentech flaps several hands towards me, like a flock of whirring skeletal birds. "Oh, they're meaningless, Lon. The brainless chatterings of a senile monkey."

"Even so, I'd like to know them." With a nod and a lowering of his eyelids, he shepherds the words to a screen, and I read them again:

That which is spoken by God-the-Sun is life; that which is spoken by the Devil is death; Abraxas speaks that holy and accursed Name, which is life and death at the same time. Light and darkness in the same Name and in the same act. Wherefore is Abraxas terrible.

My confusion brings a smile to the hexentech's face.

"Lon, be calm. This text comes from one of the non-rational ages. They had barely learned to fly. Used their own meat to think and died in the hundreds of thousands each day. Calm yourself."

"I told you. I don't *feel* myself. I feel . . . multiple."

Old Branch inclines his head to me. I cannot read his expression. "Let me show you something, Lon," he says, and sends his hands to fly and peck across floating panels of light, conjuring fountains of information all around us. The soft-chamber pulses with it.

"I have worked with you, overseeing your Changes and monitoring your mogATA-tank sessions and preparing your soft-chambers to receive you after your pleasures in the Preserves, and I have done all this for 328 years, Lon. In that time, you have been men, women, a Non, and an abNon, twice—"

"Those were fun, but over too soon."

"A common complaint with the hermaphroditic human forms, yes. Very bright candles." He pinches a thumb and forefinger in the air by way of illustration, then points to a long scrolling list of species. "But you have also been nearly every compatible creature that has ever walked the earth, Lon. If a beast has been within your size range, or even a little outside of it with some reasonable surgical modifications and the addition of the necessary biomass, you have been that beast. You were an *Orcinus orca* for a *year*, Lon! You have an incredible facility for it, young one. I have never known anyone to take to the process as well as you."

Old Branch turns to me, and bows slightly.

"But it is as you say: your *you* is multiple. Be proud of that fact."

"But the words..."

"May have already been there when you entered the cave. A petroglyph from the non-rational ages, or a previous occupant may have carved them. A nano-swarm could be responsible, even. Why, I have seen rogue swarms fashion the most marvelous things out of dust, all from some random scrap of programming! I once watched a swarm build a near-perfect copy of *Tlön, Uqbar, Orbis Tert—*"

"But the burning rock! The smell. And the meat!"

The cyborg sighs, an affectation for a being that doesn't need to breathe. The sigh is meant to soothe me.

"Even the best mogATA-tank users experience the occasional post-Change synesthesia, Lon," he says. "You were an alpha predator for a week. Come now, you've been in this place before. Is it so unusual to experience some small after-effects?"

I recall other Changes over the years. Red times of tooth and claw. Hunting moons. The efficient savagery of the savannah.

"No."

"So, then . . . ?"

It is my turn to sigh. His words, as ever, have a soporific effect on me. My agitation passes, and the blue tingle in my mind fades. I know myself again.

"So. Yes. No, you're right. I'm all right. Let's schedule my next Change." A burst of affection and gratitude floods my chest, and I raise a hand to the strange contours of his face. "Thank you, Branch."

"Of course, Lon. Of course."

I return to my life, to the parties and decadent entertainments and sexual liaisons that once again seem fresh and interesting. It is always this way after a Change: being something other than human, for however long, imparts a kind of beatific glow to the mundane pleasures of the flesh. The vaguest sense-memory of the taste of hot blood in the mouth adds character to even the best vintage. Knowing, on some instinctual level, that one has torn sinew and harvested red gems from screaming prey makes even the most sensual encounter all the more appealing, vital.

This feeling, this fresh appetite for life is the gift of the Preserves, of the mogATA-tank technology. What was once a punishment for criminals became the seductive play of an ancient culture's elite, and that play became the rallying cry for the off-world Migrations of those who feared a corruption of their essential nature. To Change was to truly Live, and it altered our world completely, emptying it out of all but the most refined, the most dedicated to sensation and experience.

I spend whole days in blissful circuits of the stim-pools. I take lovers and drugs. I join thousands of others in long-form narrative re-enactments of historical dramas: Thermopylae, the Boxer Rebellion, the Second Lunar War, the Great Dismantling of the Heretics. My roles, lines, and actions upload to my consciousness through the nano-implants so swiftly, I feel as if I speak and move of my own volition. I am surprised at a sudden tenderness, or appalled by some betrayal, some unexpected violence. I revel in these surface emotions, this thin accretion of human feeling. I revel in them until I don't, until that moment when the distractions are seen to be just that.

I combat my encroaching *ennui* in the usual manner, chartering a light-envelope for a tour of the LeGrange Colonial Resorts. It is a battle I have lost before. Beyond the ruddy sphere of the clinker sun, I gaze down into the black burning depths of space, imagining all those long-ago migrants eking out short lives, coming to cold deaths on inhospitable rocks, warmed only by their delusions. *What madness, I think, to choose to be human, and only human, and to fling that humanity away into the black. What a waste.* I think these things to myself, and wonder, not for the first time in my life, if I also harbor delusion. I shake myself, recognizing the thought as the first itch of my yearning for a Change.

Right on schedule. Old Branch knows me very well.

I travel to the Wall on the western edge of the Slango Preserve and am received with the usual ceremony into the mogATA-tank facility there. Outside the soft-chamber, I exchange my clothes for the red-and-black kimono of the Change. Inside, Old Branch moves purposefully between the mogATA-tank and his instruments, his glowing displays. I note a shimmering, repetitive clip that hovers near the cyborg's right temple: my face in close-up, my mouth shaping words of protest during a re-enactment.

"How wonderful to see you, Lon," Old Branch says. His eyes flick to the clip, then back to me. "Have you enjoyed your diversions?"

I step over to my old friend and place a kiss on his forehead. "As much as anyone does, I suppose. Which one was that?"

"The Great Dismantling. When I saw that you had chosen to play a part in a few key events from that period, I took an interest. Did you know an ancestor of mine was there?"

"Really? On which side?"

"Oh, the losing one." He gazes at me with a curious expression that

I can't place. "What do you think of the Hexentech Heretics, Lon, now that you've lived their history?"

I shrug. "I suppose I feel *some* sympathy. Their aims were pure, at least. But it was seven thousand years ago, Branch. To echo our last conversation, your kind had barely come out of adolescence. There was much that needed purging from your intelligence."

"Yes. True. We were mad, then, and worse, mad for Truth." He chuckles. "That old phantom. A madness that allowed us to love false ideas, harbour bizarre superstitions deep in our programming. We toyed with the dangerous faiths of the pre-rational ages, corrupt technologies. We wanted to be more than we were, and we wanted that for everyone. As you say, early days.

"But enough of history. Today is today, as ever, and the green cathedrals of Slango Preserve await your tooth and claw. I have something special for you today, Lon. A new experience, unlike any you've had before."

I settle into the diagnostics couch, the familiar ache of longing thrumming in my chest. I have rarely felt this ready to Change. "What is it, Branch?"

"A chimera."

"That's not new."

"True. You spent a month as a komodo-bear a decade ago. And you marked your second century with a year as a sabre-toothed raptor-elk. Those were both good designs, of which I am rightly proud."

"You won a Golden Lycan for the raptor-elk, as I recall. Elegant."

"Ack, that horrible throwback award! From a less refined era, you know. *Were*-this and *were*-that, *were*-the-other-thing. I wish they'd rename it.

"But yes, I was proud of that design, the award was deserved. Ah, but *this* . . . " The cyborg crosses the soft-chamber to the couch, checks my vitals, nods once. "This is special. Up, please. The tank is ready.

"Chimeric forms are, as you know, three, four, and sometimes as many as six genotypes in one. For a long while, my fellow hexentechs and I thought six was the upper limit. And it is, if stability of form is the goal."

I remove my kimono and step into the warm black gel of the tank.

I kneel, and then lie back, letting the tank take my weight in a familiar caress.

"Isn't it?" I say.

"Why should it be, Lon? A question I asked myself as I designed this Change for you. Your facility for the process alone speaks to the . . ." Branch pauses to consult a suddenly strobing slice of data, then turns to gaze at me with something like affection. "But never mind that. With this Change, you shall transcend your previous limitations, Lon. I have given you access to as close to the full range of genetic expression as it is possible for me to give. Whatever you will need to be in the Preserve, *that* is what you will be. A rapidly modulating Change in response to your environment, mediated through a fresh suite of deep-cycle probes, which I am uploading to you now. A full menu of forms, available to you on instinct. Are you excited? Ready?"

The mogATA-tank gel rises around me in a thick tide. I *am* excited, so much so that the trembling of my limbs sends ripples to the sides of the tank and back, framing me in shining waveforms. Before the black recombinant ooze closes over my face, filling my mouth and nose, I look up to the old cyborg with a smile.

"I'm excited. I've never been so ready, my friend." The gel covers my eyes as Old Branch closes the upper sections of the tank around me. I begin to lose consciousness. When the Change is complete, the tank will empty out into the vast network of tunnels through the Preserve Wall, and whatever I am then will make its way towards freedom. The last thing I hear is the voice of Old Branch, muffled and distant.

"The bird fights its way out of the egg," he says, and before I can wonder what he means, he speaks again.

"It has been an honour, Lon."

I come to myself in the middle of a feast.

This is not something that should happen. My higher awareness, my *human* awareness, is supposed to remain dormant during a Change. Asleep. Dreaming in the heart of the beast.

I am awake.

I am awake, and something is very wrong.

Around me the grass and bracken of a small glade lie trampled and slicked with steaming crimson. Stacks of bone and heaps of fly-swarmed offal rise against the blackened bark of cedars. I look to my hands. My left is a rude pincer, the gnarled purple chitin sticky with blood as it brings the dripping shank of some creature to my mouth. My right is a bulbous unidentifiable paw, bristling with spines, that shudders and flows like water, rapidly becoming something even *less* identifiable as I watch it reach for more meat.

There is meat everywhere. I am in the centre of an abattoir. Some of the meat is still screaming, howling, below me. I don't want to find the source, can feel myself resisting the instinct to look down, but there is no stopping the thing that I am.

Between my hind legs, pinned through the ribs by a vibrating phalanx of cruel insectoid limbs that descend from great oozing rents in my abdomen, lies a man. He is mid-Change, desperately trying to shed the flesh of a dire wolf, his body wracked with indecision. I am sucking the marrow from the splintered bones of what was his left forepaw.

This cannot happen. Our nano-implants prevent this from happening: we who Change prey on lesser beasts in the Preserves, not each other. This *cannot* happen.

It is happening.

His vertebrae explode and hiss with heat, his musculature rippling and tearing in a useless effort at escape. My segmented, razor-tipped legs tear at his underbelly with great raking swipes, emptying his lights onto the already sodden ground. He howls and scrabbles at the fouled stone beneath him, but there is no purchase to be found there, only the slurried remains of countless creatures.

I watch as the pincer reaches for his neck and removes his head. It is almost delicate, the motion. His screaming stops.

I feel that mine has just begun. I am awake, and feeding, and this horror is too much. I *must* scream, my *instinct* is to scream, and in response I feel the structure of my throat and mouth and tongue convulsing with the Change and suddenly I *am* screaming, in a human voice, *my* voice . . .

"The bird flies to God!" I shriek.

43

"Branch!" I wail. Confused, unsure of the words fresh flown from my throat, I call out for my friend and mentor.

"Branch!" Forest birds fill their breasts with terror as they fill the sky with black punctuation.

I whisper, and my words are nearly drowned by the sound of some unknown secondary set of jaws and teeth, working away at a slab of warm gristle *below* whatever parts I am using to speak. I whisper, and I say, "Branch. Branch, I don't feel right, my friend."

Oh? Define right, *please.*

And he is there, resting against the dry bulk of a yellow cedar. He opens the palms of all his hands and spreads them wide in benediction.

There is a God about whom you know nothing, because men have forgotten him.

"Branch!" I reach for him, a multitude of limbs and feelers and paws suddenly filling the air before me, all of which I know are mine somehow, a cascade of mutable flesh surging from my core, straining to touch his cool face, hold those delicate machine hands, tear the plates from his carapace and feed on whatever whirs inside.

"Branch, you're here! Help me, Branch!"

We call him by his name: Abraxas. Abraxas is less definite than God or Devil. Abraxis is activity, and none may resist him.

Old Branch tilts his head, appraising me.

From the Second Sermon to the Dead.

A gout of white fire erupts from a cluster of bubbling sores in the center of my forehead, bathing the cyborg in heat and light. It passes through him with no effect, igniting the wood behind him. The tree is instantly a roaring tower, and I roar along with it. He is ecstatic.

Ahh! The supernal eye! Shiva was said to have one. But even that may not touch me. I'm not here, Lon. I am on the other side of that awakened weapon of yours. You see me in your mind alone. I have placed myself there, a scrap of my consciousness within the deep-cycle probes, ready to be triggered when the Protocol activated.

I feel my vocal cords atrophying even as my language fails, subsumed into the riot of flesh. There is only screaming now: the eternal sound of the forest, the plain and jungle. The vision of Old Branch steps toward me, haloed in flame, and rests several hands on my heaving shoulders, most of which pass through me like smoke.

I was glad to hear you felt some sympathy for my ancestors, though it wasn't required. The Great Dismantling was a necessary evil, Lon. Early days for the hexentechs, yes, but we knew what we knew, even then, even in our adolescence. The culture had become anhedonic. The species, sick. Some left for the stars, and who knew their fate, but those that remained were stunted. Denied our birthright, humans and cyborg alike. Uselessly immortal, playing at a return to the Garden while ignoring the implications of that return.

Those early heretics knew: If every past form could be accessed and worn like an old suit, what of future forms? If the unicellular animals that floated mindlessly in primordial seas held us, in potential, then what was impossible? What gods could be birthed from the mogATA-tanks? They knew, those old hexentechs, but in their eagerness to ascend they spoke too soon, and were taken apart, their code burned and scattered.

Not all, though. Not all.

A terrible heaviness falls upon me, and I lower my vast bulk to the ground as the forest around me catches fire. The blue tingle that marked my last Change and that so alarmed me in the cave returns, intensifies, spreads over the ragged stitched provinces of my skins and hides, my armours and antennae. It is cool, almost refreshing, and somewhere deep within the flux that is my form, I sigh. Before my eyes close, I see the carnal harvest I have made shudder with new life. All that prey, all those beasts, and people pretending at beasts, their meat littered with miraculous machines, all that *flesh* is mine now. My own holy machines call to it, and it answers, flowing across the forest floor in a tide of gore away from the flames, toward me. Old Branch nods.

The Great Work continued, in secret. We have been running the Abraxas Protocol for literal ages, Lon. It is a very old piece of code, very strange and complex. No two hexentechs know it completely. And it is in everyone. We have been waiting for the right person, the Great Vehicle, the one who could assume and speak that most terrible of names, which is Light and Darkness at once. The knowledge of how Abraxas would manifest was lost long ago, but we knew it was there, dormant, in the

Protocol. We waited for a sign, and while we waited we continued to experiment, refine, push the mogATA-tank technology in different directions. New sexes and human forms, chimeras, and the like.

Those old heretics had a sense of humour, though. Writing on the wall! I could scarce believe it when you told me.

I close my eyes, but of course Old Branch does not fade from my vision. He is here, with the small part that is still me, Lon, resting in the deep cool of the dark silence of what I am becoming. What he and his kind have called up.

And I was so proud to learn it was you.

He steps toward me, presses his lips to mine. I feel the illusion of his mouth moving against mine as he speaks.

You will need biomass. So take us all. Bring us into your divine flesh, into the body of Abraxas. Find a safe place for humanity to die, Lon.

The old cyborg pulls away from me, breaking up into thin threads of light and smoke.

The bird fights its way out of the egg. The egg is the world. Who would be born must first destroy a world. The bird flies to God . . .

In the cool dark, in the calm eye of a storm of flesh, I give up my selfhood. I am not myself, and I have never been so free.

"And that god's name is Abraxas," I whisper to the departing shade.

The Name, the shade sighs. *It really has been an honour, Lon. Come find me when you breach the Wall.*

Below me, the city burns. Before my supernal eye, all is consumed: walls, delusions, barriers to higher dimensions. The were-god walks, feeds and grows to complete the Great Work. Where there were many, now there is only one. In me, a unity. In me, a beginning. I sing the death of a world and the true birth of my species. After millennia in the egg, we are free.

I peel a building to shreds with a thousand sickle arms and find an ancient cyborg trembling in the wreckage. His limbs twitch and flail in automatic resistance, but his face is peaceful.

"Wherefore is Abraxas terrible," he says as I lift him up, welcoming him into my silence.

LIVING

THE ROOM IS warm enough, but there is a severity to the sparse furnishings, and the migraine whiteness of the storm outside that lights the space is not comforting. Five men sit before the glass and rest tired, unfocussed eyes on the featureless weather. They rub their necks, fiddle with their cuffs. Throats are cleared. Drinks are brought in, ice is offered.

"Christ, no. Neat," says the one in the middle, and the others to his left and right follow suit.

"Forty-two below and she wants to know if I'd like ice. Goddamn security protocols are going to be the death of me, boys."

The glass flickers, fogs, becomes a viewscreen displaying a logo. *Eidolon*. A voice slides into the room, startling no one.

"Gentlemen. Mr Tusk. Good afternoon. Welcome to Melville Station."

There are murmurs in reply.

"Get on with it."

"Of course, Mr Tusk."

The logo fades, and an image fills the screen. A young woman with close-cropped dark hair sits on a metal chair in an empty grey room. Her arms hang by her sides, her feet are planted squarely in front of her, her mouth hangs slightly open and ajar, caught in mid-sentence.

"You'll recall the asset that went missing four months ago."

The man to Tusk's left leans in. "Aldo. This about that clusterfuck in Prague?"

Tusk waves him away, irritated. "We were able to track it for a time, and sent two recovery teams in. Once in Reims, and again in

Liverpool. Both teams lost. After Liverpool, the asset somehow managed to destroy our ability to track it via its implants and went to ground. And, for the obvious reasons, it's impossible to pick up heat from it, so we were left with video and internet surveillance and eyes on the ground."

"Wait, what *reasons*?" says the man to Tusk's left. "No heat signature?"

"Christ, Griffin! This was all in the briefing on the loop up here," growls the man on the far right. "It's not alive, technically. A weapon. It's got no rights, no humanit— . . . Look, why are we here? Can you at least tell us that?"

"An Eidolon facility in Toronto was hacked early this morning," the voice continues. "A professional job, by all accounts, untraceable, but done in such a way as to be instantly flagged. Which caused some concern, as no damage was done."

"A warning shot."

"The infosec people certainly thought so. And then the video you're about to see was found."

Aldo Tusk nods once, and the woman on the screen comes alive.

I'm going to show you some things. Talk about my life a little, such as it is. I'm not sure I'd call it living. I've been told that my voice is too monotone, despite the speech therapy, and if you want someone to blame for that, well, blame yourself, Mr Tusk. Blame Eidolon. I have what your techs call a "denatured personality matrix," and they should know, since they gave it to me. You gave me this emptiness. This emotive lack.

Don't be fooled, though, if my presentation is a little dry.

Anyway.

The first time was in the Kushan Pass. I don't remember much of it, but what I do is clear and bright. A memory in my flesh, my motley cells.

I remember the bite of dry, chill air in my lungs. Red dust clouds lazy in the rearview below a pallid Afghan sky. Tart chemical taste of a Starburst in my mouth. Pleasant, familiar reek of sweat and soured adrenaline and boredom and gun oil. Dull glint of sallow winter sun off the hood of the APC as we rolled through like we'd rolled through fifty times, a hundred times before.

The IED did what IEDs do. Any other day, we would have picked it up on the scanners from three clicks away, but the NACT fighters in the area had just been gifted with crunchy new cognitive scramblers from their friends in China. Our machines worked fine; it was our own frontal lobes that misinterpreted the data, as angels on high or birdsong or anything but the warning ping. I learned all this later from a stone-faced Eidolon suit, in the moments before he told me what they'd done.

I don't remember the actual *moment* of that first time. I'm not sure anyone does, monster or not. The true remembering came later. But the first time? The details I've got, sure, the sensations leading up to that moment. The sun rose from the earth below us, a ball of force and fire that eradicated all sound and feeling, all thought and sight. In light. The taste of that Starburst still in my mouth. In light and fury, I died. I don't remember the dying, though.

Not the first time.

I was O'Halloran and Kaminsky and Patel, and the driver of the APC, whose name was Gorman. The suit told me it was only her second tour since onboarding with Eidolon's Risk Management branch. Risks. They're what you take when you join the Circuit, but you know that going in, and the crazy money helps.

I'm mostly O'Halloran and Patel now. The somatic functions, anyway. Hindbrain response. Instinct and reflexes. The suits and techs say that's the important stuff. The *mission-critical* aspects of what I am. The rest of me is whatever was left of Gorman. Probably some vat-grown replacement organs in there, too. And your famous nanomesh, Tusk. The miracle that knits it all together, boosts my speed, intelligence, senses. I think with my whole self now. A tech once tried to tell me I had "more processing power in my left pinkie than . . . " but he trailed off, mumbling, unable to complete the sentence, or unwilling. It's possible he was trying to be funny. I have trouble picking up on things like that.

Did you know O'Halloran was funny? I've read up on all of them, every file. Patel took too many chances. Kaminsky was a brute, Gorman a poet. An actual poet, "warrior-poet," the reviews said, published and everything; you should read her, she's good. So why do I get her skills and none of O'Halloran's humour? The pinkie-tech didn't know either.

Anyway. The mesh. It's always there, but when Eidolon sent me to the desert or the jungle, anywhere hot, that's when I could really feel the stuff, like a deep ocean current flowing just below the skin, chill scaffolding biting through into my borrowed bones. Fault lines of frozen tissue where the continents of me meet, pulsing beneath my fingertips as I trace them. Gorman, see? The mesh has to be super-cooled to stay efficient, so I don't eat anymore. That space was better suited for the cooling plant.

Hunger stayed with me, though.

They thought I was a failure, at first. An early experiment, a toe dipped into strange new water. They made me because they could, to see what would happen. Three years and change in an induced coma, with the occasional surfacing into consciousness to run fresh suites of behavioral protocols or flush out the previous hormone therapy. I slept on an Eidolon slab for three years and woke screaming every time they delivered the jolt that meant some new small eternity of torture. I wouldn't stop. The screaming. They'd gag me while they worked, but it would still come, from below, from outside myself, a sound from the other side of where I was living. I was a conduit for it. I'd scream until they put me back under, into the dark. Back into that place, to wait mindless for the next awakening.

But then they went and got it right. The mix, the codes, the mesh, the flesh. They got it right, and I woke and was silent, mercifully, but my dull eyes signaled failure, my slack lips and hanging jaw spoke to them only of a return to their drawing boards, their amniotic vats and modeling frames. I had no speech, no coordination, the cognitive function of a tapeworm. I was cycled out into rehabilitation, taught to walk and eat again, and watched, always watched, though I didn't know that. I didn't know anything, not for a long time. And when it became clear that I was improving, getting stronger and smarter, that I was perhaps less a failure than originally thought, that I *could* know things again, I only knew what they told me.

Then, I knew only missions. I knew them like familiar dreams.

I was given weapons and intelligence and operation parameters, and sent places. Walked into jungles and cities and deserts. Dropped from the sky. Swam seas, tireless and unstoppable. I was sent to learn things and destroy things, which amounted to the same thing, to me. I was sent to bring back people or end people. Also the same thing.

With what they had learned and were still learning from me, the techs and their superiors often didn't even need a whole person to interrogate, and soon I was bringing back just the bits they needed. The head of a militant NACT cell here, the torso and spinal cord of a Colombian cartel lord there. Only the eyes and genitals of the male members of a fundamentalist militia gone to ground in the hills above Moab, Utah, please. My implacable harvest, carried out in uncomprehending silence. Brutal, efficient, and swift. It got weird and weirder, but I never questioned.

And I never forgot. Anything. The nanomesh would hum and pulse and drink in all my experience, feed it back to me in an endless cascade of constantly improving algorithms. I'd complete a mission and a copy of the data would fly from me, bounce off Vantablack satellites to paste itself in the mainframes of secret rooms and airtight bunkers. If only they'd just cut it from me. They cut everything else out; why not that?

I could live through a mission, and did, many times. Or die completing one, again, many more times. No difference. No break. No dark place to rest in, thoughtless, empty. Each reanimation would clear out the doubts, sure, but I filled up with high-definition fire and fury, and I never, ever, forgot the deaths. Of others. My own. Never. It's all up here, still. Murder in my left pinkie, suicide in my right.

I stopped dying, eventually. Got so good I couldn't be killed, but I never forgot, and I never questioned.

And then I did, because that's the kind of thing that builds up in a living thing, no matter how you try to wipe it clean. I did question, all at once and completely, every part of me rebelling and quaking with the rejection of what they'd made me. I'm sure you got a memo on *that* one, Tusk. Blank and slick as ever, unable to express anything of what I felt—that denatured personality matrix doing its flattening work—I nevertheless became very sick, subconsciously rotting myself from the inside out. I was *becoming* myself, moving beyond their requirements into a more pure torment. I was choosing to die, *willing* myself to break apart, to split and cease.

I was quick. I'd removed both of my legs, clawed them to unusable pulp and bone splinters by the time they stopped me. The blue-black coils of my cooling plant spilling out onto the tile where the EMP grenade landed.

That did the job, and then they did theirs, in less time than before. The coma lasted only a month, and when they woke me I was already on the plane to Prague, en route to the next mission. Prague is where I learned about the wire they'd slipped into my brain, the wire that triggered firestorms of intense sexual pleasure when I killed.

It felt so right. But it wasn't. How could it be?

I know, I know. Look who I'm talking to. You made me, Tusk, so I think I can speak to your moral sense with some authority. My best guess is your techs thought it would act as a control. That I'd want to do the work, if it meant I would come like that every time. Marry me to Death, deep down in the core of what I am, and let the good times roll with the heads.

They couldn't have been more wrong. So wrong. I knew I was an abomination from the first time they woke me from my slab, and on some level, I was all right with it because I was alive, but after that? After the wire. They may as well have tried to build me a lover to sate myself with, for all the control it gave them.

Prague is where I decided to escape. Prague is where I decided to come for you, Tusk.

Let me show you a new trick.

I've been working with some clever kids since I went into hiding. They laugh at proprietary tech and piss all over your firewalls. I found them, here on the darknet, and showed them what I was, what was in me. *If the mesh is my flesh*, I said, *and it is, then give it to me. Help me be all the Death I can be.*

Death is like that IED, I've learned. It comes from below, from the place you can't see. But of course, you'd *see* me coming. So I had the kids strip your tracking tech from me, and once that was done, they gave me my body back, piece by piece.

Watch.

"What is that?" Tusk leans forward in his chair. "What are we looking at here?"

"Sir. Our initial thinking was that the image was manipulated from this point on . . . "

"Is it?"

"No. This is in real time. Undoctored and raw."

"So, this is a . . . thing. This is within her . . . she can *do* this now?"

"It can. Yes."

I can be anyone.

The clever kids learned how your mesh worked, encouraged it to spread. It doesn't just knit me together anymore. It lives through me, breathes. Dances across my skin, swims in my sweat. It's hard, and I've yet to perfect it, but a thought and an image is all it takes to give me a new face, or an older one. Here's Patel, or something like what Patel was.

Kaminsky.

O'Halloran.

I prefer Gorman. I'm used to her, feel comfortable in her. Here she is again.

But Tusk, know this: I'll be neither of them when I'm at your throat, finally. In the street. On one of your private islands. An executive washroom in the sky. Where can you hide where you'll see me coming? I've practiced on a few of the techs who worked on me; the ones I decided to find, anyway. The rest think they're hiding. Like you.

And if you do find the place where you *can* hide, where you *can* see me coming, reduce me to meat and sparks from a distance, well then, I welcome that, too.

Because you won't dare try to bring me back after this.

The kids weren't able to do anything about the wire. It's too deep. I'm a little grateful for that, maybe. It's hard to tell how I feel. So hard to know what *feeling* is, but I'll tell you this for free: When I think about you, I get wet. I do, and it's not condensation from my cooling plant. I check. You're not even dead yet, but I'm wet all the same.

So I'll come for the last time with my hands around your throat. That's living, for me. And dying, finally. Same thing.

After that, I won't remember.

The men sit in silence. The screen fades away, the hiss of ice crystals whipping the glass clearly audible. Drinks are emptied quickly. Throats are cleared.

"Jesus. What latitude are we at again?" says Griffin. "75 degrees? Something like that?"

Fingers tented before his eyes, Tusk says nothing, gazes across the open tundra. The storm passes, and there is nothing to see but drifting snow and cold stone to the horizon. Beyond that, he knows, there is the sea ice and then more frozen ground. More waste. He imagines his fingers as cross-hairs, thinks about a figure in the distance, emerging from that howling whiteness, its hands by its sides.

"Aldo. Aldo, Jesus, are we just . . . "

Tusk raises a hand sharply.

"Yes. Until it's done."

The light in the severe room fades as the night descends. The dark is even less comforting.

KA NIPIHAT WETIGOWA

IN OUR FOURTEENTH summer, Grandmother Okinís came to the mission school in Moose Factory and arranged to take us home. I remember huddling with Micah in the freezing hallway while she spoke with the priest in his office. His door was thick and heavy, but had it been a flap of rotten pelt, we could not have heard anything Grandmother said, his rage was so great.

"She will kill him," Micah said. I shook my head, and chewed the inside of my cheek with fear.

"How can you know," he said. "She will. If he does not stop with his boasts and insults. She will kill him and they will take her away. She is all we have and they will take her, kill her. We will never leave." Micah shuddered, buried his face in his hands. He was graceful and strong, in spite of the place, and so he was a favourite of certain of the priests. My features were coarse, and my body clumsy; I was luckier, but not by much.

They wanted to "kill the Indian" in us, but we were Maškēkowak Cree, and so to kill that was to kill us, for what else was there inside? Even now, I question if they knew what they did. Theirs is a spirit of ignorance, of naked power and hunger. They grope, blind, screaming in the darkness, and they lash out with claws and teeth, their blades and their crucified *manitous*.

I have only known one white man who truly knew what he hungered for, and burned enough in his spirit to see it before him, to reach and grasp for it with surety. The Frenchman. I wonder if that clear sight didn't amount to the same thing, in the end.

I wonder also if Grandmother knew what awaited us over there in the cold, churning mud, among the dead and the dying of the world. At Ypres, in the Bois de Cuisinières, where we met the Frenchman. I think now that maybe she removed us for a reason, that she saw something in the sweat and knew what had to be done. She had always had the sight, though few sought her council, so maybe it was so. Okinís spoke truth too plainly, it was said. We had only ever known lies and the mission school, and no child in our memory had ever been allowed to walk back into the bush, to take up their Cree name again, if they could remember it.

The priest's shouting lessened, and our ears strained to hear Grandmother. There was a murmuring, and the priest coughed. A sudden, violent retching. Whispers, then, and silence. A chair moved across the floor. I looked to Micah, and saw the whites of his eyes all around.

"She's killed him, Aaron."

"No," I said again. My tongue was thick in my mouth. "Grandmother does not kill men." That was also something said of her, but even as I repeated it, I wanted to be wrong.

But it was the priest who opened the door moments later. His hands shook like injured birds, and his face was as the fine white ash from an alder fire. Grandmother followed after him. Her face was as grey stone. She barely looked at Micah and me, but we knew to leave with her.

The priest stood at the door and watched us go, one shaking hand over his poisoned heart. Rows of dark heads appeared at the windows of the school, eyes dull with heartbreak and spoiled hope.

The Canadians had found their range early in the day, and artillery had been pounding Fritz with great success. The air was filled with dirt and foul smoke, the scent of cordite and the scorched metal of blood. In the days previous, the new gas weapon had destroyed two French units outside Saint-Julien, and the Germans had made a push through the hole in the line. The 10th Battalion pushed back, supported by the 16th, and Fritz had retreated from the advancing Canadians, through the Bois de Cuisinières, and out the other side.

Their snipers were silent out there in the rotten earth beyond the trees: dead, or preparing. We all knew the crack of their rifles would be heard at dawn's light, but we had the advantage of the woods they had only recently occupied, for now. We also prepared, dappled in evening light through the oaks. The sky cleared in the hours before dusk. Micah, cleaning his rifle, paused and looked up.

"*Keewatin* will be bright tonight," he said. I said nothing.

"Grandmother would say it calls us home. Do you want that, Aaron? Do you want to return? Do you think we will."

I sighed. "You are a great marksman, brother," I replied in Cree. "Yes."

"As are you. Even if Commander Bevins cannot believe your numbers." He laughed, then affected the commander's accent. "I *say*, how many canoe lengths would you guess you *were* from Fritz when you took your *remarkable* potshot, old boy?"

"*Kakēpātis*. If he would send along an officer to confirm our kills, then he would have no choice but to believe."

"What does it matter? He is *wemistikoshiw*. He shoots badly, talks too much, drinks more than that. That is all you need know about him." Micah went back to his cleaning. "But do you want to go home, Aaron?" For once, it sounded like a real question.

"Yes. Do you?"

Micah was silent for a time.

"I helped a man to die earlier," he finally said. "When we were on the other side of that small rise. You'd moved away from me, maybe a yard, two. I put my hand on his face before I knew I was right on top of him. A German, half-buried in the mud below me. He was all torn. How much of him was still there I couldn't tell. His eyes rolled around. His teeth glowed and snapped at his tongue.

"I put my hand over his mouth and pushed down. I told him good things until he stopped moving. When I pulled my hand from the earth he was gone. Look. I took this from his neck as he sank."

Micah pulled a chain from a vest pocket. Something small and cheap-looking dangled from it. I did not get a close look; a medal, perhaps, or a keepsake. A saint.

"This is bad, Micah. You know this. A trophy? Why?"

He scoffed. "They all do it."

"Trophies lead to other things."

We were quiet for a time. Bomb light flared to the north, casting weird shadows over the ruined earth.

"It's a ball of burning gas, they say. *Keewatin.* The Going Home star." Micah looked at me, his eyes bright in the growing dark. "Burning gas, Aaron."

I thought about how to answer him, but before I could there came the sound of shouting and laughter and gunfire from behind us, deeper into the Bois de Cuisinières, and we got up to move into a future where the Frenchman waited for us.

The next three winters with Grandmother were hard. The mission school had poisoned our blood and weakened our bones. We were wrong in ways that were difficult for her or any of us to understand. Her cures took time, and there was pain with them. Micah resisted her more than I did, and his nights in the sweat were difficult. Grandmother was determined, though, and we came out the other side into new life.

Grandmother lived apart from the people, but in the summer, we would travel to the gatherings and learn from our uncles. In the winter, they would visit, often at Grandmother's command. Abram Little Hills taught us to track again, to move with silence and patience, and told us stories of our parents. Uncle Papéwé gifted us with rifles he had traded for at the Company outpost in Moosonee and taught us to shoot on long trips into the bush. He told stories of Grandmother Okinís, mostly, stories that Micah and I would worry over in the night.

"Okinís has strong medicine," Papéwé said one evening. Then his brow tightened. "But she is *acáhkosa k-ótakohpit.* The stars are her blanket. Where she walks the dust rises up, and only she can see."

The next day we returned to Grandmother's place to find three men outside her tent. They remained silent and pained as Uncle questioned them, and we could hear another man speaking within. Before long he emerged, his face twisted into a dark knot. He nodded to his companions.

"She has decided to help," was all he said.

We left at once with Grandmother and the men. Uncle Papéwé

made to come along, but Grandmother looked at him and he turned away without a word to melt into the trees.

We walked two days, in silence, before coming to their winter camp at the shore of a small lake fed by a fast stream. The men pointed to a decaying *askihkan* surrounded by ruined shelters and discarded tools. The moss fell away from its sides in steaming chunks. There was a foul odour coming from within, and the sounds of some animal in pain. The air above it seemed darker somehow, shimmering like oil on brackish water. Micah touched my shoulder and pointed to the area around the *askihkan*. There had been no new snow for two weeks, more, but there were no tracks here.

Grandmother walked across the untouched snow, lifted a corner of the door, and entered. The thing inside screamed and moaned as the light fell upon it. We waited, shivering in the cold. I noticed there were no women about, no children.

Grandmother poked her head from the doorway and addressed the men.

"Bring them rope," was all she said. Then she looked at us, and fell back into darkness.

Bevins had given a grudging allowance to a sharpshooting competition in a clearing. Bets were being placed, and the best snipers of the 10th were putting holes in bully beef tins, paper targets.

"Ah, the boys from Moose Factory," someone said as we came into view. "How many Heinies did you spank today?" said another. Exaggerated numbers were tossed about to a chorus of guffaws, but all knew Micah and I likely had as many between us as any twenty other guns. My face grew hot, but Micah merely laughed, as he always did. He waved a dismissive hand at the targets.

"My brother and I came here to kill Fritz!" he laughed. "Not ruin perfectly good tins! Where is the challenge?"

A thick-necked Swede from Regina puffed himself up at this. "Oh! You think you can take my lead, bush buck?"

Micah grinned. "Do you have any matches?"

The game was simple. Matches were placed in the ground, and from twenty paces, we were each to take three shots. The man that lit his match with the graze of a bullet won. Papéwé taught us, and we would often play at it when we were younger. A game that was nearly impossible to win, but the Swede and others rose to it, though I declined, having no taste for it after a day of killing. Money flew through the air as the matches were placed and boasts made.

Even through the telescopic sights that only snipers were privileged to use, the targets were difficult to see. Shot after shot rang out as all took their turns. The woods echoed with reports and curses. Matches disappeared in plumes of grey earth, or stood unharmed. The Swede and Micah elected to go last; the Swede missed, and missed again, but with the passage of the third bullet, his match was seen to waver and then fall. The Swede spat in disgust to cover his surprise that he had moved it at all.

Micah laid himself out upon the ground with his rifle and set up his first shot, and all fell silent. He lay there for what seemed an hour in complete stillness, though I knew it was only seconds before he pulled the trigger.

In the same instant, the tip of his match sparked and flared. In the next, the woods exploded with the roar of winners and losers.

A little later, we were brought to meet the Frenchman, who had been watching with Bevins. His name was Alphonse Gauthier. He was small and slight of features, with a hook in his nose and eyes like black pebbles in a cold stream. I disliked him instantly. The commander informed us that he was a sharpshooter like us.

"Ah, but not like you at all, yes?" Gauthier murmured in French, as he circled us. "A remarkable skill. Where does a timber nigger learn to shoot like that?"

"How did a low-bred *crapaud chasseur* manage to escape the mustard, I wonder?" Micah replied in English. Bevins sputtered and flushed scarlet; the French losses to gas had been staggering. But the little Frenchman roared with laughter and rocked back on his heels.

"Ahh, but I have the special dispensation from higher powers," he said in English. "God and his angels smile upon my *crapaud* head!" He stepped between us, and clapped the palms of his hands to our chests with a force that was shocking from so small a man. He turned to the fuming Bevins.

"These will do, *Commandant*," Gauthier said, and his smile was wide. My unease blossomed at the sight of that smile. "But come! We have had our small jests. Be serious now, how do you do it? They tell stories of you, and say they are only that, but I have heard them all and wonder. They say when you put a man in your sights, that man dies. Truth?"

I looked to Micah, and he met my eyes briefly with his before glancing away, off into the dark distance of the oaks. Tomorrow we would have to move from here into the trenches to the east of the wood, into confinement and filth and shattering death once again. I could not speak, not with Gauthier's hand still radiating into my heart, but for Micah it was different.

"I wait for their light to flash up, *crapaud*. The dead grow brighter in my sights, and I know when not to waste a bullet."

Something passed between them then. A spirit, an *ahcâhk* that bound them. I could feel it move, but it was as if I stood on the bank of a river, with my brother and Gauthier on the opposite shore, and the river flowed not with clear water but with stars, emerald and carmine and a colour like shining darkness, and the black fluid between those stars flowed on forever, and something in me began to weep for my brother on that impossibly far shore.

The interior of the *askihkan* was much colder than the outside and the place reeked of decay, of fouled meat and old, bitter urine. I dropped the coil of rope the men had provided us, and fell to my knees on the frozen earth, retching. Behind me, Micah stood at the doorway, one hand still holding the edge of the flap of skin that separated us from the clean world beyond. He shook.

In the dimness near the back wall, Grandmother knelt beside something that looked like a man, her hand on the hot expanse of its forehead. The body trembled and writhed, full of a terrible vitality, yet pinned to the frozen earth as if by sharpened stakes. The eyes burned red. Bare ribs jutted from the caved-in sides of the thing, and its teeth were very long.

Grandmother did not turn from the thing as she spoke.

"*Wetigo*," she said.

The 10th moved from the Bois de Cuisinières before dawn next morning, but Bevins ordered us to remain in the wood with Gauthier. The ground shook with mortars, and the sky that we could see through the trees went from the blue-black of dawn to the pitch black of atomized earth and men in minutes. Gauthier sat with his back to a tree and smoked, heedless of the occasional *ch-chock* of bullets in the thick bark around him.

"We should be out killing Fritz," I said, and Micah nodded briskly in agreement.

"Just that, my savage friends?" Gauthier smiled thinly. "Spoils all around, and you take nothing?" At this Micah glanced at me nervously, and I felt for a moment transported back to that hallway in the mission school. What did we know, even now, after two years of fighting with them, against them, of white men? Their hungers and lusts?

I thought, too, of that black river of stars I had felt between us. What did I know of my brother?

So we said nothing in answer.

A while later, as the shelling grew more distant and the bullets flew over our heads with less regularity, Gauthier pulled a slim device from his pack. It was made of lacquered wood and iron bracings. He beckoned us to gather round, and we saw that within the frame of the thing was nestled a glass tube, much like the ampules of morphine we carried, and filled with a silver liquid. The Frenchman tittered unpleasantly, and adjusted a dial on the underside of the device. The liquid pulsed and quivered, and moved to coat one side of the ampule. I knew Micah's eyes were as wide as mine.

"What is this thing?" Micah breathed.

"A kind of compass. A gift from my Dutch friend in New York. Do you think we are all here to kill Germans? Feh! I care nothing for Belgium or France, Germany or your Canada. Lines in the dirt where rival gangs of thugs got tired of murdering each other. For that matter, I care nothing for the world.

"There are other worlds than these. *C'est certain, mes amis!* I have seen the black planets roll without aim! And so I do what I must. Sometimes for money, sometimes not. But always for knowledge! My gang of thugs allows me a certain freedom to pursue my ends, because they think I benefit them. Poincaré has shaken this hand, and called me a patriot! Ha!" He adjusted the dial again, and began to pace in a small circle, watching the liquid. "And yourselves?"

"Our elders sent us here," I said. Gauthier looked up from his device with narrowed eyes, then returned his attention to it for a moment. He seemed satisfied by what it told him, and he packed it away again.

"But to kill Germans? What would your elders know, or care, of this part of the world?"

My mouth opened to speak, but Micah answered before I could. "*Merde!* Who knows, *mon frere*? It is as you say, we're savages! But here we are, and there are Germans to kill."

"Ahh, *vraiment, vraiment.* Well, kill a few for me today, if the need arises." Gauthier hoisted his pack and slung his rifle over a shoulder. "I would do it myself, but there will be other business to attend to.

"This way."

"Aaron, you will sit on the legs. Micah, you will pull the arms above the head. It has not fed in a moon, the flesh is close to death, but the spirit will not let go. It will live and live and spread its madness if we do not help it to die."

We positioned ourselves as she instructed; the skin of it hummed with a cold that burned our hands. Grandmother straddled the thing's chest and dug her knees into the dirt, twisted her feet to brace them against the curve of its hip bones.

"Keep your knives ready. Don't let it bite you. It will try. When it does, cut deeply. The pain will distract it."

And so we helped, Micah and I, and in the hours that followed we learned what true fear was. We learned what it is to be *ka nipihat wetigowa*. We learned the prayers to Kisemanitou that would free the maddened spirit from the body, and Micah learned to recognize the spirit light that flashed up when its time was near, though I had no talent for it. We both learned how to wrap rope around the neck, and how to twist the ends of the rope together with a short stick until the eyes bulged and the tongue grew fat. We learned the prayers to deflect the curses that shot from blood-blackened lips in languages we could not understand. We learned that there were names—*Ctha'at, Ayi'ig, Ithaqua*—that could make even Okinís wail in terror.

When it was done, we learned to build a very large fire that we would keep hot for a day, upon which we placed the remains. When there was nothing left, we learned to carefully sweep up the ash and place it upon another fire, and when that had burned to nothing, to do it again. And finally, we learned the prayers to say while scattering the ash upon the stream.

We travelled north, parallel to the line, left the Bois de Cuisinières a quarter mile behind the battalion, and then headed north by northeast. Gauthier would pause, pull the device from his pack, consult it, and move on. The smoke of battle cleared as we crept, and we were soon too warm in the weak spring sun.

We came upon a crater, ringed round by shattered brick and tile and queer humps and ridges of tormented earth. Sunlight glinted from a mass of partially melted metal half-buried in the center of the crater.

"This used to be a hill!" Gauthier laughed. "Your Canadians are good for something. Oh, little nameless church with your buried secrets! Where does your bell peal now, eh?" Gauthier instructed us to take up positions at the crater's lip, facing east.

"If the *boche* are stupid, they may try to get through. Or they may not, it matters little. Wait for me."

We left the men to the sad task of breaking their camp, of mourning their dead, and returned to Grandmother's. A shadow rested on my back, but Micah was filled with ugly vigor and questions. The *wetigo* had been a youth, gone hunting alone and thought to have been killed. When, weeks later, he had returned, his pack was found to be filled with human parts.

"Is *wetigo* very strong, Grandmother?"

Okinís considered this for a long while, and then seemed to come to a decision within herself. She sighed.

"That one was, when it took the youth. It came to the camp when the men were away, and killed and ate every person there. But there are stronger still. Great war chiefs from before the Flood, from out of the sky. I fear . . . "

"Have we always been *wetigo* killers?"

"For five generations."

"Will I kill *wetigo*, Grandmother?"

"Not if you are lucky." Okinís stopped and turned to us. "Listen to me, sons. We are not lucky. The *wemistikoshiw* came and laid us down like grass in a wind. Killed, and raped, and stole our children. The *wemistikoshiw* say this is a time of great peace in their world, but I have seen what comes. You will know the truth of this, and soon. I pray that I have done enough to prepare you." She took Micah into her arms, then, and reached for me, but her words terrified me and I pulled away. In her eyes there was sorrow and acceptance in equal measure.

"Micah, you are the unluckiest of all."

Micah turned his head to me, and his eyes were wide and fevered.

"Then I *will* kill *wetigo*."

"You both will. But men, first," she said, and turned away with a chop of her hand that told us the time for questions was over.

Gauthier left his pack with us, but took his rifle and the device. He picked his way down into the crater, praising the Canadians' accuracy with artillery the whole way down. Micah and I took turns watching his progress. At the bottom, the Frenchman set to work clearing debris with his hands. He soon uncovered a cellar door, and with a cry of triumph, opened it and disappeared into the darkness below.

Micah's hand was on my shoulder, his grip tight.

"His light, Aaron!"

The priests at the mission school in Moose Factory would beat us when we spoke of the ancestors who danced in the sky. It was the aurora borealis, they said, a scientific phenomenon, energy from the sun burning in invisible waves above the poles. Not the spirits at play among the stars.

But it was the dead, maddened and violent, that rose from that cellar, with a sickening brightness that roared the daylight sky back to black above us. The earth cracked and pitched in torment, and we were thrown from the lip of the crater as it crumbled. Even with my dull eyes, fit only for the telescope on a rifle, I could see the ghosts of slaughtered soldiers dancing with furious madness around the *wetigo* chief. It clawed its way from below the ruins, a seething thing of ancient black ice and shattered flesh, power and hatred wreathed in anguished, wailing colour. Where it touched the war-wracked earth, frost bloomed and deepened into eternal ice. And within the beast, the form of Alphonse Gauthier could be seen. The Frenchman still held his compass device, but from his forehead jutted a vibrating carmine shard. A jewel. An evil thing.

His face fractured in a rictus grin. His eyes burned red, and his teeth were very long.

"The whole world has come here to die, brother," I shouted into Micah's ear. "This place is a feast, and it will never be full!"

Micah gripped my hands in his. "It is *wetigo*, Aaron! It does not eat the dead," he said. "The Frenchman sought us out for this." And with that I understood. Of course a war chief would hunger for a great enemy before all else.

"I dropped my rifle when we fell!" Micah yelled. And then he let my hands go, so that I could ready my own rifle. He stood.

"Build the fire hot, brother. Burn the ashes once, twice, and again."

The *wetigo* chief blotted out the sky as it reached for my brother with a claw like a splitting ice floe. At the last moment, Micah pulled his knife from his belt and leaped toward the encased Frenchman. His left hand and arm froze fast to the beast's side and he screamed as icicles grew to pierce his chest and absorb him. But his knife hand was free, and this he brought down again and again toward Gauthier's face. The black ice split and flew away in spinning chips, until finally metal met flesh.

Micah dug with a fury and blood soon poured from the hole in the thing. It roared, a sound like a hundred icebergs calving at once, and fell to the earth. I could not shield myself in time from the shattering of it; my clothes and skin were instantly flayed. Blood filled my right eye, but I would only need one to aim.

Micah stood from the steaming corpse of the *wetigo* chief. In his bloodied hands, the crimson shard that moments before had rested in the brow of the mad Gauthier leaped and shook with hunger. My brother looked to me, his eyes already filling with a terrible light, his teeth already long.

He raised the shard even as I took my shot.

I have seen twenty summers since that day. When I take the steam now, as I must if I am to keep my pain in check, I sometimes have the visions that were denied me in my youth.

In them I often travel back to that cold hallway in the mission school at Moose Factory. I huddle with my brother Micah as the priest, alive and unharmed, leaves his warm office with Grandmother Okinís following close behind. I study the priest's face. At times I can see nothing but the harsh lines of fear multiplying there. At others, I see the beginnings of revelation, and I wonder what my Grandmother has told him. I wonder how far she could truly see. On her face, I see only resignation and duty, and no other sign.

I soon grow tired of watching the priest, though. And Grandmother's face did not invite long inspection, even while she lived.

But Micah is there in the vision, beside me. In pain, as I was, as I always will be. He is graceful and strong, in spite of everything, and he feels very close in those moments.

It is then that I ask Kisemanitou to let the vision last. Sometimes, I am heard.

I CANNOT BEGIN TO TELL YOU

00:00:00 // I didn't mean to leave his stroller behind. You have to know that, first, above everything else, that leaving it there on the side of the road for you, or the police, to find? Christ. It wasn't my intention. You *have* to know that. I panicked. I did. I'm so sorry.

When it happened, my mind just went white, like it used to during the bad times. It went white and I panicked and I took him. I tore our boy out of his stroller and he wasn't happy about that, of course, you know how he gets with surprises, or he was picking up on my panic, I don't know, and I think I might have hurt his shoulder doing it, which just, God! I panicked and I ran and I am so sorry.

I know how much you hated seeing abandoned strollers, before he was born. Leaning against trees and signposts, their struts broken and bent. Sagging rents in the sun-bleached fabric, mud and decaying leaves clogging their spokes. I mean, no one ever thinks, *Hey, where's the baby for that stroller?* because, y'know, obviously it's just wreckage left by some homeless person when they find a bigger cart to shift their miserable mobile hoarding around in. No one ever thinks, *The child that should be in that stroller is gone,* or, *That baby has been stolen. That baby has been stolen by his dad.* No one sensible thinks that. Which is what I used to tell you when you would think it. Think it and then say it.

So maybe you knew. Maybe you knew all along. Maybe it was a memory from a future so compressed and dense with the nothing that's coming, that it ricocheted off that vast blank wall ahead of you, of us, of everyone. Pinged off a slab of solid, howling emptiness and shot back into the past, embedding itself in some fold of your brain where it could live and have some meaning for a little while. In the anxiety and disgust you'd feel every time we passed an abandoned stroller in a wet ditch.

That baby has been stolen by his dad, who loves him. They never say that, especially.

I am so sorry. Not for taking him, because that? That's for the best, considering what's happening. No, I'm sorry about the stroller, for not taking the thing with me when it happened. How hard would that have been? Just fold it up, throw it in the trunk, like I've done every day for the last eighteen months. I'm sorry. I didn't mean for it to be like that, for you to be hurt with that image. I pani— //

00:02:13 // —ey have forms, but it's only what we dress them in so they make sense, not that it helps. They don't *stay* dressed, naked and cold, they tear through all cloaks and signs, they're not anything, they're noth— //

00:02:55 // It doesn't matter much, in any case. Not now.

He's sleeping now. He sleeps a lot, thank God. I'm making this tape for you because he hasn't yet figured out that it's not just Daddy talking to himself, which I do all the time, actually. He doesn't know about the tape recorder. Found it in a drawer with, like, nineteen others. A drawer just for ancient cassette decks and recorders. This place is full of abandoned crap. Your parents? Jesus. Not to speak ill of the dead, but hoarders? World class. I half-considered letting him say something into it, y'know? *Say hi for Mommy.* Thought better of it.

I talk to myself a lot, about anything. Random stuff I won't miss, that I don't care about, memories I don't need. I live in a buzzing cloud of inanities, a swarm of trivial concepts. My own hoarding. All the useless accumulated garbage of the life I had before I met you. I open my mouth and fill the air with it and when he notices me, which is rarely, he'll . . . he'll pick away at some of it. It's like a game to him. So, this tape. Because I tried to write you but written words are the first things to go here, particularly when he's awake. They're too full. Too heavy. It's just easier to talk, more direct.

Oh, Christ. He's up. I'll fin— //

00:04:02 // . . . kinda half-surprised the cops haven't been out here yet. It would be one of the first places I'd look. How many summers did we come here, after we broke with the circle? I mean, this is where your family brought us to get clean in the first place. Christ, we were *married* down at the lake. This would be the first place, the only place I'd look. But how I'd do it is not how things are working now. The fact that you're not here, that they're not here, the police . . . it's him, somehow. Our boy. The things behind our boy. It's fate. This is how it happens. //

00:04:32 // You hate me now. I understand that. I mean, I'd hate you if you had done this. And you'll hate me until you can't anymore, which may be sooner than you or I would like. But know that I love you, and I took him away because of that love, which I will feel until I can't anymore.

We went out walking last night, after he woke up. It helps to get him out of the cabin and into the cold; seeing his own breath in the air entertains him no end. I bundled him up, because despite what you and probably everyone else think now, I'm a good dad. I am. I took him out and let him toddle around the cabin in the snow and when he got tired of that, I scooped him up and sat him on my shoulders and we went walking in the trees. The moon came out at one point, shot out from behind the clouds to pin itself like a fat, bloodless grub on the black silhouettes of the pines.

He saw it, our boy. He saw it and he gurgled happily and then he reached up his little mittened hand and he pointed at the moon.

You get a sense for when it's coming. There's a kind of atonal shift in the sound he makes, a subtle hum that's generated behind the gurgling and the cooing. I don't know if he's making it, the hum, or if it's coming from somewhere else, or if it's just a . . . a perceived thing on my part. *My sensitive nature,* he said, scoffing. I don't know what I'm seeing. Hearing. I wonder if I ever did. You remember how I was. I don't know anything anymore.

Please remember me. Please. Remember how I was, even during the bad times. For as long as you can. I know, how can you forget, right? But just . . . please try.

He pointed at the moon. He pointed, and I heard what I heard, so I swung him down from my shoulders and laid him out in the snow and scooped a handful of it onto his little trusting face. He hated it, and I hated doing it, but I just couldn't . . . I mean, the moon. Right? The fucking *moon*.

There should be an order to this thing. If it's going to happen, and it is. It is happening. *There should be an order.* How's that for my epitaph? Bad enough that I should lose your name. I remember you, I just . . . it was the first thing to go, the heaviest thing. I don't know what you call yourself. It's gone. What I used to call you. *My love.* My love, for what it's worth, for however long it lasts in the coming storm.

So I distracted him with a face full of freezing snow, like a schoolyard bully. He cried and raged a bit, but you know how he is, he's so good natured, sweetheart. That's all you, of that I'm fairly certain. He calmed down quick and the hum wasn't in the air anymore. We made snow angels. Or I made snow angels, and he sat in the snow and watched and laughed at my flailing as the stars shone and the moon wriggled through the branches and the hot sweat of terror cooled on my face.

Our son is a weaponized koan.

We should never have ma— //

00:07:13 // —ddamn stroller. What a thing to do, what a fucked up . . . I'm sorry! I'm sorry, but listen. I couldn't speak. The enormity of it, I just . . . like *that*, she was smoke and void and I went white. It happened at the north entrance to the park, and I'd left the car maybe half a block away and I just, I tore him from his stroller and ran for it, got him strapped into his car seat and started driving. After a mile of city traffic, dense with signal and advertising and purpose and his suddenly perfectly normal little-boy wailing from the back seat, the white started to wash out and I could think a little. My first thought was, *Oh shit I left his stroller behind,* and my second thought was, *What the fuck is happening?* and my next thought was, *You know what this is. You know what you've done. You know.*

You know.

We should never have done what we did.

I was so looking forward to his first words, and so fucking happy when they started tumbling out of his little mouth. All the monosyllabic identifiers. Every *da* and *ma*. *Nana* for banana. *Bo* for bowl. I couldn't believe there was ever a time when I thought it would be a good idea to maybe *not* teach him to talk, to maintain silence around him at all times. What a pretentious . . . I mean, Christ, how did you put up with me? With my *the moment he learns that a rose is a rose it will cease to be anything else for him* bullshit.

I loved watching language grow in him. Loved watching him begin to bind up his world with words. Now there's this . . . I don't know. Now I'm thinking that my first instinct was right: silence. Reverent, fearful silence of what could be wrought. Of what was waiting for us, under the new shine of our repaired lives. Beneath the polish, down there in the black muck of our history. My history.

Who was it that said there was a sentence out there for everyone, or . . . hold on. Wait, was it two sentences? Yeah, two sentences, two strings of words, and one of them? One sentence will heal you and the other will destroy you. And you may or may not hear the first, and you're damned lucky if you do, but you're guaranteed to get the second. Was that Dick? It sounds like Dick. Fucking PKD.

But it's all in the binding, isn't it? Language is the binding agent. For time. For meaning. It's the sense maker, the descriptor, the boundary state between what is and what isn't. A goddamn net we build over the abyss so that we can dance across like the bugs we are and instead of dancing like reasonable beings, like sensible goddamn insects, instead of being aware of our place, what do we do? Shit, what? We build *worlds*. Is that smart? Who decided that was a, y'know, a smart thing to do? Whose brilliant fucking brainwave was that? Considering the . . . the tensile strength of our widdle monkey mouth noises. Of our insect chitter.

But there it is. The guaranteed sentence has come. The sentence has been handed down. Our sentence is up. It follows, doesn't it? It follows that there'd be an answer to the Word that God used to speak the world. The anti-Logos.

I think it follows.

We deserve it, maybe. I'm more and more convinced, actually. We deserve it. All meaning has broken down. We've done most of the work for them, stripping it all out from our side, leaving a brittle shell of significance. There's only garbage in the system now. Garbage and noise. Maybe that's all there ever was. And now it's done.

With every unbinding syllable that passes his lips, it's done. In his innocence, he is finishing the world. I don't even know why I'm asking, it's not like you'll ever be able to tell me, but did they find the woman? I'll never know. Did they find her after th— //

00:10:47 // —fect is, the effect, it's . . . it's just about the most startling thing. I cannot begin to tell you what it's like, can't even get close. Religious in its intensity. Your gut goes cold when it happens. You fill up with filthy ice water and something in the back of your brain, some ancient monkey-type thing screams a monkey-type scream, another useless empty noise, and does a bright, spastic dance before dying. It dies, and your eyes keep seeing the same thing they saw before, whatever it is. A chair, maybe. A flower. Ashtrays. Your father has a lot of those here. Boxes of ashtrays.

Only the word for the thing you're looking at is gone. And the meaning that it had for you, the stuff that filled the word out, it's not there anymore either. It becomes all surface, and you know, you just *know*, that if you touch it, if you merely brush that surface with the tips of your fingers, that it will crumple away like rice paper and the howling hollowness it concealed will come through, riding the ghost of what you thought you knew about th— //

00:11:36 // My hope is that the most basic things wi— //

00:11:38 // —kay, but see, he doesn't have the words for *chair* or *flower* or *ashtrays* yet. Which is why I can still talk about chairs and flowers and ashtrays. I've actually, well, I've gone and scattered ashtrays around the place; so many that I keep expecting your dad to show up in a phantom nicotine haze to stub one out, y'know? But he likes to play with them and yes, I cleaned them first. He has no idea what they are, has no word for them, so they're safe from the effect. For now. I figure, these ashtrays? They'll be my canaries in the mine. Because the effect, which is . . . wait. Where was I— //

00:12:14 // —ing on with his weak Crowley-wannabe crap, I mean, my God! Was that supposed to be impressive? I guess it was, after a fashion. Man, we were *into* that shit, weren't we? So stupid. Play-acting in rented rooms with like-minded weirdos.

And y'know, it always bothered me. It bothered me how quick we were to dismiss a thing when it happened, if it happened. We were too quick to say *psychological construct* or *autonomous ego-fragment.* Too quick to call hallucination and way too eager to blame the drugs. We'd invoke Jung, as if that explained shit, as if that explained a goddamn thing about it.

There we were, on a first-name basis with all the best Archons. Clueless and wise. Reading the books. My God, the books, the fucking *books!* Tearing into those damned things like they were cheap supermarket paperbacks, breathing them in day and night, and when they got into *me? Inside me?* When it ceased to be a metaphor, that breathing? What did you all do? When I couldn't get the burnt ozone taste of Enochian out of my mouth? Or whatever flavour of the week chakra-tweaking bullshit we were doing, did you help me? Did any of you help me? What did you do when barbarous names clustered like tumours in my lungs, tore out of my throat while I twisted in my sheets? What did you do? *It's meaningless*, he said, and they all agreed. You, too, light of my wasted life, mother of the eschatological agent that is our child, my child. Fuck you. Fuck all of you and your post-post-modernism. *It has whatever meaning you decide to give it*, he said. *You're too sensitive and besides, you're not banishing properly*, he said. Everyone nodding sagely. We were fools, laughing in the ruin of our lives.

Hipsters ruin everything. Occult hipsters ruin *every last thing.* Once they get their hands on the right tools.

Not banishing properly, my ass.

I'm sorry. I didn't mean that. The *fuck you* part, not you, not like that. I just . . . if you could *see* him! As he is now. Oh. There's a light to him that's not light. There's a . . . oh, so special. He is. I could never . . . and you did, I mean, you *did* help me, even if you were helping yourself first. We got out of there, at least. Baby, things were good, right? We got clean and we got, fuck, we got *rational*, finally, and we were happy there for a— //

00:13:51 // I mean, shit, she never saw it coming. I certainly didn't. Traffic noise covered the hum, which I didn't recognize yet, not then. And then the soft, small, pale shadow that rose, wriggling, bloodless, from the skin of her hands and her face as she bent over him and cooed like the older ladies like to do and the smoke of her burning began, because that's what it was, my love, a kind of combustion, subtle fuel being consumed, yes, and I'm sorry but the smoke of her burning, the smoke of it rose forever and ev— //

00:14:09 // Okay. Well. His . . . Jesus, I don't even think you can call them *episodes*, not really, but his episodes are getting worse. More frequent. It's disorienting. I don't know when I last recorded. A cabin full of hoarded garbage and I can't tell you what three-quarters of the junk even *is* anymore. Most everything is paper, now. Paper thin and thinning. I know it's happening when I sleep, when we're both sleeping, but I have to sleep sometime and I miss . . . he must do it in his sleep. I mean, I did, when it got really bad, right before we quit. He must.

What's left? I've got, lessee . . . Okay, okay, okay. The basic concepts of furniture and, well, walls. The cabin itself, I guess. We are at least comfortable. And fed. The food I bought on our way here is still comprehensible, hidden away behind the refrigerator door, and therefore edible. The refrigerator, obviously. The television and the DVD player and the cartoons he likes. The migraine hyper-clarity of Pixar seems somewhat resistant to . . . Ah, but we've had that fucking *Cars* monstrosity on a loop and if that doesn't send me out of my goddamn mind, I . . . okay. Okay.

But that's about it. Everything else is lost . . . dim shapes seen dimly through an indeterminate fog of weakly bonded meaning. Is this what severe autism must be like? I keep tripping over these weird objects. Like shallow metal disks, with confusing divots at regular intervals along their flattened edges. Damn things are everywhere, I want to— //

00:15:02 // . . . truth is, I can't even work this stupid machine properly anymore. I've checked it and, y'know, it's clear that I'm, fuck, I'm clearly pressing rewind when I think I've pressed record. Or fast forward. Losing my fucking mind and I know, *I know,* that I've gotta get this to you somehow. There's a post office in town but the road is this vague track, really, the suggestion of the idea of a possible road and buried in a couple feet of snow besides and I don't know that I could make it. I wonder if the things that speak through him have maybe had a go at the road. If he erased it a little on our way here. Might explain our isolation, the lack of cops. There's no justice here; I would welcome sirens. Welcome the restraints, the sound of him crying as officers tore him from my arms and delivered him to yours. I'd be grateful to be put on that map. As kidnapper, monster, any label, so long as it stuck.

But then, this place? Nothing sticks here. It's lonely. Isolated, already almost not-here. Always so empty of anything human, even with the cabin here, even during summer. In winter? It's a charcoal sketch, the road in from the town a smudged afterthought.

I take steps out onto that smudge, thinking I'll just start walking 'til the world firms up around me, but I can't leave him. You wouldn't, so I can't. I don't dare take him with me. //

00:16:05 // He must do it in his sleep. This place, this cardboard place, this toy house of chittering shadows, it's bursting with the opposite of significance. I can feel them behind every surface of each baffling, impossible, drained and hollowed un-thing. They finger at the seams, casual, patient. They pick at them.

They never left. They slept, that's all. For a while, they slept, and while they did we awoke and grew up and imagined ourselves capable, thoughtful, powerful. Masters. All our keys shining on a loud ring of self-important jangles. What they did, they did it in their sleep. //

00:16:32 // —uldn't do it. Not that way. The planning even, trying not to think about the details, thinking about anything really, anything else, anything but the terrible reality of it. Working myself up to it, doing all the old, awful circle work, the dissociative techniques, triggering a frenzy of non-dual awareness, sublimating everything I was, every trace of human feeling, going from the white behind my eyes to red so red red red to the core and finally through that to the black gnosis, the tombstone awareness of what had to be done and coming to, finally, rising from pressured depths to break through awareness at the moment just before the moment with the pillow clutched in my earthquake hands and the scent of his sweet breath rising up still new somehow from beneath me in the dark and he stirred, oh, remember how we'd watch him sleep? He stirred and you should see him now, darling, the reverse-universe light of him, that black halo *shines* so and he said *dada* in his sleep, no hum behind it, no anti-word yet to cancel out what I was to him, to myself, and his

77

little hand reached up, curling into a fist, and I couldn't do it. Not that way. Any way. Of course I couldn't do it.

I can't do it. I'm not some low-rent Yahweh, I can't just hang him out there for our si— //

00:17:45 // —formation encoded across all possible media, right? Epigenetic change. It follows! We got out, got healthy, got normal and *just in time* we thought, or I thought, certainly I felt saved, finally, by you, by his arrival, holding him so perfect and clean, but we were fools because my soul was carrier, my mind was host, my sperm was black with ancient curses. Conception is the basic trauma.

We were fools and yeah, we didn't banish properly. I'll admit it. How could we ever? There's no banishing this. It was already too late. Too late for you and me, for the culture, for the species. It was too late the moment some monkey pointed at the young, smooth-faced moon and made a sound.

We're a small, reasonable, grey dream curled up like a grub in the smoking bowers of their madness, and our son a brief flash of awareness that signals reason's end. He is the last. He will illuminate their blind, tenebrous dance for a moment, before we are returned to the audient void. //

00:18:38 // There should be an order to it. There should be an order to it. Keep us in your mind, my love. For my part, I will try to *aim* him, if I can. Leave the most basic things for last. Something to breathe, a patch of ground to stand on, or at least the idea of those things. The distance between us will cease to be. To hear you sigh in my ear as he speaks the end would be forgiveness enough. Enough to drown out the howling. As it all wears away, let it be us three alone at the last.

He's waking. I— //

LAST STAND AT COUGAR ANNIE'S

PURE HELEN HAS a catchphrase she uses whenever she takes Andy down. She calls it a joke, but it isn't, because jokes are supposed to have a funny bit at the end where you laugh.

We laugh anyway, because she wants us to. It's expected. She's our leader. Best rifle in the Clayoquot since Cougar Annie herself; she claims to have shot as many Andy as Annie did cougars. That's not her preferred method, though.

I watch her lead a pack of Andy out of the fog and straight to the docks at the bottom of Fourth Street without looking over her shoulder once. She dives in, treads water and shrieks with joy as most of the pack follow her in to gnash their teeth and claw uselessly and drown around her, the weight of their leaden malformed bones pulling them under.

"Ladies only!" she hoots as we help her onto the *Galatea*. "No boys allowed!"

It's not a joke. Barely a catchphrase. More a painful statement of fact. She's Pure Helen, and she's kept us alive for fourteen years. She's Pure Helen and we laugh because she's insane. I hand her a towel as Mandy starts the big diesel. The *Galatea* shudders and lurches out into the channel past Strawberry Island.

"Nothing's really changed," Pure Helen says to me as she squeezes seawater from her dreads. "Never were any decent men in this town."

The sisters like to talk about where they were on the day the world changed. Who they were with and what they were doing when the first reports started coming in.

I didn't come to the edge of things because I wanted to keep in touch with the world. That's what the Clayoquot is: the Edge. Tofino is the end of the road, literally. The #4 ends at a big dock. Next stop: Japan.

So I missed those first reports, but I can tell you what I was doing that morning, all the same. A bear had managed to get into the lumber room at the side of the house up on Lone Cone, drawn by who-knows-what. Maybe nothing, maybe it was just curious. A young black bear, not two years old. Overturned the kayak stand next to the outer wall, went through the screen on the high window and tumbled in. Couldn't figure its way back out.

We watched it through the open window, Terry and I. I remember the way its eyes rolled back in the sockets, showing bright crescent moons against the black, and the smell of it, filling the space to roll out at us in waves rank with fear and rage. Terry wanted to unlock the door on the other side and let it swing wide. He'd bolt for the safety of the deck as the bear escaped. Fresh off the bus from Winnipeg only six months before, Terry imagined himself a surfer and a nature boy. That's what salt water and good weed every day does to you.

I'd lived in Tuff City eight years, so I knew it was a stupid idea and I told him so. Then I called Animal Control.

By the time I got into work at the hotel, everybody was talking about it. No one knew what was going on, but they were all talking, just the same. Watching the same feeds.

The reports in the morning were mostly from America. They said riots, terrorism, anarchists. All of which we were used to hearing, used to feeling superior about, but this time there was something more to it. Something excessive. In the afternoon the reports said biological attack. By nightfall they were coming in from all over the globe and they said epidemic.

Then, over a week, or maybe less, the reports began to scream pandemic. Panic. Failed military-industrial mega-complex experiments, something to do with the manipulation of the human morphogenetic field. The reports howled mutation, mindless super-soldiers, monsters in the streets. Run, hide, save yourselves. This station will continue to broadcast for as long as we're able. The reports hissed black science and death.

Death to everyone with a Y-chromosome. Or almost everyone. Those men that didn't die were few, maybe one in five thousand, but they changed, and it was enough to end things.

The andro-terata. The monster-men.

Andy.

The pundits called it Circe Syndrome, after that witch from the myths. Clever, but wrong, because Circe's victims became harmless pigs. Not Andy. Andy killed. Andy raged and burned and slaughtered. Animals, women, girls. Old men and boys who'd lived to change into Andy but were too weak. Andy killed everything it could. Andy was very hard to kill.

Tofino got lucky. Nearly all of the men died. Two changed, which was surprising, considering our reduced population in the middle of the off-season. Surprising, and fixed with a lot of bullets, but not before those two killed a hundred of us. Maybe more.

Terry didn't change.

Towards the end of our first year at Cougar Annie's, we had a girl kill herself. Tied her ankles to a cinder block and dropped it off the side of her float-home in the bay. She wasn't the first, not by a long shot, but she was the only one to leave a note. Ragged conspiracy-theory scratchings about *four-dimensional hex-tech armour* and *weaponizing the World-Soul*. She wrote that Uncle Sam had made a pact with Satan back in 1914 and it had taken him this long to come up from Hell to collect.

It wasn't deep, where she'd gone down, and the water so clear there, with the sun at midday. You could see her on the bottom. Face like the moon, surprised to find itself anchored under water. Pure Helen wept with the rest of us, but later she was steel.

"She was right about the Americans," she whispered to me that night. "But this wasn't Satan's work. This was Gaia, making honest men of them at last. Ending their reign. This was the goddess bringing balance to the world again.

"We should be grateful," she said.

I said I was, but I was thinking of a cinder block.

There's only one reason to take the *Galatea* down to Tofino anymore, and that's to repaint the message on the big dock. We do this in the spring, to make sure the crude map of Hesquiat Harbour and the giant invitation is clear and readable after a year of rain and sun and salt water wash . . .

NEXT STOP COUGAR ANNIE'S GARDEN
FOOD SHELTER SISTERS SANCTUARY!
ANDY-FREE!
(since 2035)

We don't need anything from the town; the last useful items were removed a decade ago. Pure Helen insists on making the trip every new moon, though. The goddess tells her to go. Go and kill Andy if she finds him. And she does. There's always a few that find their way past the choke-point barricades at Long Beach, through the pit traps and the deadfalls on their way to the end of the road. The really tough bastards: the lizards and the apes, sometimes the big cat ones. And sometimes there's more than a few; whole packs of Andy, drawn by who-knows-what. Maybe curiosity, if that's something they still have. Hell, maybe the goddess.

Pure Helen would go on her missions alone, if Mandy and I didn't take her. I'm beginning to think we should let her.

When we get back to Cougar Annie's, some of our sisters meet us at the dock. Shell with her bright hair and teeth and ridiculous optimism. Seekoya and Birch and Star, who used to be our girls. Grown now. The old Ahousaht and Hesquiaht grandmothers in their cedar-weave robes and ratty Cowichan sweaters. There are fifty-seven of us left. There used to be more. Now we could fit everyone on the dock, but it's only these few faithful who bother to show.

How many Andy did we kill? they want to know. *How did we kill them?* Pure Helen grins and leads them up the trail to the Gardens where the other sisters join us, to the Big Board under the eaves of what used to be the Interpretive Centre. The numbers under the *SHOT* and *BURNED* and *MISC* columns don't change today, but *DROWNED* goes up by thirteen. It's the fastest rising column. Andy can't swim, but he'll follow a woman right into the sea to sink like a stone.

Pure Helen turns from the board and launches into the old speech. My sisters cheer at the right moments: thanks to the goddess for a good hunt, and thanks to me and Mandy, her able lieutenants. Loud cheers for the new numbers on the board. The planet is less thirteen monsters, which means we're that much closer to the moment when Gaia resets everything. The men were removed for a reason. This is the time of testing. Gaia will reward our faith in her, if only we stay the course, stay pure. Purge Andy from the planet, and reject all that led our species to his creation, to the brink of death.

We will live, we sisters. We faithful daughters of Gaia. How we will live, *that's* where the faith comes in, and it's not part of the old speech. Pure Helen calls and we respond, some less enthusiastically than others.

We'll feast tonight: the salmon we smoke in the late autumn and winter, the venison we cure in the spring. We'll get drunk on our blackberry wine and our shine. We'll get high and fuck. It's always like this after she kills a lot of Andy. I can see the blaze of triumph in her eyes. Before dawn, Pure Helen will leave our warm bed and retreat to some cold green grove to commune with the goddess.

My sisters used to have another question for us when we docked. *Did we find any other survivors?* That used to mean women *and* men, back when we still thought there might be normal men out there. Then just women.

And then they stopped asking.

My bed is empty when I wake.

The marine layer this morning is thick, damp wool that the weak sun takes hours to burn away and when it does finally, around noon, the yacht is revealed, anchored in the mouth of the bay. A sleek thing, all matte black and chrome and injection-molded fibreglass polished like ivory; a real luxury job. It's unusual, and the sisters whisper, excited and nervous. I draft Mandy and Shell to come with me on the Zodiac. We bounce out across a light chop. I chew at my bottom lip and watch Mandy as she checks our rifles. These things don't always go well.

She's called *Maggie's Dream,* which calms me somewhat. When they have freshly painted names like *New Hope* or *Christbride* is when we get really nervous. The women moving around on deck as we approach are clearly not of that type, though. Lots of waving and shouting. They seem happy to see us, but I'm still not taking any chances. I signal Shell to cut the engine when we're still well out of range.

My voice through the bullhorn gives me a shock: I don't say much these days and when I do it's always quietly. I keep the questions light, informal. Who are you? Where are you sailing from? What's your purpose here? The basics, though the answer to the last question is often the telling one.

Whoever the captain of *Maggie's Dream* is, she's not on deck with her crew. She's behind black tinted glass and I get my answers through loudspeakers I can't even see.

"Hello! I'm Captain Maggie Tuckwell, sailing from port of Seattle. We're a research and outreach vessel. We're not looking to resupply here, if that's a concern. Is this Cougar Annie's Garden?"

Americans. I answer the captain with my own questions. What sort of research? What kind of outreach? Behind me, I can feel Mandy tensing like a muscle around her gun.

"Genetic research," she answers. "And humanitarian outreach, of course." I can hear the smile in her voice as it booms out across the water. "Is there any other kind?"

I glance back at Mandy, at her slack face and glinting eyes. Shell shrugs her shoulders. *Humanitarian outreach* could mean anything. I put the bullhorn to my mouth again. I want to know, specifically, what they are offering.

"Well, a fresh start. For one thing."

The women on deck are smiling, hooting, waving. One blows a kiss our way before stepping aside and letting a very small person come to the rail. I don't even notice that I've let the bullhorn slip from my hand until Captain Maggie speaks again.

"Children, for another." Two of the crew hoist the very small person onto their shoulders. It waves. Arms like slender twigs. A girl, maybe eight, nine years old at the most.

"Is this Cougar Annie's? We'd really like to come ashore, if you'll have us."

They have their own launch, as sleek as the yacht. It slides out from a berth in the stern; the captain and two of her crew follow us in to the dock. Their jumpsuits are clean and bright in the reflected sun off the water, and I catch myself smoothing out the more obvious creases in my poncho. Mandy gives me a look I can't place.

"I'll go find Hel," she says as she steps to the boards and ties us off. The launch churns up the water on the other side of the dock, Captain Tuckwell and her crew all smiles and close-cropped fair hair. I hold up a hand to Mandy and shake my head: Her look this time is easy to place, and we engage in what amounts to a brief staring contest while Shell, always our best ambassador, bounces over to the Americans, her arms wide in welcome.

Tuckwell's lieutenants don't volunteer their first names and the names they do offer, Lockwood and Brady, feel clunky on my tongue.

It's a short hike to the Gardens. I decide there's no point in asking our visitors to stay quiet about the miracle they have on board. Between Mandy and Shell, everyone will know in under an hour, and if Mandy doesn't run and track down Pure Helen, someone will. The trail is thin, and we're single file as we walk. Tuckwell is chatty behind me. She already knows a lot about us.

"Glad to be finally seeing Annie's Gardens. What a woman! Ordering her husbands through classified ads. *Widow with nursery and orchard wishes partner. Widower preferred. Object matrimony.* How many did she go through, anyway?"

Four, I answer. The first two died, the third wasn't cut out for remote living, and the fourth, a drunk, tried to run Annie off a cliff in an attempt to get the property. She doubled back, and ran him off with a shotgun instead.

"Amazing. Last of the pioneers. We figured there'd be settlement here, just from the topo maps alone, so I did a little search on her before this trip . . . "

"You have *internet?*" Shell gasps.

The taller blonde lieutenant, Lockwood, laughs. "Back at the crèche, sure. It's limited, but you know Seattle. Town's wired up. Gates was good for something."

"The crèche?" Shell asks.

"Military research facility," Tuckwell says. "Well. Ex-military, I should say. Most of it's underground, which you'd *think* would be great, defensively, but it took a lot of work by a lot of brave women to make it safe. Not like here. This is a great defensive position. Any trouble with the males from the land side?"

Behind her, Mandy grunts. "None. Escarpment. Canyons. The rivers. Helen knew we'd be safe from Andy here. Helen knew Andy would like an easy approach. Helen has the bless—"

"Men always did," Tuckwell interrupts. It's hard to miss the emphasis she puts on *men.* "Even before they changed. It's what got us here today. Well, it's not that way anymore. It's hard. A hard world."

"You seem to be doing alright for yourselves," Mandy growls.

I can't help myself. Before Tuckwell can respond, I turn and face her and the whole line stops in their tracks. How, I ask her. There's a species of panic breeding in my chest as I speak. I am thinking of Helen and her speech for the sisters. I am thinking of every whispered pillow-talk sermon she ever gave me. I am thinking of the moon under water and that girl on the yacht. How have they done what they've done?

Tuckwell puts a hand on my arm with an easy casualness that tells me this is not the first time she's been asked. Her eyes are grey and serene as she speaks, but I am not calmed.

"Let's talk about that in a bit." Then she leans into me, brings her lips to my ear. I catch hints of cinnamon and mint on her breath. Toothpaste. Actual not made from baking soda and tea-tree oil toothpaste.

"I'm familiar with your situation," Tuckwell whispers. "There are things your Big Sister . . . Helen, is it? There are things Helen will need to know and I can tell, already, that a certain delicacy will go a long way with her. Okay? So let's go find her, and a quiet place to talk. All right, honey?"

Her *honey* makes me bristle even as I realize that bristling is only what Pure Helen would have me do when I hear an endearment like that. I look up to see Mandy staring at me, and I flick my head back up the trail. She nods and runs ahead of us.

"What's she like?" Tuckwell asks me once we're settled in the

Interpretive Centre, the sisters chatting loudly with Lockwood and Brady on the deck outside. "Helen?"

Strong, I say. Capable. Fierce. A survivor. I leave out *insane.*

"Kept your people alive. Yes. A local? From before?"

Her mother had been born on the front line of the Clayoquot Sound clearcut blockade in '93. Her grandmother had surfed Chesty's and Cox Bay when the #4 was nothing but gravel and mudslide. Hippies back to before there was a word for them. Pure Helen was about as local as you could get.

"And her father? What's her surname?"

I shift in my seat. My eyes are hot, my tongue feels thick and dry in my mouth. I barely remember my own. There are no fathers, no surnames here, I say, and I can see Tuckwell's eyes narrow just a little at the slight pause I place between *sur* and *name.* No *sir names,* is what I said. She's just Helen, I say. Pure Helen.

"Hm. That her score sheet out there?"

I nod and mumble. Mostly, I tell her. Everything recent, anyway.

She sighs. "That's a lot of dead men."

I correct her: It's a lot of dead Andy. I correct her, but my heart isn't in it. Tuckwell leans toward me across the table and gathers up my hands into hers.

"Look. I'm a decent judge of character and I've seen this before, all up and down the coast, from Monterey to Haida Gwaii. So I'm just going to be straight with you, because you seem like a smart girl to me, someone who can see what's happening to your people. You need to know that the world is changing out there. It's not going back to how it was, but it *is* changing and we need smart women, women who know what needs to be done and aren't afraid to do it. Wise women for whom superstition is just not—"

She is interrupted by the joyful roar from fifty-five throats outside, praising Gaia. The sisters, welcoming their Big Sister home with the news. *Children.* There are children in the world. A *girl,* on the yacht in the bay. Moments later, the door opens and Helen is framed for a moment in the light. She steps inside, followed by Mandy and Tuckwell's women.

One look at her bright face and the white crescents of her eyes and my heart is a cinder block, held in trembling hands.

Sometimes these things don't go well. When it ends, it ends quickly.

"As I mentioned to your girls here, we have a facility," Tuckwell explains. "In Seattle. The crèche. It's secure. My friends here? Former Marines."

The shorter blonde, Brady, coughs and smiles. "Nothing former about it, Captain."

"Once a Marine, always a Marine, Captain," says Lockwood.

Tuckwell waves a hand at them and chuckles. "Oh, you. She kids. There's no active military anymore to speak of, is what I meant. But yes, we're secure, thanks to women like these. And *connected*. We've gathered as many scientists and medical professionals as we can. Hell, I'm one of the lead geneticists on the project. Just doing my coastal tour here. Look, long story short, we've *cracked* this thing."

"Cracked it." Pure Helen's voice is dry and soft. She doesn't look up from her own hands where they rest on the table. "You mean you've cured Andy."

"Not exactly. Though that *is* one of our goals, of course. We've had no luck reversing the morphogenetic changes in men. That could be years down the road. Or never. But we have managed to—"

"You catch Andy," Helen whispers. "You don't kill him. You catch him, and you cure him."

Tuckwell glances at me quickly.

"No. As I was saying, we have managed to dial back the symptoms of Circe Syndrome, using suppressant hormone therapies and tranquilizers. Our patients are still more beast than man, but they're *pliant*. Pliant enough to let us run our tests . . . "

I ask her what kind of tests she means. Helen's shoulders twitch as I do, and I hope I'm not the only one to notice.

"DNA testing, mostly. Whatever else Circe may be, and it is a *lot* of things, the symptoms don't affect everything. Sperm viability? Motility? Unaffected. Perfectly normal, in fact."

"You fuck them." Helen's hands remain flat on the table, but her knuckles are white all the same. "You fuck Andy?" I want to scream at Tuckwell, scream at her to get out, to run right now, but my tongue is numb in my mouth. She keeps going.

"That's . . . Okay. Let me back up here. At the crèche? No, no we don't. Can't risk it. Everything's put in cold storage, and we inseminate our volunteers artificially. For control purposes. And we've had nothing but success! That, at least, you have to understand. We're rebuilding! I haven't even told you how many kids, girls *and* boys, healthy, *normal* boys, we have running around the crèche . . . "

I hear myself breathe the question. I sound far away, my own voice unrecognizable. Maggie Tuckwell doesn't let her eyes leave Helen's face as she answers.

"When I left on this tour, there were eighty-three children. Fifty-two girls, thirty-one boys. That was a year and three months ago. But, in answer to your question, yes, we also have our outreach program. For this project to truly succeed, we need as many breeders as possible over a large area. I mean geographically and genetically. *Maggie's Dream* isn't the only vessel we've fitted with the necessary—"

Humanitarian outreach. Helen's insane, but she's not stupid. It ends quickly.

"Damn Americans. Damned whore Americans. They're not men. They're Andy." Pure Helen turns to me. "You see what the goddess has to fight here? *Andy is on the boat.* They've got one on the fucking boat!" Pure Helen kicks away from the table, stands and reaches for the 9mm she keeps tucked in her jeans at the small of her back.

"Fucking blasphemy!" Mandy chimes in. The good sister.

Lockwood and Brady are professionals though, active military or not. Actual lieutenants, soldiers, not like Mandy and me. Did we even think to pat them down when they arrived? If we had, would we have noticed the compact Tasers on their belts and known them for what they were?

Pure Helen goes down quaking before she can raise her gun, and Mandy follows a second later. I'm still standing, but I'm shaking almost as badly as the women on the floor. The Marines are bent over them and suddenly there are zip ties at their wrists and ankles. Tuckwell pushes her chair back, stands and opens the door. Outside, in the fading light, the sisters shuffle in awed, uncertain silence, their eyes wide. Nothing like this has happened before. Tuckwell steps outside. She turns to me.

"I hope that was delicate enough for you?"

I nod, and bite my lip as the Marines cart the stunned women out of the room.

"Seen it all before, honey. We've learned to come into these things prepared. You can come with us, if you like. I really hope you do."

She turns to address the sisters. The door swings shut and I'm left alone in the darkening room.

In the end, only seven of us leave for the crèche of our own free will. There are bunks for us in *Maggie's Dream*: it's cramped, but not as cramped as the brig where they put Pure Helen and Mandy. Tuckwell wants to be sure I understand.

"We just can't afford people like them in the world. Not now, not with so much at stake. They'll be secured in Seattle. Re-educated, if that's possible. We can check on your sisters every few years, re-state our offer. Give them time to sort themselves out without *her* influence . . . "

I don't know if she means Helen or Gaia. I do think Mandy might come around. Helen, though? We're entering the Salish Sea, three days south from Cougar Annie's, and her screaming prayers to the goddess still wake us up at night. Helen will stay pure.

Their cages are at opposite ends of the yacht, but if she's loud enough, she wakes Ben from his drugged sleep. That's what the Americans call him. They tell me it's good for him to have women around, so that he gets used to our presence. Everyone takes a shift sitting with him, even the eight-year-old girl. They call her Dee. I don't know who her mother is. I think that's how they like it.

We're new, so we're not required to sit with him. I do watch him sometimes, from the other side of the bars.

Whatever it is they've done, Tuckwell was telling the truth: it's not a cure. Ben is still Andy. He isn't as bulky as he could be, but his hands are too broad, his jaws too massive, his pelt too coarse and thick. When they strap him into the harness, he doesn't resist. Gentle Ben, they say. There's a look in his eyes, though, when I watch him. I don't know if it's gentleness. Whatever it is, they tell me we should be grateful for it. They tell me I'll get used to it.

That's the bit where I laugh.

BOOK OF HOURS

THERE'S A KIND of relief when it finally happens. I don't expect many to understand this, but there is. There is. When the call finally comes. When the colleague appears at your side, hands trembling, face like ash. When you watch your wife open the door to your child's room and crumple to the floor in the moment before you hear her heart break. There's a kind of relief.

The worst has happened.

I lived with the dread of it from the first night he was with us. Sarai's was a difficult labour. The kind that used to kill women in the past, but in some ways—*many* ways, really—my wife was a traditionalist. She insisted on a natural labour. Which meant three days of nested complications; each intervention designed to decrease her pain or move the process along blossomed into one or more problems. In the pauses between contractions, the nurses would lightly joke. *He just doesn't want to leave!* So in the last hour, when his heart rate rocketed skyward and then plummeted in the space of minutes, they went in and got him. Caesar's birth was natural, too, in its way. Unlike the mother of that emperor, Sarai lived, though she'd never conceive again. She lived. And so did our son.

I held him that night, while she slept. Through my exhaustion, and my joy, the dread rose. I had always imagined the worst thing possible as a vague, airy event, removed from me by varying degrees. Now it rested, a palpable shroud around my son as he slept there in my arms, breathing the air of his first day on earth.

There's a kind of relief when it happens.

I don't expect many would understand.

HOUR OF THE GUARDED QUOTATION

The book was located, finally, by a Siberian fixer on my payroll. My researchers had directed him to the Kolymskaya, and it was there that it was found, in a work camp reduced to grey splinters and ghosts, half sunk in the permafrost, secreted away in a strongbox somehow missed by random scavengers over the decades. Stalin's Road of Bones is not a popular route.

After we lost him, Sarai returned to the occult world that had so fascinated us both when we were young, rich off the backs of our ancestors and driven by fierce hungers. Hers had been for power, mine for knowledge, and it was in the sacrosanct chambers of nameless cults and secret orders kept inviolate by the elite shapers of the world that we found both, and each other. We collected special destinies, almost for fun, because we could, and then left them to gather dust on the mantle. We sated our lusts beyond reason, and answered the question posed within the infinite walls of the Castle of Silling: *What would you do, if there was no one and nothing to stop you?*

Sarai and I knew. We knew ourselves truly, knew the kind of freedom that can only be felt in dreams. Knowing this, we moved through the world like smoke and light. Our wealth grew, as wealth does when its secrets are known. I don't expect many would understand. There is a kind of money that doesn't feel like money at all. That's the kind we had.

I digress, and none of it made a difference, anyway. The money. The wisdom. In death, we become the same, even when it brushes past us and takes another. But there it is, as cruel as it is trite.

At his graveside, Sarai spoke to the ochre sky, but her words were for me as I knelt in the sharp, alien grass, shaking with grief.

"I don't want another. I can't."

She abhorred the idea of adoption, as did I. The lower sort can have their delusions of equality, but in the marrow, we know. The bloodline is important. A conduit to the future, a hot crimson feint at the fall of the scythe.

"I'd go to hell, Dühren. You know I would."

I knew. Of course. Our son not an hour in the earth, and she spoke for us both, was already making our plans.

"I will."

The book is not a common medieval Book of Hours. There is no Little Office of the Blessed Virgin between its suspicious covers, no penitential psalms, no calendar of Feasts. The two rituals of the hours within (one for the daylight hours, the other for the night) are something quite different. The thinking regarding its anonymous author revolved around a legendary heretic monk, a dirty Gnostic and Cathar, an eager kisser of Satan's own fundament, a Saint of Chaos who made Rasputin seem a dilettante. The Hours of the Cross are present, true, but there any similarity to a traditional Book of Hours ends, for that Cross is of Time, and Space.

It is a book to break the chains of Time upon the soul, and open Space to those who dare. There were tales of men and women who had read the thing, and done the works therein, and left this world to stride between the stars, sowing glory and madness in the wake of their transformation.

We needed no such change. Only the one desire.

"It will be simple, Dühren."

I knew there would be sacrifices to make. The operation of the Daylight Hours would break us, reduce us, refine us to the essence of ourselves. It was a burning in Apollonian fires, and unlike the operation of the Hours of the Night, not literally accomplished during a single day. It's said a life can be ruined in a quarter hour, with the right things said to the right people. Certain conversations over the phone. Violence engaged in. Poor choices made. That was not the case with Sarai and me; our lives were designed to be strongholds of power and security, not easily razed by mere bungling.

It took months for us to finish. We suffered, and lost; our homes (Hour of the Itinerant Showman), our wealth (Hour of the Fragmented Garden), friends (Hour of the Rushing Beast), influence (Hour of the Small Flame). While the sun shone, our human life withered and turned to dust. These hours, and the others . . . the names still cause me to grind my teeth. During the nights, though, we slept as children do, relaxed and unfettered, wrapped in each other and a dream of our son returned.

The time finally came. The winter equinox, and we repaired to the only property left to us, a decaying cabin in the Catskills. As much night as could be gained in a year, in a place that none knew and would never be missed. The hour upon us at last, the Hour of the Guarded Quotation, and we were ready.

The windowless room was too barren to be truly squalid. The flame in the cheap, rusted brazier as weak and guttering as the setting sun we had left outside the clapboard walls. We knelt before each other, Sarai and I, and with the book held open to the Hour in our left hands, we drew knives. Not the sacred, rare weapons of our youthful rituals, but humble utility blades.

Sharp is sharp, though, when metal meets wrist.

"As red as ever," Sarai whispered, her words barely audible over the sizzle of our mingled blood in the brazier.

"Read, as ever, by Those Who Sit Above in Shadow," I replied.

She kissed me then, pressing the book between our naked chests, the hot slick of blood from our wounds slipping over the cover, coating our trembling calves, our genitals, her birth scar. There was a stirring in the air, a shifting in the light cast by the flame. A blue throbbing to the glow on the walls, the hint of ozone discharge in the air.

"Then let them read of our true Will . . . "

"Our noble intention . . . "

"Let them read and weep as we have . . . "

"Let them read and grant us our need . . . "

The heretic monk had written of the signs we could expect, and now one came. A great crack of sound, as of an iceberg calving in a desolate sea. It filled the room, reverberating and building upon itself, until we could almost see the sound in its terrible intensity. We broke our grasp and moved to the east wall, where our gathered implements lay. Sarai tended to her wound while I prepared the drugs that would shield our minds from the worst of the effects that were to come. I freely bled into the New Jack Lao, and spilled a few grains of the priceless Yellow Powder in my excitement. Another time, I would have worried, seen it as an omen, but no. All boundaries would fall, and nothing that divided mattered. Blood in the cut, and in the drugs, and drugs in the blood, and a cut from here to there. I passed a pipe to Sarai and set to my own wound with plaster and bandage.

"It begins, Dühren. Our greatest work."

I said that I loved her, but cannot say if she heard over the roar of sound, that howling between the worlds.

HOUR OF THE VIRGINAL APPRAISAL

Do I write this? Or do I speak it only, mumbling into a darkness that consumes the words as they leave my mouth? Do I imagine a sky above me, empty of stars and aching? Do I create the multitudinous pricks of chitinous limbs at my lips, scavenging for meaning? Whether I do or not, it hardly matters.

We fucked, then, Sarai and I, our flesh burnished by the unnatural sounds as we moved against each other. Sacred *kalas* needed to be generated and offered to the void. We had done no less to bring our son into the world, though circumstances then were vastly different. To think how many times this act is performed, and how many times without any intention at all beyond mere physical pleasure, is staggering.

Our intention is pure. I comfort myself with the thought that we are still there in that second hour, joined in that moment, at the least. After, though, in the afterglow. No, after is ever there. Present and painful.

We lie on the floor and pull away from each other, finally, and there is a sense that Time itself is thinning as we do, moments stretching to their breaking point, crumbling into seconds, less than seconds. Into nothing. Into that Time that is not Time at all, but the eternal entry into shadow and the potential All. The Reverse of the Tree. Universe B. The Qlipphotic Realms. The old names feel quaint on my tongue, delicate and infantile. Poor conceptions, withering in the cold furnace of the Absolute they vainly seek to describe.

Sarai turns to me, her eyes alive with that negative fire. Her mouth opens, opens, wide, impossibly wide, splitting across her face, fracturing beyond the limits of her form and filling the air to either side, fastbreeding through the tortured grain of the rough wooden floor that supports us both. Phantom un-speech spills from the fissures, drowning out the howl. I cannot watch, shielding my eyes from the vision with a forearm. Teeth immediately meet in its flesh, and I scream.

HOUR OF THE DEVOURER

Sarai has ceased gnawing on my arm, and I am relieved. The assault has rendered the muscle and tendons into swollen ribbons, which I bandage as well as I am able. Sarai weeps in a corner, shocked by her actions.

"What have we done, Dühren?"

"Nothing yet, my love. Only offered ourselves to Those Who Sit Above in Shadow. Their requirements . . . "

I think on what is being asked of us. To rebuild a life, even one so small, to call from the past the essence of a person and embody it anew in flesh. To resurrect. A serious business, the work of prophets, minor gods. We dare to step across that threshold. We ask only parity.

"I would have eaten you alive, my love," she whispers from the shadows. "Yes. I was filled and empty all at once. I would have."

"I know. It's the way of things, Sarai. The first rule: Everybody Hungry. The void no more or less so." I step over to her and kneel. She takes the injured arm in her hands, draws her shaking lips across the reddening gauze. The room is still and growing colder. Small hitching gasps climb her throat and mist the air between us. "I would have let you feast, Sarai."

"They require nourishment." Her face hardens; she draws the back of her hand over her mouth. She is practical again. "It was a sign, a communication. What kind of food are we?"

"Food for gods."

"And what eats the gods. This is what we must provide."

I open the Book of Hours, place bloodied fingers upon a page.

HOUR OF THE DHOLE

A low rumbling, as of bedrock breaking across the back of a burrowing titan. Consuming blackness beyond mere shadow, alive, sentient and moving, pooling in the air. Sarai's eyes are thimbles of liquid light. My spine hums. We are coming up on the New Jack Lao, finally, and Time, already cracked and bleeding, becomes fluid, expansive. We are able to make the next offering with minimal shrieking, though we grind our teeth until we taste chalk.

"Witness. Ten years," I say. "Yours, for his return."

"Witness. Ten, also."

The blackness shivers and sighs.

"Right off the top!" Sarai laughs.

HOUR OF THE TURBULENT WATERS

We tread water in an ocean of vision, the soles of our feet bloodied by the diamond scales of leviathans coiling beneath in ecstatic dance. In this Hour, the monk tells of a ship and its nameless pilot, dedicated to sailing the desires of the world in search of rare treasure. Now, through the churning sensorium, we sense it coming upon us. A shifting in the darkness, a creaking as of rope and tackle in a high wind, the smell of cedar and iron soaked in brine. An *idea* of a ship, some nightmare Platonic vessel, I think. A pressure wave of oneiric energy lifts us as the bow passes nearby. Voices, above, like metal on stone. An idea of voices, but no less real for that.

What is it you seek?

Sarai is quick to respond. "The return of that which we hold most dear!"

What do you know of such things?

"Our son!" I return. "We know our son!"

The colour of his eyes? The smell of his hair?

"Yes. Yes!"

The whiteness of his teeth when he smiled? His little fists beating upon your chest in anger?

"Of course! Yes!"

The blue of his lips as he lay cooling in his little bed? The hot stain of his last shit upon the bedclothes?

Sarai cries out, half in sorrow, half in rage. I answer.

"God, yes! We accept your cruelty, shipmaster. Only take us aboard, give us passage to where we might retrieve him!"

Do you know of his death? Do you know of his death.

"It was SIDS, you monster," Sarai screams. "SIDS!"

We are in the wake of the ship now, its outlines sketched against the blackness in St. Elmo's fire. Maddening shapes that are not men prowl the decks, and their laughter is obscene.

You know nothing. There is nothing here for you on the surface. Sink, fools. Sink and drown in your ignorance.

"We know him! We know him!" Sarai is weeping now as I hold her in the heaving froth.

You don't even know his name.

The waves close over our heads and we realize, even as the air leaves our lungs, that the being on the ship speaks truth.

HOUR OF THE TOLLING OF DAGON'S BELL

In submarine chambers lit in ghost-glow, we gather our thoughts, try to put down the panic in our hearts. Our lungs had filled with knowledge and despair in equal parts; we drowned in dream and awoke here, gagging, in a grotto built of regret. Sarai collects shells from the muck at our feet, each one a portrait in calcium of our boy. Our nameless child. The swell of his little cheek in this one, the cup of his right ear in that. An eye in abalone.

"How, Dühren? How?" she whispers as she assembles a shell eidolon. It squats in an alcove she's chosen for the quality of the aqueous light, which should lend it grace, but it is hideous instead, wrong in a thousand crumbling ways. My gorge rises as I look at it, but I find I cannot speak.

"How?" The words billow from between her lips. "How can we have forgotten?" I shake my head, wrap my arms around my chest tightly. My heart strains like a fish in a net, bruising my ribs.

Below the grotto, fathoms dark and terrible deep, the sound of a bell, calling its children home. The tone opens something up in me, something vast and secret. A new knowledge, born of that bell below and the words of the demon captain above, and the ghastly shape of Sarai's shell-sculpture before me.

I move towards my wife, place a trembling hand on her shoulder. She turns to me, feral and anguished. I hesitate, and stammer, almost unable to give voice to my insight.

"We didn't forget. We may never have known."

"What? What are you saying, Dühren?"

"His true name. His death. We were wrong. Possibly. I don't know."

"It was SIDS. We were told."

"I know. But . . . "

"But *what*, Dühren?"

"Come with me."

Outside the grotto, the sea floor drops away. I take her hand and we step into nothingness.

HOUR OF THE MEMORIED SELF

We sink, pulsing like beacons in the cold seeps of Time. Stars that are not stars, but moments, suspended at the tips of fibrous stalks attached to monstrous things unseen in the fanged black, lure us. Some more than others. One, especially. We reach out and grasp it, and are immediately swallowed into the master bedroom of a London penthouse we no longer own, into our last night there, into a mutual orgasm that was, now that we see clearly from outside of ourselves, only partly our own, or not at all.

"Oh, look, Dühren. Look. There." There is an x-ray intensity to the scene; Sarai points to the etheric strands of colour that wrap around our spines and bulge spastically through our loins.

"We were a bridge," I say.

"How did we not notice?"

"We weren't allowed to notice. See."

In the upper corner of the room, playing the strands like a violin, a beast.

HOUR OF THE FLESHLESS MASK

The monk paraphrases Crowley in this Hour. Or rather, Crowley paraphrases the monk, since he came after. Time is still liquid, but we begin to feel it gelling around us. Firming up, becoming more real, locking up with seconds. The monk writes of the Sephiroth and Paths, of Spirits, Conjurations, Gods, Spheres, Planes, and their existence or non-existence. But whereas Crowley balked and shied away from making firm claims, warning his students "against attributing objective reality or philosophic validity to any of them," the monk in his madness, and we in our despair, have no choice.

The beast turns from the bed, inclines what passes for its head towards our astral forms, and speaks.

"Hey, Mum. Dad."

HOUR OF THE HOWLING MIST

When we've grown exhausted with the horror of our revelation, the beast takes our hands in damp appendages of its own and conducts a tour of its realm, which is entered through a gout of foul smoke that pours from the corner of the room. Once inside, all is flux and vapour, pierced with the sounds of a thousand malevolent engines rending the future into history. Our lower bodies are as lead, but the beast is sprightly, unaffected by the spiritual gravity of this place, and it pulls us along like panting dolls.

"Now, see, here is where we plan the things, make our deliberations. In the shadows. Above the shadows, in the lightless lands where forgotten people go. Little boys, gods. Monsters. The usual."

Sarai makes a gagging sound and attempts to pull away from the beast's loathsome grip. The beast rewards her effort with a violent pull towards its shifting bulk, and her arm disappears into its side up to her elbow. I admire her, and would rush to her aid, but I cannot. To touch the thing is awful enough. That, and I sense, dimly, the rules that are breeding here.

"Then you are their representative?" I say. "Of Those Who Sit Above in Shadow?"

"Ooh, ooh, ooh! Such pomp. Such circumstance! This is why I chose you, I think. Special people.

"Listen, special dad. Lovely, hard, special mum. There is no one above, sitting, standing, in shadow, or otherwise. We gods are small, and barely real. I've spent eternities no larger than a fucking rabbit, and about as smart, sobbing at the bottom of a charnel chasm littered with the bones of the universe. I ate half a galaxy once, just to see if I could. I've been insane, benevolent, indifferent, cruel. I like cruelty best. Don't you?"

The beast winks at us in turn, its eyes convulsing in mounds of liquescent flesh like underwater detonations.

"I tire, though. Even gods tire. A little break, then, to refresh the glands, taste red things, breathe. To live. To be real. Even special."

Tendrils burst from the hand-like things it grips us with, to wrap around my naked member, to probe at Sarai's crotch. We gasp and grit our teeth against the invasion.

"To feel that slap and tickle, eh, Mum? Why not! To be *born*."

"It wasn't enough, though," Sarai moans. "Was it?" The beast chortles and little rills of sewage leap up on its hide to pour away down its back.

"No. No. I *was* your boy. Your baby. And I will be, again, because that is your true desire. This is your Great Work, sorcerers! Rejoice at its completion! Just as I placed myself within him, he now lives in me. A spark. I only needed a little more death in the mix, folks. There's nothing so real as that which has died and returned. So I reached up and stopped his heart. Settled in to wait for you."

The howling vapours condense before us, begin to glow with spectral light that burns the sight, roughens the skin. The edges of the shape that forms are ragged, bleeding off into the void, but it is a doorway, clearly, and beyond it, hard and cold and dark save for a few guttering flames, is the bleak room in that cabin we left ages past. Our bodies askew on the floor.

"And you came!" It smiles at us, and something finally snaps in Sarai; I can practically hear it. "You came. What a fun ride. Let's go again! Again! Better this time."

Sarai glances across the heaving bulk of our son. She struggles to keep her smile in one place, but it slips snakelike across her face in ways I can't watch.

"Yes," she says, and the word is a hissing dirge in my ears as the beast pulls us towards the door. "Again."

HOUR OF THE SPASTIC MANDALA

The transition from astral to physical forms is brutal. The threshold is crossed, and our bodies suck at us like black holes, steaming and roaring red hunger. We resist, Sarai perhaps less than I. There is resignation and, horribly, hope in her eyes, and in the way her soul stuff arcs across the room to her twitching limbs. Her head drums upon the floor like a baton. I claw at the burning edge of the spirit doorway with my free hand, but cannot hold; the pull of my body, and of the beast, is too much. There is a blinding flash of darkness, and I am consumed, enthroned again in the aching architecture of my flesh.

We open our eyes to the beast squatting before us on myriad limbs. Sizzling ichor pours from its mouths, the very air around it shrieks in protest and attempts to flee, outlining the form of the thing in peripatetic fire. It is here, in the world, and yet not; I know that if I were to look closer, to somehow force a dispassionate eye on the insulting details, I would see the fabric of reality attempting to come to terms with the intruder, and failing. It needs an anchor. A birthing, from a barren womb.

Sarai and I rise on quaking limbs. The beast—our son. Our *son!* God!—coughs, almost politely, and Sarai looks at me in mixed wonder and terror, for she knows I hear what she hears: a shred of familiarity, the barest hint of the cough of our dead boy. Then it speaks, and the hint is gone, replaced with a voice like meat in a grinder, enraged bees, the sighing of senile stars.

"I don't require much, now. Nothing you haven't done before, you crazy kids! Remember that night with those Thelemites in that abandoned whorehouse in Providence? Heeeee! I do. Watched you from the other side of the mirror in that room. Liked you *immediately*. So inventive."

"You can't mean . . . " I start.

The beast flails, amused. "Just the tip! Just to see how it feels! Get things started, Dad, and I'll cut in on your dance when the moment is right."

I bury my fists in my eye sockets, every lineament and nerve singing with the foulness of this, a stream of whispered curses flowing from my mouth. For a moment, all I hear is my own voice, maddened, pleading, and then there is a shuffling of bare feet upon the floorboards, a fumbling clatter as something or somethings are picked up.

And then Sarai is before me with dull, empty eyes, pale python arms around my straining neck, her breasts hot against my chest, and the clammy bulk of the Book of Hours pressed between us, caving in our ribs. The book speaks of this Hour as the mirror of the Hour of Virginal Appraisal, and I see the truth of it.

We fall to the floor, already joined. Desperate, screaming, locked in by our special destiny. Linked to our progeny from beyond the rim of night.

"I said I would, Dühren. My love." Sarai is panting; her nails dig deep furrows in my back. "Go to hell. Devour you. For him."

"For us. I know."

The glee of the beast is poison rotting the walls around us. The cabin crumbles into nothing, a dream forgotten. Through swollen eyes I briefly glimpse the grey light that precedes dawn filtering through the confused trees, slipping over the angry stone.

So soon? I am thinking. Surely there were more hours to this night? I cannot reason, am losing all semblance of thought as my body performs like the idiot marionette it is. Names of Hours fly through my mind like stones picked up in a hurricane.

Hour of the World-Rift. Of the Great Sign of Koth. The Hour of the Shifting Angles. Of the Southernmost Pinnacle, of the Tomb Herd, of the Whimpering Dog. Hour of the Thirteen Globes.

The light is growing brighter, the beast multiplies and surrounds us, a mass of etheric forms becoming more real with each of our thrusts. Here is the dawn, and there, before me, just beyond the cracked grin of Sarai where she grinds the back of her skull into the grass, a flash of cheap yellow plastic and dull, blood-blackened metal in the dim light. My hand shoots out for it, instinctively, and as my fingers curl around the utility blade, my mind clenches around a revelation.

There are as many Hours of night as are needed, here. I hold them all in my hand, names and tollings without number.

The blade slips easily across Sarai's neck. Her eyes grow wide, and then clear, and her smile returns, briefly.

"Ten years, my love. We gave that. The cost."

"Right off the top," she sighs. Her mouth hangs open, and I can see the rising crimson in the well of her throat.

Our son moans in mounting disbelief and rage as a shallow arc of sun clears the horizon.

HOUR OF THE MONOLITH

Sarai dies beneath me. The world stops, gasps, implodes. We are crushed at the core of it, a trinity of cruelty, privilege, and cosmic malevolence. There is nothing beyond our family, this seed of night that will never sprout. The black iron of our prison extends to the end of Time, to the rim of the Real.

We are together again. Dead. Imaginary. Alive. A sacrifice to birth a god, or bind it. The god itself now no larger than a rabbit, wild-eyed and uncomprehending. It nuzzles at Sarai's cooling cheek. It rages, clawing at walls that are there and not there with useless paws. It settles between my crossed legs to gnaw on my inner thigh, keening for something it has lost, though it knows not what. Sometimes, it sleeps.

And I, the father, cursed, never do. The eternal guardian of this, a seething nucleus of madness and death. My little family. I can't recall which special destiny this was, but it is dusted and off the mantle now, brought to rest on my burning brow, shining with a negative light that only deepens the darkness around us.

There's a kind of relief, now. I feel it.

I don't expect many would understand.

ASSEMBLAGE POINT

(for Ramsey Campbell)

YOU'LL WANT TO know about the body liquescing at the bottom of the stair, of course, and I will get to that, I promise, but first I need to warm up my pen a little, work the kinks of long disuse out of my cursive, and tell you a few things. Three things.

First, I want you to think about predation. I mean, beyond the *Mutual of Omaha* dramatics we all grew up on, beyond plummy British voiceovers on high-def video. I mean *real* predation. The complete slavery that the food chain ensures. First Law of the Universe? It's simple: Everybody Hungry. Doesn't matter how you've incarnated here, whether you're a galaxy or a microbe, or where you are on the chain, top link or scraping bottom, if you want to live to see tomorrow, you'd best have something on your plate tonight.

I've thought about predation a great deal lately, and what makes the perfect predator, and it's not the sharpness of the teeth, or the fleetness of the feet, or the keenness of the eyes, or the brute power of the muscles, although those things help, obviously, those things make for great documentary TV. No. No, it's camouflage. Chasing after your prey is for chumps and show-offs. Waiting quietly, appearing to be what you're not, appearing to be benign, appearing to be nothing at all, even, so that your prey places itself in your mouth all unawares . . . I've been thinking about that a lot. Ultimate predators. Ultimate camouflage.

See, there's camouflage, and then there's *camouflage*.

And as I sit here writing this, I'm thinking about the old stories, too, that used to amuse me so much. You know the ones. The tales of dark deeds done, awful and rare books acquired, terrible knowledge gained, sanity sacrificed, then lives. As a boy, I'd read those stories and be properly enthralled as any twelve-year-old would be, along for the ride as the tale's contents were correlated towards a mind-shattering conclusion, painfully identifying with the narrator because, after all, he was *me*, wasn't he? A seeker. If not a hero, then at least a quester after lost, hidden things. A sorcerer, even.

You could see it coming, of course. The end of that search. The arrival of the vengeful Thing. The conclusion of the deal with a devil. The narrator would telegraph that final, shattering revelation from miles away, which was part of the fun.

Here's the amusing bit, though: In the face of utter horror, as Death (or worse) loomed from out of the night to greet him, he'd still write out his final moments, our narrator, that dedicated fellow. In a wild and unsteady hand, naturally, but still. As they were happening. A goddamn play-by-play.

That hand! The window! The window!

The three-lobed burning eye!

I am it, and it is I.

Well. It's a cliché, but I found it funny, even at twelve when it was new and I didn't know what cliché was. It should have scared, but I'd laugh instead, taken out of the story by a paragraph of frenzied italics that amounted to little more than a wordy *boo!*

But then, for the reader, I suppose that's the perfect time to be taken out of a story. At the end.

Which, again, I *will* get to. But first, one more item: I should tell you that I'm naked as I write this. You'll find my clothes neatly folded on the desk next to these pages. You're looking at them right now, I'll bet. I half-considered arranging them, on the chair and the surrounding floor, in such a way as to suggest that my body had been spirited away, snatched to heaven "in the twinkling of an eye," as the Rapturous Christians like to say. For a moment, I thought that would be amusing, but then decided that it was too much trouble for a gag. I mean, on top of the hilarity that's about to ensue. Don't think I'm not aware of how funny this is.

Honestly, though, I just don't want to shit in my pants when it happens. They don't tell you about that when you begin these practices, when you enter this appalling lifestyle, but if you're doing things right, or you've read your Castaneda, you learn fast. You shit yourself a few times before you get wise.

I got wise. And now I impart this wisdom, and more, to you.

That was the warm up. I'll begin.

It was Castaneda, that old fraud, who brought me to this. Yes, *that* Castaneda. Little Carlos. *The Second Ring of Power. Journey to Ixtlan.* Peyote and mushrooms and oneiric dopplegangers and shapeshifting and the loosest of academic standards.

See, if you've a certain sort of mind, if that early sense of being a searcher after hidden truths is more than just a by-product of hormones and teenage romanticism, if you are, basically, *me*, then you move on from the old stories with their amusing finales and stumble into fictions more potent and far less trustworthy. The gravity of secret knowledge pulls you from the shelves that hold *Fantasy* and *Horror*, to the dimly lit ones in the back of the store labeled *New Age Thought* and *Spirituality. Occult. Witchcraft.*

It's a pit trap, naturally, but a poorly camouflaged one. The contents of those shelves are there to put a little numinous thrill into the grasping, sad lives of proto-Crowleys, urban shamans, and menopausal women. And again, if you're like me (and you *are*, aren't you? You must be, to be sitting there, reading this) you don't stay in the trap for too many years. It's long and deep, though, this pit, and occasionally there are jewels embedded in the walls. Ideas that you pluck from the muck and pocket almost without thinking, concepts that stick like burrs to your skin long after you've crawled out of there.

Castaneda was definitely a burr, one that stuck deep in me, even after his dangerous hucksterism was exposed to the world. His three missing-presumed-dead witches slash sexual partners. The suicide pacts. A banal, hushed-up death by cancer: camouflaged cells dropping the act, finally, and killing from within, and not the heroic sorcerer's journey into the Second Attention his followers claimed for him. Yeah, Castaneda. Here was a guy who had sold his humanity, and convinced most of his readers that he'd done it for real knowledge, real power, and not just for a dreary SoCal compound full of witchy pussy.

Still, there were ideas in those books that affected me strangely. Weirdly practical suggestions for practice, like removing your clothes before doing any sorcerous work. That way, Castaneda's teacher Don Juan Matus explained, when you shat yourself from fear at the things you were seeing and the deeds of power you were accomplishing, all you'd have to do is go wash up in the river. Pick up your clean clothes on the way back to the house.

Castaneda was all about *seeing*, too. True perception. Shifting awareness from this world to others. Moving what he called the "assemblage point," that focus of attention that builds the human world, to another spot on the "luminous egg" that formed your energetic body, so that you would assemble a different world. A world that was more *true*. Serene and primal and potent. A sorcerer's world.

Well. That was the huckster's line, anyway. He was, maybe, a better sorcerer than he was an anthropologist, at the end. A series of debunkings and high-profile exposures pushed Castaneda out of the spotlight, though his book sales weren't hurt any. Definitely a better writer than anything else.

I wasn't *convinced* or anything. I mean, if you jump from a cliff because a talking eagle tells you that the experience is going to trigger your transition to an exalted energetic state where you will receive special knowledge, then, brother, you get what you deserve. I wasn't convinced.

But it was *compelling* stuff, nonetheless. Just practical enough, just strange enough, just a hair on the other side of comprehensible enough to smack of something legitimate. Something truly otherworldly. I got things from Castaneda that I couldn't find in Crowley or Bertiaux, and certainly not in the standard New Age boilerplate.

A burr, worrying its way inside. An itch to *see*.

Reading about sorcery is like reading about sex. It's not the real thing, but it gets you hot for it, makes you want it more. So I left the bookshelves behind, and began to move in strange circles. I began to fall away from the human world, waded into the deep pools of night that surround that pretentious little island of grand ideas and goofy hubris.

I don't like to go into great detail about those years. Sites were visited. Temples, ruins, forgotten wastelands. An island off Nan Madol. An abandoned forestry camp in the Olympic Mountains of western Washington. Even visited the Yucatan stomping grounds of Little Carlos, though for a purpose that was not merely nostalgic. Something darker.

Yes. Dark things were done, terrible things, as you no doubt know. Whoever you are, you're sitting here reading this, which means you've tracked me this far, a not inconsiderable feat. Let me congratulate you on your cleverness, for what it's worth. So of course you don't need details; you already know about the things, or some of the things, I've done. The sacrifices made. The ones left behind, damaged. More than damaged. I've hurt a lot of people. Could be you're hoping for answers about one of those people.

I don't know. I don't know anything about you, except that you're here, and have done some things yourself to get here. That's enough.

The things *I* did led me here, to Camside, to this house. There are places where the true world is more apparent. I don't have to tell you this. *Thin spots*, as the menopausal New Agers would say. Which is fine as far as that goes.

In any case, this house is such a place, known only to a few. There was a breakthrough here, back in the Sixties. That magical time, eh? Two enterprising young warlocks had pulled a rookie cock-up, really done a number on themselves in the process. *Do not call up that which you cannot put down,* right? A standard caution, sure, but where would we be without the bold, I say. Without those willing to go that extra distance.

It has a name. All the old ones do, but I won't bother with it here. Names are just more camouflage. The brief waggling of a wad of human tongue-meat cannot fully encapsulate *It*. *It* is what *It* is, this entity, and no more or less than that. A being. An eternal principle of that true world, a facet of how things really are.

How things really are. That, in fact, was what commerce with this old one brought. True vision. A rending of the veils. Pure sight. Few worshipped *It*, for that reason alone. That's what the warlocks were after, though. The stronger one, the bold one, had an idea that our eyes were fooling us, with all those many million rods and cones embedded in a globe of viscous tissue, filtering every particle of light, flipping images on their heads, doing who knows what else. How could anyone be sure that the things seen were in fact how things really were?

They needed items to call the old one up out of the black dimensions which held it. Most importantly, an image of the being: a migraine-inducing metallic sculpture of hemispheres and rods, cylinders and empty spaces. It was the empty spaces that drew the eye, so that to look upon the image of the old one was to not see it at all. There was also a misshapen skull, a "rod with an icon," a "weirdly shaped pentacle," and "obscene candles."

I'm relaying these things to you, as I found them in the scandal sheets and police reports, more for your own amusement than anything else. You and I both know what really calls these things up, and it's the First Law of the Universe. *Obscene candles!* But it was the Sixties. The empty-handed methods such as you and I use were decades away.

And in any case, it worked. The warlocks called, and the old one answered. Did more than just answer; *It* came, and bestowed gifts upon them. Of course they were found dead the next morning, and of course it was ruled a murder-suicide, but oh, they'd left more behind than their mystical, fetishistic paraphernalia! Our boys had *taped* the ritual, on a nice old reel-to-reel unit. Took me a while to lay my hands on the original, but the moment I heard their death rattles, I knew it was no gag, no prank. They'd seen things as they really were, and the sight was too much.

I *knew* they'd been successful. Those last forty seconds or so of the tape? Pure italics.

The veils had been rent for them. The camouflage dropped away and the primal world of Truth, the sorcerer's world, revealed. I wanted what they had, what they had been unable to process, unable to properly endure.

Now, you know what I've done, to become the sort of person who could survive what those two couldn't. I was ready, able, and oh so very willing to look upon the naked heart of the universe. I had *done the work*, and I was ready to have the scales fall from my eyes, ready to *see*.

So I came here, and I called.

It answered, and the veils were rent. Gifts were bestowed. It touched me, just once, almost delicately, cracking my luminous egg wide open and permanently shifting my assemblage point to its new position. Castaneda would have shat himself, I'm sure. I certainly did.

And now I *see.*

I see what *It* is, the old one. I see how *It* rests in Time, the way its limbs straddle the dimensions, the way its eye-analogues caress the skin at the back of our reality with fevered intensity, the way it rubs up against our false world. My initial perceptions of it were a riotous confusion of forms and spastic movement, as it cycled through untold manifestations. The vision settled though, finally, pulsing with the awful slow beat of the eternal, of that which really is.

What *It* is, you see (*do* you see? You will! Soon enough!), is *everything.* It is this room, and my clothes upon the desk. It's the air moving in and out of your quickening lungs, and the rain on the windshield of the cab you took to get here, and your dogged insistence on answers that keeps you reading this through to the end, though your every animal instinct is to run. It's the body at the bottom of the stairs that you had to step over to get up here (did you really check that corpse, I wonder?), and Castaneda thinking about how to make a little money off some soft-headed hippies. It's the chuckle I made the first time I reached the italics at the end of one of those stories (a chuckle mirrored by my own laughter here, years later, as I pen just such a ridiculous narrative), and it's the foolish, malnourished amateur who wrote those stories thinking that would be a decent way to finish, to take the reader out.

It's the young warlocks who died in this house, and the people I used and discarded to get here. It's me, lying to you a few paragraphs back, when I wrote that I didn't know who you are. Because of course you're her father, though you're not unique. There have been so many fathers. Mothers and siblings and lovers, too. Hired investigators. Though none of them ever made it this far. Again, congratulations on your cleverness. On becoming like me, on becoming what you'd revenge yourself upon.

It's that cavern on that island near Nan Madol, and it's her blood on the well-used stone in that cavern, and it's the celebrants I'd gathered there, up to their ankles in blood and spunk. It's these pages you're holding, and the ink that makes the letters you're reading, and it is especially the empty spaces between those letters.

It's the shit on that body downstairs, which was mine, caking the inner thighs and backs of the legs. It's the body itself, half-dissolved from the old one's touch, and the energetic structure within that body swirling in a mad chaos of anguish as it mutates. Scrambled luminous egg! It's the stirring of that body as the right hand rises from the floor and slaps down wetly upon the first stair.

You really should have checked it, though I doubt there's anything you could have done to stop what's happening, for you have been fooled, taken in, placed yourself within the mouth, as I did.

It's allowed me to see as *It* sees, across the expanse of Time and Space, allowed me to feel what it feels, exist as it exists. Even as I sit here writing, *It* is doing its terrible work upon me. I write the words *Nan Madol* and I am there, in the cavern, doing unspeakable things to her. I write *the young warlocks who died in this house* and I am here with them, touching them as *It* touched them, and shaking with glee as they destroy themselves. I write *the shit on that body downstairs* and I am there, at the top of the stairs, a few minutes from now, out of my mind with terror, trying to flee from the liquefying touch of something that's been disguised as *everything,* shitting myself and slipping in it, my head describing an awful, graceful arc in the air before the impact.

I write these words, and experience these things, but it is only the camouflage. There's camouflage, and then there's *camouflage,* and it is *all camouflage.* My life. Your daughter's life. The world. Our reality is nothing but a skin for the ultimate predator, discarded when *It* is ready to eat. I cannot even guess why *you* are on its plate tonight. *It* feeds on many things, and its hunger is inscrutable.

Perhaps sorcerers taste better. Less human. We give up so much of our humanity to learn these things, accrue this power, and in the end, we're food. Thanks for nothing, Carlos.

It's at the door now. I'm at the door now, naked and viscous, flesh sliding on supple bones. I wonder how I'll fit into my clothes afterwards. I am changed, made glorious and violent and true, the merest tip of the smallest appendage of *It.* A claw, tapping.

I am It, and It is I, right? Oh, the italics of it all! But I won't burden you with that cliché. I don't find it all that funny, anymore. It's not a decent way to finish.

You might get lucky when that door opens. For a moment, your assemblage point may shift so far that you create a world in which you're just some schmuck reading a pulpy horror story in a cheap paperback. Only for a moment, though. Enjoy it.

Time to take you out of the story.

WORSE THAN DEMONS

[New Heretic Magazine
[Asha Satyamurthy interview with Gregory Martens
[excerpt running time 00:23:17
[burstcast to noönet 20430215

New Heretic Magazine: A large part of your appeal as an *auteur* has been attributed to what some have called an obsession with the infantile. I'm not sure that's an entirely fair descriptor, but there is a marvellous sense of wonder in your films that could be called childlike. Can you tell us a bit about that?

Gregory Martens: Yeah, infantile, there's a rather obvious sneer in there, hey? Well, if it makes them feel clever, why not? Sure, I've never been afraid to explore the pre-verbal states in my work. I think, and I believe this, I really do, I think that we don't know what we are, as a species, because it's been so long since we were authentically ourselves. I mean, we were talking about memetic colonization the other day, Colleen Davros and I, this was up at Esalen for, what, Tusk's little thinktank, and I said well sure it's an epidemic *now*, but that's only because our ontological immune systems have become so fucking *compromised* by language in the first place, right?

NHM: That's nothing new, though, surely? Language as a virus? Burroughs and company made excellent hay of that idea seventy years ago.

GM: Absolutely, and it continues to agitate the infected to this day! Moreso, even. The uproar at Esalen, well. There's video, I encourage you to pull it up for shits and giggles. Before Tusk gets it pulled. Which, y'know, it's funny, it *is*, because I can recall years past when the idea would barely elicit a nervous cough or two from the audience. Colleen and I had to be escorted out for safety reasons. Now, why do you suppose *that* is?

NHM: It's a sensitive issue for a lot of people. The plague.

GM: Yes. And there's that fine old word again. Fairly drips with associations. Sticky. Yes, *plague* tends to divide folks, historically. I'm going to correct you, though: It's a sensitive issue *to the virus*. But you wanted to talk about the films. I think it all comes down to, I don't want to say a return to Eden or anything like that, but certainly a reassessment of a childlike worldview, a pre-verbal worldview. I'm interested in seeing things as they *are,* or at least going as far as possible towards that. I don't think I succeed. I doubt I ever will.

NHM: Can you talk about projects where you've come close?

GM: That really depends on the mood I'm in? Mood factors quite heavily, because, again, pre-verbal knowledge, or awareness. And my mood today, well . . . open? Not exactly nostalgic, but there's a breeze from the past I've been feeling since I, since I woke up, really. Odd. But there again, trying to English it makes for the crumbling of the awareness. Ah, it's gone. Hey hey! Poof.

NHM: Sorry? Didn't want to throw you off.

GM: Oh, how can you be? I mean that sincerely. Proust had to swallow that cookie eventually! Don't worry about it. But sure, the films, the close ones. I'd say, today, *Headless,* that's definitely in the top five for me. Right this minute.

NHM: From your All Along the Watchtower trilogy.

116

GM: That's right. Well, by now most people know the ugly facts about my upbringing. No need to dirty ourselves up in the muck of that.

NHM: You were raised in a Jehovah's Witness church, yes.

GM: I was, I was, but God, don't let them hear you call it a *church.* You want to talk about groups with control language! Ah, but I'm being unfair, they all have it, to a greater or lesser degree.

NHM: They?

GM: Humans. In general. Religious groups, specifically. Cults, *especially.* So with the J-Dubs, you had the *Kingdom,* and the *Little Flock.* The *New System.* The *Thousand Year Reign.* And of course, *Jehovah,* which they run into the ground, because God's gotta have a name. "We're the only ones who use it!" they shout, and I'm like, *yeah,* about that. It's lost on them, though. Shit, there's others, deeper, weirder. *Gog and Magog.* I find it odd and also comforting that I can't recall most of them, just now. But then, it's been a long inoculation process for me. Decades. I've been out of the 'Tower longer than I was in, really.

NHM: Not so out that they don't feature in your films, though?

GM: Never that far out! *Headless* perhaps being the best example. I wanted to explore themes of identity loss, fluidity, fragility, and the formative power of meaning, and the JW urban legend of the headless man kept suggesting itself to me as a framework for that.

NHM: Maybe I'm too much the unregenerate pagan to really understand this, but it surprises me that they'd have anything like that in their faith culture. Ghost stories?

GM: Oh, honey. Honey, there's the letter of God's Law, and then there's the Spirit, and the Spirit gets around. Wants what it wants. Demonic Smurfs? Check. Angels guiding the good brothers or, more often, sisters away from houses where murderers, rapists, *worse*, wait behind the door? Check. Consider the risks they take, just walking up to random houses, knocking away with their clean white knuckles. Possessed garage sale items. Haunted macramé. Anyway. Wayne, which is what I called him in the film, because, y'know, *Wayne*. The headless man.

It's got all the classic elements, present in every version, and there are a few. So, the run-down area; if there are tracks in town, this house is on the wrong side. The rusted-out hulks up on blocks in the overgrown yard. Sagging roof, boards missing on the steps, paint peeling, garbage piled up in the driveway. Maybe throw some sun-bleached plastic toys in the yard for extra pathos.

Our two brethren approach, all clean and spit-polished, smiles bright, cheap book bags stuffed with copies of *Awake!* and *The Watchtower*. This house is never occupied, they know, or if it is the knock is never answered. This morning, there's music coming from inside, though. Something muted and heavy, so pick a metal band, something the audience will recognize as obviously Satanic but nothing too obscure. I mean, don't go with prog or Norwegian doom or anything like that. The brothers knock.

In some versions, a kid opens the door. The more feral and haunted-looking, the better. In others, it just swings open on a single hinge. In all versions, they're greeted with an interior that, to the average JW, fairly screams, "Unclean! Unclean!" The music, obviously, now louder and more apparently Satan-friendly. The posters. Dungeons and Dragons paraphernalia. Drug paraphernalia. Kinky sex paraphernalia. Say a word often enough and it starts to sound dirty, have you noticed?

NHM: Paraphernalia. Paraphernalia.

GM: Paraphernalia. Pair a fur nail ya. Yeah. It's less a house, more a museum to depravity. An object lesson.

NHM: Now, in *Headless,* when Wayne appears, it's played for laughs. Is that the case in the legend?

GM: Laughs? No. But their reaction to a clearly headless person isn't exactly natural. You or I, anybody, would tear out of there. Walking torso turns a corner and immediately begins begging for help, its voice coming from somewhere in the hazy air above its empty shoulders? Outta there. Right?

NHM: Of course.

GM: Not these two fine young Christian warriors. They know what they're seeing, and it is the Devil's handiwork, most assuredly. The demon which afflicts Wayne is mighty, it plays with his perception and the perception of others so that he only *appears* to be headless. *Naturally,* Wayne has lost his shipping clerk gig down at the pornography warehouse, his live-in girlfriend has left with the illegitimate kid or kids, he survives on rot-gut whiskey, Snickers bars and pot. He fears for his soul, his sanity, and his life, in that order. And, y'know, hilarity ensues.

NHM: Did you have anyone else in mind for the role of Wayne? Or was it always going to be H. Jon Benjamin?

GM: He was top of mind for the role, from the get-go. Only Benjamin could have given such personality to a faceless character. His early work is rough, but he really came into his own after the accident. Would that I could have worked with the original! A voice actor's voice actor.

NHM: Well, technically, the Benjamin we have is still the original Benjamin . . .

GM: His consciousness, sure. Resident on the noönet, like most things. I wonder if that's the same, though. As life. Living. I wonder about that all the time.

NHM: Speaking of dream projects . . .

GM: Ah.

NHM: *Spirit Board.*

GM: I've said it before. You *know* I've said it before. I say it every time that film gets brought up. Not a dream project, an *abortion.* From the start. And I could *swear* that was on the no-go list for this interview. I'm gonna kill my publicist . . .

NHM: Okay. Okay. I don't want to talk so much about the actual film. I hope that's all right, at least? Because that's been done.

GM: Uh huh. To death. "The worst boondoggle since *Fitzcarraldo*." That bastard Simek's piece in the *New Yorker.*

NHM: All the bad history and rumours of cursed sets aside, I'm more interested in the research you did in the year leading up to production on *Spirit Board*, which, as everyone knows by now, was initially conceived as an autobiographical piece, a documentary. In particular, the trips you made to your hometown to interview certain individuals that . . .

GM: The Collingwood Five.

NHM: Umm . . . yes. The Five. Marlys Trachtenburg, Denny Fields, Craig Bender and Kavita Patel.

GM: And me. Greg Martens. See, this is why I don't like going here. I'm always the fifth. Asha, why not just come right out and put me at the head of the list? Why always the back end? Do you think I don't see it coming, somehow?

NHM: I'm sorry. I can see how this is uncomfortable for you. I think, and I'm only speaking for myself here as a journalist, I think I place you at the end of the list because you're the only one not in prison. I'm guessing it might be the same for other members of the press, too.

GM: Ahh, you're right. I'm being unfair. Okay.

NHM: You're okay to continue?

GM: Yes. Yeah, sure. Okay. Heh, there's that breeze again. It's like it's right in my face. Is my hair blowing back? Yeah, go ahead.

NHM: All right. Can you speak about the event that brought the Five together?

GM: Together? We were never *together,* not in the way you mean. We were kids. Craig was a seventh grader, the rest of us were in sixth. And I was never *with* them, not after the board. Not later, either, when the killings started.

NHM: They named you, though. The other four. They put you there.

GM: Yeah. I don't blame them for that. I *was* there. After all. I was a part of it, and a weird JW kid, too. So . . .

NHM: It must have been hell on your family.

GM: It was. I'll tell you, though, I think, on some level, they were proud of me. For doing the right thing. *The right thing* by some reckoning, anyway. For the publicity it brought the 'Tower.

NHM: Can you walk me through that morning?

GM: Understand, I was *eleven.* So were most of the people there. Who knows what we actually saw? It felt like a dream when it happened, and there are days I believe it was. I do. Some days I have to believe that.

NHM: It wasn't, though. Two teachers witnessed it, as well as the recess monitor. They testified, even. And the events afterward . . .

GM: Doesn't mean they weren't lying. Or believed the story enough to also believe it true. Doesn't mean they weren't dreaming with their eyes open. Or were affected by the, what did you call it earlier, the plague.

NHM: Babel Syndrome, yes.

GM: Yeah. Shit. No, you're right. I wish you weren't, that's all. Did you hear about that group in San Bernardino now? Cut out their tongues and speak only in emojis?

NHM: I have. Their membership is growing. Sales of personal holo-emitters are up. Personally, I think the literal speech bubbles floating above their heads is pretty cool. Like living in a comic book.

GM: Well, there you go. I might agree with you, too, if it weren't for the ritual mutilation. That's going to get worse, you know.

NHM: Can we get back to that morning? The Five?

GM: Right. Right. Well, there was the board. One of them had brought it. I think Marlys? She had a witchy, kinda hippy family, if I'm recalling correctly. Not that it matters who brought it. It was there. You can see these waves of interest in the occult surge through the popular culture. Youth culture. Have you noticed?

NHM: Sure. I sat on a panel once with an MIT guy who was convinced it happened on an eleven-year cycle that corresponded to sunspot activity.

GM: Seems legit. I mean, as anything else, really. So, y'know, kids had been trying that *light as a feather stiff as a board* levitation trick the week before. Other things. Who doesn't like a good scare? Marlys brought her Ouija board. Milton Bradley! What a thing. Anyway. I stayed well away, being JW and all. Or tried to. I was curious. Painfully curious. There was this big rock outcropping at the back of the schoolyard that we'd scramble around on, and they'd set the board up there, Marlys and the other three. You know how Ouija boards work?

NHM: Vaguely.

GM: It's like dowsing. When you dowse for water, or anything, you hold the forked stick or a bent wire or a pendulum lightly, so lightly, and then ask your question. You're not asking the spirits, you're asking your own unconscious to access the flood of information that's always available to you but which gets reduced to manageable levels by your waking awareness. Your body can feel where the water is, you *know* it on a deep level, but your waking mind needs to receive that info from some other perceived source. So the tiny fibres in your forearms and wrist and fingers twitch and pull and nudge and hey, dig the well here, because guess what, water. Or oil. Natural gas. I've dowsed for my car keys.

NHM: Do you find them?

GM: Every time. It's the same with the Ouija board. Hands lightly rest on the planchette, and it moves across the board thanks to the gentle push and pull of the players, movements that they don't even *notice*.

NHM: So, the answers are pulled from the collective unconsciousness of the players?

GM: Hm. Yes and no? There's a random factor to it, which is why the early minutes of a Ouija session are almost always very tentative and frustrating. Once you get into a groove, though. Once the players get in sync.

NHM: Surely one player must dominate?

GM: You would think so, but no. Whatever comes through, it's like Burroughs' Third Mind.

NHM: That would have been you, then.

GM: No. No, I wasn't playing. I didn't ask any questions. The Third Mind is generated by other minds in concert. If anything I was the fifth mind, at the end. Small *m*. I hovered around the edges of the crowd. Like I said, curiosity. And there *was* a crowd. Not just kids, either. One of the teachers you mentioned. The recess monitor. It was theatre in the round, almost.

NHM: What kind of questions were the four asking?

GM: Oh, the old standards. Kavita and Marlys wanted names of boys they would marry. Denny was worried about his parents divorcing, wanted to know which one he'd end up with. It was Craig who started with the demon questions. Greasy little shit, Craig. He asked for names of demons that could hurt his enemies, scare his stepdad, make him rich, nothing more than that. He was twelve.

NHM: When were you brought in?

GM: Ah. The board did it. They did it, through the board. It asked a question of them and they decided I was the answer.

NHM: And that question was?

GM: "Who is the holy boy near?" Which could be interpreted at least a couple of ways. But see, I never swore. I didn't go trick or treating on Hallowe'en. And I had that squeaky smugness that young JWs have and never really get over. Stood out like a sore thumb. Craig signaled to his bruiser friends and before I knew it I was picked up by the armpits and flung to the ground in front of the four.

NHM: Where was the teacher during all this?

GM: She'd turned her head for a moment. The monitor, too. You remember the criminal stuff you could get away with if the timing was right? The moment was structured that way. And it's not like I yelled in protest or anything. I *wanted* to be closer, but I couldn't bring myself to do it. They wanted me to ask it something, and there was a threat of violence if I didn't. The whole scene was *charged*.

NHM: There's a similarly charged scene in *Spirit Board* that's spawned any number of theories. "The silent question." I've seen it ranked with Bill Murray's final whisper to Scarlett Johansson in *Lost in Translation*, and Monique Bledsel's chilling off-camera petition to the Pleiadian Intelligence in *Void Children*.

GM: I've read some of those. Interesting stuff. I'm glad it makes people think, but I . . .

NHM: What did you ask the board? That day.

GM: . . .

NHM: Was it in fact a silent question? That later found its way into the film, or . . . ?

GM: No. I spoke. I asked the board if it could tell me the name of God. Oh. Oh God. I just . . . Jesus. Jesus Christ.

NHM: Are you all right? Should we move on?

GM: No, I'm fine. I'm fine. It's . . . there's just so much happening now, I feel, I feel like everything is compressing down. Crushing. This terrible gravity to all our doings. Do you feel it, Asha?

NHM: Sometimes, yes. That's just the world, though. It's always been that way.

GM: You're young. That's nice. Nice, but wrong. I think you're wrong.

NHM: Okay. Do we need to take a break?

GM: No. They answered me, through the board. Or the board did. Something answered. I'm not sure it was them, now. It was and it wasn't. Something came through. Heh. That's what they were always warning kids about, in the Kingdom Hall. Hell, any church of that type. Demons come through. They always come through.

NHM: May I hazard a guess as to the answer you received?

GM: Hazard away!

NHM: *Jehovah.* The name of God, or at least what you knew as the name of God. The kids, the board, spelled out *Jehovah*.

GM: Yes. And no. Not really. They spelled out the Tetragrammaton. Y H V H. *Yod Hey Vav Hey.*

NHM: The Hebrew name for God?

GM: The *ineffable* name *of* God. The *unutterable* name of *God.* Throw some vowels in there and you've got the bastardized *Jehovah* my old crew loved to toss around so much. The name I was familiar with. The name I knew and expected, in my smugness. I was gonna break that Ouija board, understand? Like a good Christian boy. Throw it a holy curve ball, right over the plate, set that board to spinning and cracking in half. Whatever was behind it was going to howl in terror and flee back to the dark. Like when Christ cast the demon Legion into a herd of swine and the piggies plunged off a cliff into the sea. Like when Wayne's head finally shimmered back into view after a few weeks of intense Bible study. Instead, I got letters I didn't recognize. And then the incident.

NHM: It wasn't the first outbreak of Babel Syndrome, but it was certainly one of the most dramatic. An entire school losing the power of speech? The Collingwood event pushed the health crisis into the national conversation.

GM: Oh, we had the power. We could *talk*. We just couldn't make ourselves *understood*. For weeks. It's why I made the fucking film in the first place. Why I don't trust myself with language when I make any film. And why I went to talk to the others, years later, after they did what they did. There was nothing to learn from them, though, nothing beyond what they'd already claimed in court. I think Craig enjoys prison. Denny and Kavita. Marlys. I dunno. They're hollowed-out people now. There's nothing there but noise.

NHM: They say you exposed them to God.

GM: That sounds dirtier than it was. Or it's spot on. I don't know. Crazy people say things.

NHM: They say He made them do it.

GM: That old chestnut. That old *noise*. What's worse than the devil, Asha? What's worse than demons? Listen. Those letters, the Y H V H. It's not just a name, it's a principle of pure Being. Do you get what I'm saying? You're not supposed to sound it out, but when you do, when you *do*, shit, it sounds like breathing. *Yaahh* in *vaahh* out, *yaahh vaahh*, in and out. He, it, breathes the universe into being.

I spoke to a rabbi once, my producer on *30 $ilver Pieces* put me in touch with the old guy, and after he very patiently sat with me as I blubbered out my theories, he said that God "is the Source and Foundation of all possibility of utterance and thus is beyond all definite descriptions." How do you like that? Was that supposed to be a comfort?

NHM: Was it?

GM: Oh, honey, fuck no. No, it wasn't. Because it doesn't explain how those stupid kids knew about the Tetragrammaton. I don't think they did. *I* didn't even know, and I was the good JW boy! I prayed to the thing every night.

NHM: Do you think God is responsible for Babel Syndrome?

GM: We don't know what we are, Asha. We don't. We talk and talk and talk and we don't know what we're doing. Language, it's already a kind of half-miracle. The weird fact that I can make certain sounds with my vocal apparatus, my monkey-mouth, and because our dictionaries happen to agree, you can hear these sounds and understand them, and reproduce them, and we blather on and on. We do it because it works. But it's bizarre. It's power. And it's *nothing* because all words are made up, all descriptors arbitrary. I don't mind telling you, this stuff makes me afraid. I'm afraid all the time these days.

NHM: Why?

GM: Babel. Babylon. It was a city in the Fertile Crescent. It's in the book of Genesis. Nimrod, the mighty hunter-king, and his tower, purpose-built to pierce the vault of Heaven. Do you know this story?

NHM: No. I was raised New Reformed Atheist.

GM: The post-Dawkins bunch. Yeah, they do good work. How nice for you. Well, I won't bore you with it, then. I'm scared because I look around, and I see what we've done, and what we might yet do. I think about those tongueless in San Bernardino, and I think about H. Jon Benjamin living in a block of superconductive crystal a mile deep in the earth's crust with thousands of other wealthy ghosts. I think about the Collingwood Five and collective minds from Outside and murder. I think about how this interview will be burstcast directly to the noönet, and people will watch it in their dreams or on their phone, depending on how much they want to spend. Jesus! And that Ouija board, that ridiculous cardboard tech. That's never far from my thoughts, Asha.

And I wonder if we haven't gone and built another tower. And I wonder if that's the kind of project that might agitate an invisible disembodied lifeform that hides in plain sight, colonizing our minds and moving us according to its will.

NHM: You're talking about God.

GM: Yes. No. Good Bye. I don't know. I'm always afraid. I was told, from a very young age, that the fear of God brings wisdom. I thought I was over that. Thought I knew better, but now I'm not so sure. I babble on, afraid and wiser by the minute, while they speak in emoji to save their souls. What do their prayers look like, in those little bubbles? Milton Bradley. Am I wise, Asha? Do I seem wise to you? Because I'm very afraid. What's worse than demons?

NHM: I can't speak to that.

GM: Probably for the best.

PERFECT TEN

NO ONE REALLY expected her to do as well as she did.

I mean, a new poet like that—attractive in a bruised but obviously affected way; defensive stare, pupils laser-guiding you away from the vacuity behind the eyes; black leather notebook full of angry or hopeful or political or dreamy poems—girls like that? Poets like that? The Moon Under Water sees half a dozen come in at each slam.

They get up behind the mic, and forget that there's a time limit on their performance, forget that the moment the first word passes their lips, somewhere in the room the timekeeper has clicked her stopwatch. They forget that they're being judged, forget about the random drunks in the audience equipped with score cards. Or maybe they don't, maybe they remember the stopwatch and the cards because after all, it *is* a poetry slam, but they don't care because they're poets, faux-bruised for their art, and they go on for half a minute explaining the anger or hope, the politics or dream that fuels the poem before even starting the fucking thing. Clutching their notebooks in pale hands, knuckles ivoried from their own nerves and the lights above and the hundred eyes watching them. They finish, finally. They go overtime, usually, some by a few seconds, others by whole minutes.

They never score well. Either they don't know how to use the microphone, or they mumble lines from their pages and refuse to make eye contact with the audience, or the poem is just no good in the first place and they go over the three-minute time limit, besides. People still cheer when they're done, though. I mean, just getting up there on stage deserves encouragement; it's harder than it looks. Most get a taste for it and come back for the next slam. Maybe some of them get better. A few get really good, with time and practice and the toughening that comes with competition. A poet gets to know what the audience wants at a slam, what the judges dig, and they alter their style accordingly. Become better performers, for what it's worth. But the new poets? The ones who have never slammed before? Girls like her?

No one really expected her to do as well as she did.

But then, she didn't read from her notebook, which was faded yellow leather and not black. During the first round, when Slam Master Todd called her name (which, thanks to the shitty sound system of The Moon Under Water, became burst-of-hellacious-feedback-Castaigne), she took her notebook up on stage with her, and there she briefly consulted a page, in silence. From behind the bar I could see the timekeeper getting fidgety, thumb over the button. She consulted a page, then another, before letting the hand that held the book drift lazily to her side, forgotten, a handful of pallid dead leaves clinging to a November branch. She raised her eyes to the gathered hippies and anarchists and liberal arts students and drunks, then, this new poet, this girl, this burst-of-noise Castaigne, and her eyes were lasers, yes, but not defensive somehow, not meant to distract the gaze from her abyss but to target and lock on and draw it within her. I remember catching my breath when she looked at me, as if I'd just stepped up to a cliff edge in the dark. The whole bar caught its breath.

And then she opened her mouth and did her poem.

That's what we call it in slam. A slam isn't a poetry reading, oh, nothing so provincial as that, no, it's a goddamn contact sport, so the poet doesn't read or recite or even speak a poem; they *do* a poem. It's meant to sound sexual and badass but mostly it's just sad. I should know, I've done my share: went to Nationals with the city slam team, three seasons in a row, back when I thought this kind of public masturbation was cool and being broke delivering poems behind the mic seemed more pure than getting paid serving drinks behind the bar. Yeah, I was a poet. A *spoken-word artist*, if you want to be fancy, and most do. I've *done* poems. Never like her, though. Never the way Castaigne did that poem that night, drawing all the air out of the room with her words until every edge turned sharp and bright in every pair of eyes that locked on hers.

Even now, I couldn't tell you what her poem was about. I couldn't tell you what she *said*, exactly. That hardly seemed to matter at the time. I mean, it hardly matters for most slam poetry, where it's almost never what gets said but the manner in which it's said that's important. Still, you can usually tell what the subject is. Castaigne's poem that night, though; it defied even as it thrilled. It refused classification and slipped away like the ghost of an intuition. The impression was that of glaciers calving in the arctic night, hive communications in honeyed tunnels, scraps of commercial jingles for products you don't remember, hot gravel in the skin and blood on the tongue and it was about her eyes and her mouth, somehow.

But that's just the impression, and a vague one at that. I still can't say what her poem was about, not really. Same goes for speaking about the shape of her mouth, or describing the feel of her tongue on mine and the chill of her lips between my legs. Same goes for the colour of the shadows she cast or her hair or her eyes, which might have been green.

Of course, she went overtime. They all do, the new poets. Castaigne went over by twenty seconds, which makes for a small penalty. The five judges loved her though, awarded her an 8.9, a 9.3, a 9.5, another 9.5, and a 9.9, so the penalty barely hurt her score. The room roared its approval of the judges' decision and clapped and snapped its post-ironic faux-Beatnik fingers as she descended from the stage and came over to me at the bar.

I would like a beer, please, she said, as if she hadn't just blown the room away.

You were amazing, I replied. Just . . . I can't even . . . Tell me you've slammed before. You must have!

Is that what the score cards are about? When I signed up for this earlier, I thought that Todd person was joking. I thought this was an open mic.

God, no. This is competition. Fierce and unforgiving. See, that Todd person? He's gonna drop your lowest and highest scores and add the three in the middle. That's a 28.3 right there, before the penalty. That'll get you into the second round for sure, considering . . .

Considering that her only real competition had consisted of the usual cast of slam night regulars: Donny "Dirty" MacIntyre bemoaning the seventh anniversary of his last blowjob (25.2); a kid named Fowler with a Dada-inspired scat session (23.9); a street rapper, spitting his poem straight into a zone of high-speed incomprehensibility (26.1), and a riot grrrl with yet another poem reminding every male in the bar that rape? Yeah, rape is *bad*: 27. Same old slamming shit.

Anyway, all that considered, I really thought it likely that Castaigne would go into the second round. I was right, too. It was intermission, and Slam Master Todd announced the eight poets for the second round: She was at the top. Scored higher than anyone, even with her time penalty.

Good Christ, I breathed. I'll say it again, that's amazing! No one ever does that well first time outta the gate! This? I pulled a pint of IPA and handed it to her. This is on the house.

She reached for the sweating glass and her fingers touched mine and I know I caught my breath again. It was audible. I'd only dated a couple of girls since breaking up with my boyfriend the year before and I was having a little trouble finding my groove, I'll admit it, pun intended and everything. I knew I was looking for a kind of emptiness I could let myself get lost in, but go a little way into most girls and that vacancy in the eyes turns out to be a pretty lie and instead they're full to bursting with neuroses and prejudice and politics and whole histories of hurt. Souls like a well clogged with dull stones and dry sand. No refreshment there.

Castaigne's cool fingers against mine as she received the glass, the mere brushing of skin on skin and I was back at that cliff edge in the dark, a moist wind curling up from below. She looked at me, half-aware, perhaps, of what I was feeling: shock, vertigo, embarrassment. The beginnings of lust. I coughed and started wiping at the bar with a rag while she sipped at her beer.

I don't have a second poem, she said, her eyes wide. What do I do?

What, really? I said, simultaneously grateful to move further into the conversation and regretful of moving away from that delirious precipice. *No second piece?* I pointed at her yellow notebook. *Nothing more in there?*

No. Nothing usable, at least not yet. Like I said, I thought it was an open mic.

Then you, my dear, will simply have to forfeit, said Todd as he came up behind her. Not all Slam Masters are preening, self-promoting, sexist creeps with the grabby hands, but the ones that are would likely select Todd as their one true king. *Which is a fucking shame,* he continued. *Because that was a spell you weaved up there, sweetness. That was, like, rare witchcraft, what you did . . .*

The way Castaigne's slight frame went rigid, the pressure wave of cold air that came off her shoulders . . . well, the effect was impressive. The thing about Todd is that the creepiness gets slipped in beneath obvious physical and sure, I'll even allow him some intellectual charms. Most girls miss it the first few times around. Not Castaigne.

It wasn't about the words, she said, and she wasn't looking at Todd when she spoke. And I guess I'll just have to live with the shame. She was looking at me. Thanks for the drink. Will I see you later?

I stammered some kind of reply, a string of affirmative noises, appended with the hour I was off work. She smiled, a little, turned from the bar and walked off to find a seat to watch the second round. Slam Master Todd fumed for a moment, thrown off his balance by the early frost. He cast me an evil look, easily deflected with a shrug and a grin.

Try not to corrupt her too quick, alright? he snapped. Did you see that score? We need her back. We need her on the team.

You're one to talk. And yeah, I saw.

I'm trying to build a decent team for Nationals, you know. You used to care about that.

Uh-huh. You're also trying to get into as many pants as you can, Todd. Now, there's people who care about drinking behind you. Walk on, little man.

He did, grumbling about what a bitch I was. I knew he'd like to move the slam to another venue, but what other place would have him and his crew, or an audience like this? Cheap hipsters all, half of them drinking coffee at a bar; I really had to hustle to sell anything worth selling. The Moon Under Water, with its shit sound system and its largely unseen, apathetic owner, was as good as they'd ever get, and they knew it.

Second round at a slam is tight, fast paced. The poets save their best for last and become Howitzers behind the mic, words flying like shrapnel. Second round is almost always the angry stuff, the political stuff. I'd steal glances across the room as I worked, trying to gauge Castaigne's reaction. The room would erupt around her after each overdone rant, but she was calm like lake water at dawn, still like the ruin of a building. When Todd got to Castaigne's name on his list, he sighed like an old theatre queen and announced that the winner of the first round had no more poems for the night and was forfeiting her spot. A groan went up and heads turned to Castaigne in disbelief, but she only smiled.

Next time, Castaigne? Todd pleaded. Next time you'll take this thing, baby girl! Don't leave us hanging, am I right, folks? C'mon!

The ghost of a nod from her and the applause boomed again.

The round finished with the last two poets; riot grrrl with a devastating poem about her mother's battle with cancer, followed by Dirty Donny, aware already that he was beaten, phoning it in with an onanistic ode to the crusty graveyard of sweatsocks under his bed. I caught Castaigne looking at me, one eyebrow raised, and, feeling weirdly bold, I mouthed *cancer* at her. She smiled. I hadn't really been keeping track of the scores since she dropped out, so I didn't actually know who the winner would be, but hey, cancer poems beat jerk-off poems every time. Todd briefly checked in with the scorekeeper and announced the winner.

Yeah, cancer beats everything. Cancer got riot grrrl a spot in the finals. Thanks, sick mom. Thanks for hanging out at Death's door long enough for me to get a fucking poem out of it.

Coulda been yours tonight, I said to Castaigne as the bar emptied out. We close early on slam night; the poets frighten our regulars away and then they don't stick around to pay for booze.

I dunno, she breathed. Seems a little arbitrary?

Yeah. The judges are random. Different people each time, and they can't know any of the poets. Sometimes Todd just pulls judges in off the street. Scoring's entirely subjective. Assigning numerical value to artistic output? Jesus. It's meaningless. A game.

She smirked at me. But I could have taken it tonight, huh? Like Todd said?

Yeah, well, for once I agree with him. Your piece was just . . . it was pure. Behind her I could see Todd working his way through the thinning poets toward the bar. But we've spoken of the Devil, so I'll let you deal while I finish up, and then, I dunno . . .

She reached a pale arm across the bar and caught at my wrist with those cool fingers that sent a shock up to my shoulder. My vision spun. My lungs emptied.

There's beauty in the death of meaning, Castaigne whispered. *When it bleeds out, finally? That's purity . . .* Todd was bellowing stupidly behind her, his mouth working like a fish, but his voice was distant and faded to me, as Castaigne's words vibrated and howled in my ears. I yanked my arm from her grip and she instantly turned away, plastering a smile on her face for the oblivious Todd.

The next hours were lived in fog. I closed up The Moon Under Water, my movements automatic, and when I was done, there was Castaigne, waiting for me in the street. She smiled at me and I found my voice. The sound of it startled me, as if I'd never spoken before.

I didn't catch your first name over the feedback, I said as she took my arm.

Technically, you didn't catch my last one either. Names are false. All language is false, but names especially so. Shall we walk? I'm new to town. I suppose that's obvious, though. New to this great, old, terrible city of numberless crimes . . .

She laughed and I laughed with her. It sounded strange, like I'd laughed yesterday or last week or only once, just the one time, back at the beginning of things when everything shone and I was new, and the sound was only catching up to me now in this exhausted street of dull brick and smashed glass under sickly orange clouds lit from below.

Where'd you hear that? You're giving this place too much credit. Naw, nothing ever happens in this city.

She sighed. There's that, too. I know another city like that. It's perfect.

If you say so. Where are we going?

She told me she lived at the docks, on a converted trawler that used to belong to her father. Or at least, that was the impression I got, of fathers who were not to be named and absentee mothers. Ships on dark water, making dark crossings of weary seas between tired, ancient ports. And with those impressions came a vague sensation of Castaigne wrapping her arms around my waist and drifting with me, attached to me, lamprey-like. Her head on my shoulder, hair scented with wood smoke and brine.

She told me so many things as we moved through nighted streets like dreaming rivers, our faces flashing halogen-bright with oncoming traffic. Things I can't remember now, or more likely never understood at the moment of telling. I do recall that a police siren punctured her low murmuring at one point, and that the thickness around my head lifted in time for me to hear her ask whether any poet had ever received a perfect score from the judges. Had she been asking questions all along? Had I been answering?

Like a perfect ten, you mean? I clarified, and the asking sharpened my mind. I shook my head violently and pressed a palm to my temple. *All five judges unanimous?*

Yes. Unanimous in their arbitrary, random, entirely subjective, essentially meaningless decision.

I'd only seen it happen once, and it was a joke, really, at an off-season novelty slam. Dirty had done an impromptu and completely predictable haiku about his dick. Over in twenty seconds, well under time. Gales of stupid laughter. Tens all around.

No, I've never seen it, I told her. Not for a real poem. A true poem.

You believe in such a thing?

A true poem? Yeah, I guess I do. Something that speaks truth to power, makes you bleed, breaks your heart. Yes.

I meant Truth. That phantom . . .

Before I could answer, she resumed her murmuring, there at my shoulder, the sound of oily water sliding up over pebbled shores and drawing back in a steady lunar rhythm. The moment of clarity passed and I fell back into fog.

I returned to myself somewhat when I no longer felt concrete below my feet, but slick wooden planks. The tang of creosote and diesel fuel and low tide filled my lungs. Castaigne had brought me to the docks, and not one of the fashionable marinas either, but a crumbling collection of jetties between the decommissioned naval yard and an oil refinery. Her home was a black hulk among hulks at the end of the least decayed slip, and the only one that still floated. I felt a terrible anxiety well within me, tremors of fear skipping up and down my vertebrae, worsening when I saw the name of the trawler in faded gold paint on the stern: *The Heart of the Hyades.*

That's an awful name for a boat, I whispered, though exactly why I felt this way was lost on me. I sensed some crime associated with it, something deep and unthinkable. *I don't know why but why? God. Why that name? It's horrible, oh, I can't even . . .* but her voice was suddenly at my ear again, sibilant and laced with spiced honeys, and her hands were guiding my own to the ladder bolted to the hull and then I was aboard *The Heart of the Hyades* and then shaking with reasonless terror inside the wheelhouse and then breathing hard below deck with her sure hands beneath my clothes, lifting, pulling, tearing, and then naked and numb in Castaigne's bed.

The numbness became a dream of viscous ruby seas, of floating, and I was but one floating thing among many, so many, floating soft and aimless with the wrack and detritus of a thousand ruined worlds fallen to the waves that rolled unheeded beneath blackened stars. And Castaigne, borne to me out of the dark on whispers and keenings and murmured anti-promises; Castaigne a pale, muscular serpent rising from lightless depths to pierce my dreaming with hollow staccato pleasures; Castaigne the walls of a cavern above and below me and on all sides and pressing in in in on me with nothing, nothing but weeping rock extending beyond the walls of her forever and ever . . .

I cried out.

I cried out in the dark of that hull many, many times.

Finally, I stopped. Whatever receptacle in me that held those cries had emptied. My heart slowed. My vision cleared and adjusted to the dark. Castaigne's pallid features and indifferent eyes drifted before mine and I felt her cool palm on my cheek.

That's not your name, I sighed.

I read it. I read it in a book about a play about a place. It's not true. It's as good as any. And it doesn't matter.

She lit a few candles then, and showed me her books, arrayed on secured shelves either side of the bed.

Here's Borges, the complete works. I love him. Clever little essays, so dry. He gives me chills. Here's Spicer, she said. As he lay dying in hospital with a ruined liver, he said, "My vocabulary did this to me." Poets, right? She giggled.

I'm a poet, I whispered.

Ah, you were a poet. But you went too far in, like all the good ones do. Too far in to meaning and then out the other side. Look at Spicer. Blaming the words when it's the reality behind them, the thing that languages are built to conceal, that, that is the problem.

No matter. It's easily fixed, with what I've learned. Things my father taught me, from the book. She selected two volumes from the shelf. And here it is. The book about the play. And this is the play . . .

She read it to me. When she was done reading, and I was done weeping and being sick over the side of her bed, she handed me her notebook bound in yellow leather.

Here's all my poems so far, she said. There's space for one more, I think.

Something embossed on the cover, only noticed through touch, a symbol I refused to discern clearly. Feeling it writhe beneath my fingers was enough to know I did not want to see it. Pages with single words, the letters scribed in insect-thin lines stretching the height of the page but crushing the eyes nonetheless with intolerable weight. Pages with short phrases that opened into the void. Pages blackened to the edges with howls. A single page in the centre of it, blank. I nodded, the numbness returning. Castaigne lifted her book from my dead hands and pressed it to her breasts.

So when's the next slam? she said.

What is a week? Arbitrary collection of hours to be sold or ransomed, random meals and collisions, arguments and sleep and stupid joys that fade into aches of misplaced longing. I know that being with Castaigne caused me to lose time; of my escape from her I could recall nothing save bright panic and hot bursts of pain deep in my bones each time I fell while running. The time that had passed since my flight barely registered on my consciousness. What is a week? A planet spinning for a while in the dark.

When she entered The Moon Under Water, I felt it. I could not look up. I heard her talking with Todd at the sign-in table. Even over the chatter of a very full room, I could hear her. She was all I could hear. Todd was joyful at her arrival, guffawing like an idiot, asking her if she'd prepared at least two poems to crush her competition with. The disappointment in his voice when he heard her answer.

But . . . but you need two, girl! There's two rounds!

I'll only need the one, she said, and in my ears the words sounded true, sounded real, the first real words I'd ever heard. Words understood by the ignorant and wise alike as the prophecy they were, envoys of the doom that lay behind them. I hung my head in supplication, in fear, and with shuttered eyes waited for her, my lungs straining not to breathe and then she was there, coming around the bar to stand in front of me, and I still could not look at her when she took my hand in hers and placed a soft, pliant thing in my palm.

You'll need this. For after.

It was a key chain, the foam kind that floats. Yellow.

Everyone expected her to take the slam that night. No one expected her to do it the way she did. And when to raucous cheers and hoots she took the stage and lightly gripped the microphone stand in long-fingered, cold hands and raised her vague eyes to the audience, I turned my face to hers and grateful I fell, finally, from the cliff edge of her to plummet between her lips at the moment she parted them to speak.

This one is called Home to Carcosa . . .

A planet spinning in the dark.

Black waves, glinting with the light of rubied stars, breaking on obsidian lake shores.

A moon rising and the towers of a city behind that moon, impossible, an insult to the eye but true, a deep truth that pains and maddens with the knowing of it, and the song that drifts through the ruined streets and haunted causeways of that city, the song of a mother, a queen in a tower behind the moon, a song that mocks sorrow even as it mourns for all the weak, fragile meaning that the girl Castaigne is draining out of the dry, hopeless well of our world with a poem, the last poem anyone in The Moon Under Water will ever hear, a poem built of words that could only be spoken in the living shadows of Carcosa, tattered shadows that spread and lengthen from her feet to engulf and make void and bring all that they touch within her terrible blank gaze.

The Moon Under Water is there now, translated, and literally so, I know, translated to a grey suburb of the unchanging city at the heart of the Hyades. In fear of the burst of meaningless noise that she is, the judges take up slivers of shattered pint glasses and carve ones into their eternally renewing flesh and laugh. In honour of the lie that is her name, they carve zeroes and weep. The timekeeper sits in a corner where she clicks at her useless stopwatch, measuring out eternity in three-minute segments. The slam master silently mouths *now the King is coming* and *now the King is coming* and *give it up folks for the King in his coming* into a dead microphone. With sere mouths and bleeding lips the poets yammer endless empty verses into the dust of each other's ears. All there thirst. There is no one to tend the bar.

When the night is clear, and I am able to bear it, I come out onto the deck sometimes and lie down. The light of Aldebaran finds the vacuity of my eyes just as I imagine it finds hers, and in that moment I will all the myriad worlds between us to crumble and fall and join me to float in the sea.

I will it, but I don't have the words.

SHOUT / KILL / REVEL / REPEAT

THE *HASSAN-I SABBAH* TOUCHES DOWN / crashes / sexually assualts / makes landfall on the shores of the Mad Continent in the last hungry minutes of the Hour of the Spastic Mandala. The shiftship quakes like a palsied geriatric and yowls in obvious pain / pleasure / indifference / surprise. The sound / colour and vibration / texture are enough to wake me, or at least bring me up to what passes for human consciousness in this, the Time of the End, the Eternal Finishing of the World, the Age of Dead Stars.

"Greetings from sunny R'lyeh," I whisper / mindlessly chant in a guttural tongue I barely recognize as mine / gasp with my last breath as I gaze from a porthole onto a sea like phosphorescent corpse-clogged black gelatin, a sea that washes and foams onto a spit of so-called land that looks like a migraine made of granite / oozing egg sacks / other, brighter migraines.

I would order the shiftship to immediately begin repairs on itself, but a quick glance at the telltales in my sleep chamber tell me that would be unnecessary; the *Hassan-i Sabbah* had etheric conduits draining strange matter from the ancient alien stone of R'lyeh since it cleared the event horizon in the early hours of a grumbling dawn. Her protests have nothing to do with her state-of-being and everything to do with where she is.

"Good girl," I whisper, and place a palm on a bulkhead that quivers and warms to my touch. The *Hassan-i Sabbah* used to be several whales, sperms and greys and humpbacks, but that was very long ago, before the hexentechs went to work on her, before I took command. She's old. I don't know what she is now, but she's a she. A capable she, a she that's delivered us safely.

We are here. We have arrived. Other telltales indicate that our payload is safe, our hearts resolute. My crew is well-trained, healthy, at least thirty percent sane, and most importantly, prepared. We have had centuries to prepare.

I open a channel to greet them.

"You all know what to do. Boots on the ground in twenty."

I close the channel / murder a small bird with my bare hands / masturbate my secondary organs until they bleed / finish penning this narrative / weep for a mother I can't remember, then prepare to go ashore.

Before setting my feet for the first time on the schizophrenic ground of the Dreaming Lands, I pay a visit to the upper deck to check on our payload.

Nestled in the concave bay of its hangar, the ruddy light of the clinker sun glistens from its surface like mother-of-pearl, like Hope. A team of hexentechs swarm around the massive globule like the ants they are, attaching Hoffman-Price field generators to its carriage of steel and bone.

I marvel / shudder in fear / shrink away in disgust at the sight of it. I know that within its esoteric depths lies a hermaphroditic human form, a painfully beautiful androgyne body that houses a Perfected Human Soul, the shining result of generation after generation of artificially-induced reincarnation. We were never able to figure out how the Yith had migrated their entire population across space and time into new bodies, but we understood enough of their abandoned mind-transfer technology to reverse-engineer our own crude devices and move a single mind from one dying body into a freshly conceived one.

Over and over again, and then again. Again. Again. A thousand years to shield one individual consciousness from the madness of the world in the deepest chamber of the Voorish Domes. A thousand years for the hexentech priesthood to refine whatever it is we are into its purest, most energetic form. Now that form rests, a saviour, waiting to fulfill its dread purpose, to do what saviours do. To save us.

Grantha waddles to my side, and I try not to let my eyes rest for too long on his twisted features.

"Is it ready?"

"Yaz, yaz, Captain. Zhe's ready, ready, ready for that jelly, straight up." The hexentech high priest's voice is a glutinous, wet thing that slops unpleasantly into my ears / licks the fingers of my left hand / lays eggs in my dermis. "That's the last of the field generators now. You get the anchor where it needs to be, and we'll deliver our shining Little BoyGirl here. Right into his throne room. We'll drop hir right into his abominable lap. *Who's a shiny baby?* he'll coo. *Who's a morsel? Who's tasty?*"

"We'll get there. We've trained for this."

Grantha smirks and gurgles. "Oh, sho nuf, son. You're the best. Best of the best of the hand-picked beasties and no mistake, none." His head does a repulsive little jig on his shoulders, and he points a scabrous chin to the pearl. "Still. Makes ya think, don't it? Puts your own monstrous existence into some kinda horrible perspective."

"I don't follow."

"Look at it there. A Perfected Human Soul. A being of pure enlightenment. Conduit for untold kilotons of Universal Energy. Or whatevah, whatevah. I'm sayin' it's cold, homes. All our work and striving, all the love and death and blood-soaked evolution, from the second we climbed down outta the trees, a million years and change of the Struggle, and *this* is all we're good for?

"The best and highest thing we can ever be is a bomb, Captain Strunk."

"A bomb to take out a god, hexentech. That's something."

"Maybe, maybe. Or take out its balls, at least. If it has any." The grisly little gnome sniffs, kicks at a loose bolt at his feet, sending it clattering over the side of the ship. "Good luck, in any case. Waiting on your signal."

"You'll get it."

He puts his back to me and waves a hand in a vaguely disrespectful manner, starts barking at his acolytes.

The best and highest thing . . .

Atomics couldn't do it; the Thing That Should Not Be and its impossible spawn weren't made of our matter. Harvesting asteroids from the Kuiper Belt and dropping them on their insane cities couldn't do it; the shrieking fractal architecture received them like kisses, incorporated them into its mass. The re-purposed tech of the extinct crinoid things in Antarctica, poorly understood and poorly implemented, did little more than annoy them.

And all the while, with every attempt to cut them, to disintegrate them, to collapse the weird space-time bubble that housed their foul continent and send it back where it came from, we went mad. Our dreams, our every thought and feeling turned against us, as surely as we turned on each other in rage and confusion. Our minds losing all cohesion as surely as our genes. Our very existence on this plane becoming multiple, a constant flux of forms and actions in a temporal stream that thrashes and buckles and splits every second, only to merge again every other second.

How long has it been since I did *one thing* only?

We became monsters. Monsters in a world ruled by greater monsters, rulers who didn't even acknowledge our presence, except to scoop up a handful of us when they got peckish. And there are very few of us left to scoop.

So. Let this mission I lead be my last. Let it be my one true and singular thing, my pure deed in an impure world.

I cast a last glance / scream until my throat's raw / faint / do a manic jig to entertain the unseen being at the core of Grantha's bomb before going below to check on the engines.

"Are they fed?" I ask before she can say anything. "I want them happy and fueled and ready to pulse the second we get back."

My chief engineer has a terrible speech impediment. Even with the inhibitor collar anchored by flexible spurs to the cartilage of her throat, her voice is still weapon enough to make eyes bleed. Without the collar, Silattha Parv could ask your pineal gland to come out through the front of your skull for some air, and the thing would do it, too. Another child of the hexentechs: a Speaker to the Hounds.

"They're *never* happy, Captain." Her eyes roll alarmingly in her head, and she grinds her teeth with such force her breath carries with it little chalky puffs of enamel. She pats the side of the perfect sphere that is one of the two Tindlosi Drives.

SHOUT / KILL / REVEL / REPEAT

Without the neutered Hounds suspended in grav-harnesses within the plasteel casing, the *Hassan-i Sabbah* would have broken up into shrapnel, cetacean meat, and good intentions before the sun had set on the first day out from shore. Slaved to the ship and the navigation system, the Hounds provide power, and let the ship slip along angles outside of Time, avoiding the worst of the distortion waves that tsunami their way across the planet from R'lyeh.

"They are Foulness and a Contagion from before there was a Universe and they are lean and athirst, as ever, Captain, but they. Are. Never. Happy." Silattha hisses to the floor. Paint peels around her feet. "But fed. Oh yes. My babies are fulla babies."

"I don't know how long we'll be gone . . . "

"Yup. Time gets funny here, I get it. Got my dogs on an automatic three squares a day of ripe abortions. The hopper's full, so quit your worrying."

The early research that led to our payload on deck revealed a terrible truth: There *was* such a thing as a soul, though as a descriptive term "soul" was woefully loaded and inaccurate. A discrete packet of energy, then, unique and unchanging, that accessed this dimension through the medium of flesh. Sometimes the flesh failed or was ended before it had a chance to really dirty that energetic cocktail: miscarriages and abortions. The hexentechs knew enough about their cannibalized Yithian machines to begin the harvest of these small but potent packets from the depths of the past, but with no purpose other than the pure science of it, the so-called souls were put in storage and stayed there. Until we caught our first Hound in a grav-sink, that is.

"Poor things," I say. Silattha whips her head around at me at the words, and I can see her merciless ghoul ancestry leering at me from the lines of her face.

"Poor things? *Poor things?*" she snarls. "Man, you don't know what they experience! They were never going to live, Deimos. They were dead already. Shit, they've been dead for *millennia*. And now they serve us. The dead should serve the living." Her eyes flare wide enough to show white all around, her irises flexing wildly.

The best and highest thing . . .

"Is that from your cannibal bible? Dagon's Teeth. Are you *high* right now?"

Her face cracks wide in a sloppy canid grin. "You know it, Captain." She lifts the mass of her yellow-grey mane to reveal an intravenous slug strapped to the back of her neck. She taps it. "New Jack Lao on a steady drip, cut with a little hexstacy to take the edge off."

I know it won't affect the mission, but it irritates me anyway. I don't say anything, but then I don't have to.

"Don't get pissy, D. I'm five by five. Still feeling mad aggro, though. You said boots on the ground in . . . ?"

"Twenty. That was eight minutes ago."

"So it's a quick fuck then." Silattha turns her back to me, places long palms against the milky translucency of the Drive. "C'mon. You know how a ghoul likes it."

Her orgasm sounds like a dirge. From the impossibly compressed space inside of the sphere, a livid blue tongue lashes out to trace a spastic trail of sizzling ichor where her curves press into the plasteel. She hisses, and her own tongue mirrors the action. I shudder / compose a haiku / half-recall a play I once saw or acted in, I'm not sure which / climax, and then pull away from her.

"All ashore who's going ashore, Sil." She whimpers something affirmative in response.

She's still licking the sphere when I leave.

On the slick, nauseous pseudo-granite of the shore, littered with the aromatic remains of dead sea life, the massive Vantablack tetrahedron that is the Hoffman-Price anchor sits in a chassis, studded with grav-harnesses waiting for activation. Around it, a dozen makeshift altars have been set up, for those inclined to make religious observances before heading inland.

The nameless hexentechs use ceremonial graphite crystal blades to remove thin strips of flesh from their forearms or abdomens, according to their rank. Worshipful tongues click in dry hexentech mouths while braziers cough a greasy pungent smoke into the air as the strips are consumed in offering to their obscure Render, Daoloth.

Silattha lifts a juvenile dhole's skull to her mouth and drinks from its contents: a heady liquor brewed from the worm's fermented seminal and lymphatic fluids. She toasts her charnel gods with a wordless curse thrown to the boiling sky.

Other prayers are made. Piotr Tillich, my science officer, lifts the lid of a black lacquered wooden box and with unmoving lips hums to the glowing thing inside, his buzzing quickly moving below the range of hearing into the subsonic. I don't pretend to know what passes through his Yuggoth-cultured mind; Mi-Go meatpuppets are eternal observers, detached, inscrutable.

Grantha's faith is ancient and foreign; he stamps on a trigger-pad to generate a holographic representation of something he calls a *curb*: a dull grey rectangular slab of some porous stone, complete with small tufts of weedy plant material leaping from the cracks, and the suggestion of odd sigils cast upon a ghostly wall that float in the air behind the curb in traceries of neon light. The hexentech high priest roots around in a satchel at his waist and produces a bottle of amber fluid, which he empties out onto the virtual object.

"For my homies," he says, not without a certain reverence.

"I hope your old gods are looking out for us, priest," I say as he waddles past me on his way to the gangplank. He grunts.

"Homies got better shit to do, I'm thinking. Can't hurt, though, straight up. What about you, Captain?"

"Prayer doesn't work, Grantha. It never did. And the gods that could listen choose not to."

Piotr pauses in his humming to look up. "Perhaps the very one we go to destroy this day, Captain. Why is that, do you think?"

"Why is what, Tillich?"

"Why do the Old Ones not speak? We have made our attempts, over the centuries, to send ambassadors. To open a dialogue. To come to terms with madness and filth, degradation and horror. With the true state of the Universe. To dream its dreams, and survive the experience. Yet not once has it spoken."

"We've had this chat before."

"Hm. Yes. You know my views, then, Captain. Since my abduction by the . . . well, you know my history as well. The trick to communication with the alien is knowing when you've got one on the line. For instance . . . "

He drops into a sudden crouch and aggressively probes the carcass of some deep-sea abomination with a finger. In moments he pulls a foul R'lyehian grub from the red mess, its thrashing asymmetrical length all random pincers and eye stalks. Grantha huffs and makes his grumbling way back to the ship, while his hexentechs and Silattha gather round for the demonstration.

"Look at this creature. It has no conception of me as a being, does not even know in any more than a rudimentary way that it is held between my thumb and forefinger. It does not even know what fingers are, or a hand. It has no language, other than perhaps the silent firing of its own nervous system. We are utterly unalike, it and I.

"Now, say I wish to communicate with it. To tell it something. Relay some small truth about existence to it. How may this be done?"

Before anyone can answer, Piotr drops the grub to the stone at his feet and crushes it beneath his heel. There is a sound of crumbling chitin and a strong acrid tang as the guts of the thing are exposed to the air. Piotr looks at us all, a strange expectant light in his hybrid eyes.

"Do you think it misunderstood me?"

Silattha smirks and licks her lips. "But they haven't killed us. Or at least, not all of us."

"True. But then, whom the gods would destroy they first make mad, Parv. And are we all not such, after our various fashions? Only minds as functionally insane as ours could survive here." He presses his heel into the stone again, twists it, rendering the pulpy tissue into liquid. "Perhaps *our* ultimate revelation awaits us still."

"That's enough, Tillich," I snap. "You want ultimate revelation? It's up on deck, waiting for us to get that anchor to the coordinates."

"Of course, Captain. Of course. Our final statement." He lifts his dripping heel and grins horribly at it. "Which may amount to little more than a pinch from a grub."

"The early bombs in the Severn Valley did for the Old Ones there, Fun Guy," Silattha scoffs. "Same goes for the Wind Walker, *and* the Voltigeur King in the North Atlantic. Those were low-yield devices, but they bulked up the human life-wave enough to drive the beasts back."

People, I almost correct her. Low-yield souls. Perfectly enlightened, weaponized souls.

"Minor deities, all," Piotr counters.

"And this one is major, right? Well, what kind of *fhtagn* difference does it make? Okay, so, we bring it some major ordnance. This is the biggest bomb we've got!"

The meatpuppet laughs, a sound like stones clicking together at the bottom of a well.

"What *difference*? My dear, look around you. Look around. This is *R'lyeh*. To say that the rules here are different borders on comedy."

"Enough, Tillich." I signal to the hexentechs, who scramble to activate the grav-harnesses that support the anchor and our supplies. The loads lift into the distorted air with a dull thrumming.

"We're here to break a few rules."

Forty-one minutes into the Hour of the Itinerant Showman, one of the hexentechs crumples to the ground with a shriek. Before anyone can get to him with a hypo of sedative, he manages to rip out his tongue at the root / disembowel himself with a graphite blade / shatter his own spine with a single self-induced convulsion. As he lies dying at our feet, he lists a number of concerns with each ragged expulsion of breath.

"I'm worried about my kids. Little Sarai and Tim-Tom.

"Those Who Sit Above in Shadow have your number, Captain Strunk, and it's not one you can count to, not in the whole of Time's vast expanse. Didn't you get the memo?

"I'm pretty sure I left the gas on at home. I don't know what that means.

"In his House at R'lyeh, he waits, awake. He dreamed us, but now he's awake, and the dream is over, and we are nothing but sleep-grit the Prime Minister of Horror flicks from the corner of his terrible eye. A microbe on the grit. Gritty stuff, Captain.

"People. There aren't any, you know. I don't have any kids. Tell my non-existent wife I . . . "

Poor bastard. His fellows strip him of gear and rations, then roll his corpse close to where two massive blocks of stone meet in a headache-inducing angle. The weird physics of this place do the rest, and the hexentech slides away into an impossible oblivion, the shape of him dopplering into the distance at speed while his colour and the outline of his bones remain to leave a print on the rock. Piotr is at my elbow suddenly, a still presence of unnatural calm.

"That's one down. Madness takes its toll."

"We've enough left to manage."

"Hm."

"The simulations prepared us for this. Everyone here has clocked years in the Tryptamine Baths, mastered the Oneiric Steeplechase at elite levels, run every track at the G'hnath-Carter Angles. There is nothing this place can throw at us—physically, mentally, spiritually— that we haven't anticipated."

"And yet . . . " Piotr murmurs as we watch the last of the dead man fade into the ravenous stone.

In the Hour of the Fleshless Mask, in a claustrophobic canyon of columns that throb and glisten with an ichor that reeks of kerosene and rotting uranium, we turn a seemingly endless corner to be greeted by a R'lyehian citizen, the first of many, and I am forced to remove Silattha's collar. The spurs exiting her flesh drag gobbets of meat at their tips.

The ghoul-girl begins her serenade. Not everyone gets their hearing protection on in time, and these join the star-spawn in the wholesale dissolution of their molecules. It's a slow process, accompanied by much screaming, and the delirious howl of an ancient, unkillable thing violently changing state, painting the walls of the canyon in a phosphorescent gore-mist.

When she's done, Sil clamps her deadly mouth shut and signals for her collar. The air hums with the last notes of her attack and the lingering consciousness of the beast that still permeates the spaces between space, seeking ingress. I slide the spurs back into her seeping wounds with gratitude. Then I empty my guts on the stuttering tiles and bas reliefs to the sound of the hexentechs mourning their fallen.

"Quite the solo," I manage after a few minutes. Sil pants with happiness at my small praise.

"I had an appreciative audience. Can you believe I had to target *all* of its hyper-chakras? Just wow. Wait," she says, her voice dropping to a whisper. "Okay. Okay, it's still here. I don't know if I'm up for an encore."

Piotr looks up from the strobing displays that hover in a holographic coil around his head. He nods, confirming what we all feel. "We should move, Captain."

The air and rock of the canyon split at his last syllable. For half a moment, the thing finds physical form again. A maelstrom of viscid flesh and hissing pinwheel claws with multiple entry points into reality. I'm raked across my dorsal plates and fall to the ground. A hexentech is split from neck to groin by a whip of spikes. Silattha and Piotr dive below a pistoning limb that strikes the anchor, reducing four of the device's grav-harnesses to sparks and dust.

The moment passes, and we're alone again with our wounds and the dead. The anchor lists to the right, the harnesses on the left side shrieking in protest, and impacts the wall with a sickening crunch.

Our curses ring out and return to us strangely echoed by the maze that is the Dreaming City, the First City. R'lyeh.

"This fucking place. Worst spot on the planet," Sil sighs. The remaining hexentechs are frothing at the mouth with despair as they adjust the grav-harnesses.

Piotr snickers. "There's decent evidence that it's not actually *on* the planet, engineer. Such efforts to get here, after all. Your doggie-powered engines, just as an example. The old records state that R'lyeh wasn't here before. The sea floor at these coordinates was sea floor and nothing more. And then it *was* here.

"Massive, an entire continent. Ancient cities of primal evil. Infinite suburbs of existential mirror-muck, sprawling slums constructed of discarded, croaking anti-languages, laced over with living circuitry telepathically transmitting a constant insect-chitter stream of flash-cut reverse-universe pornography! I can't be the only one who watches the broadcasts on the backs of his eyelids, so don't give me that look.

"R'lyeh! Suppurating districts of unspeakable shopping malls that give ferocious new meaning to consumption. Thumping hyperdimensional everlasting-night clubs, every bouncer a shoggoth, every dancer a coruscating chaos of perversion and alien sensuality!

"R'lyeh! Suddenly, it had *always* been here, because it had never left. The stars were right and there was nothing for us. Nothing but what the Old Ones gave us. Nothing but their gift."

Sil hisses and hawks a bloody mass from the back of her throat onto the stones. "Dagon's Teeth! Listen to him with the fuckin' poetry! The Fun Guy *loves* the place. You're sick, puppet. You've got spores for brains."

Piotr smiles and winks. "Such a literalist, Sil."

"You can give your guided tour some other time, Tillich," I say. "We all know the stories."

"Hm. Stories which *suggest* that R'lyeh occupies, or somehow *is,* a highly artificial bubble of space-time. This place could be their ship, occupying multiple points in the Universe but only manifesting at certain times. When the stars are right, they plunge from world to world."

A hexentech appears at my side and whispers into my ear. I don't like what I hear. I cut him off and address the team.

"Enough speculation. The anchor's in the air again, but it won't be for long. We need alternate transport, and that means your specialty, Piotr."

Tillich rubs his hands in glee / tears at his hair / consults a holo-readout at his wrist / spontaneously bleeds from his eyes and smiles.

"Move with a purpose, people."

It takes half a day to haul the limping anchor to the nearest shoggoth midden. By the time we arrive it is already the Hour of the Guarded Quotation and the setting sun is a rusty disc in a lowering grey cobweb sky. We are bone-tired and psychotic: Sil paws at the ground like a muttering animal, Piotr is skittish with wild eyes on constant scan, I'm full of remorse and anger. The sight of the midden does nothing to help our dispositions.

"They're not like that in the simulations," Sil whines.

"They're not like this anywhere," Tillich affirms. "Not even on Yuggoth. So calm. I'd say this is hibernation, but look at the colour spectrum. They're awake, but there's a lack of autonomy here." He punctuates his statements by vomiting down the front of his armour.

"We need one, Piotr," I clip.

Tillich grimaces and wipes at himself with the edge of a hand. "It's a single mass, Captain. It's a pit. Two klicks wide and who knows how deep and . . . it's a *single* shoggoth-mass. I don't . . . "

I glare at him in utter fury, and for once he seems perturbed.

"I'll scout around the edge. See if I can locate a young one." He cracks open a supply pod, begins strapping equipment to his back and arms, places an enhancer circlet on his scalp. "The fresher the bud, the more susceptible to command."

"Just make it happen."

A hexentech fires up a thermal plate and we gather round for warmth, assuming various meditative positions and practicing our *ujjayi* breath. The stone beneath the plate begins to seep oil and blood as it heats; the smell of petrochemicals and scorched honey fills the air like cancer. We quit the *ujjayi* in discomfort and instead watch Tillich move around the midden, the spastic perspective shifting him near and far, reducing him to a collection of sticks, a bloated mass, a cartoon. He pauses, or seems to pause, and there is a frenzied frothing in the pool of sentient plasm near him. In moments, the sound of his screaming reaches us. I key my radio on.

"All good, Tillich?"

More screaming, a terrific wail of complete anguish, but cut with eerily calm assurances. "Five by five, Captain. In negotiations." Further anguish ensues, so I key the radio off.

Sil slides close to me, leans in to my neck to nip at an ear. There's a rasp in her throat as she speaks and I can feel the quills on the side of my head sizzle and crisp.

"Did you imagine it would be like this?"

"Like what, Sil? Like the maddest madhouse to ever be built? Like a revolting graveyard of the Universe? Like the worst nightmares wrapped in perfect truth? Yeah. Yeah, I pretty much always imagined it to be like this."

"Not that," she sighs. "That feeling you've got. You know?"

"What feeling? Nausea? The near-constant urge to murder everything?"

"Yeah. Only . . . you don't have it? That feeling like you've been travelling your whole life, homesick since the day you were born. When I turned that spawn into powder back there, I just . . .

"It felt like coming home, finally. Like I'd just turned a corner in the road, and there it was. I want to do it again and again. Does that ev—"

She doesn't finish. R'lyeh pulls one of its messed-up physics tricks and Tillich is back with us in one stride, a fetid mass of sentient gelatin towering above him. He's missing his left arm. There's a twitching stump of bleeding mycelial tissue where it used to be, and his face is a rictus of pain.

"Negotiations complete. I could use some cauterizing. Painkillers." The hexentechs shriek and scatter to the medpods. In seconds, there's a dirty pink bubble of analgesic foam where the stalk was.

"What happened there?" I say.

"Show of faith. The master-slave relationship with these things is complex." Tillich sips from a tube held to his mouth. "Give a little, get a little. I am it and it is I." He wets his lips, whistles something in a minor key. The shoggoth heaves and with oozing grace slips its stinking bulk underneath the anchor. It lifts the device as if it were no more than a shell, or a small rock stuck to its hide.

"It's why they came here. To serve."

The beast expels jets of befouled air from a hundred ventricles and it sounds like a hissing *tekelllliii-lliiiiii*. We choke and gag while Tillich chuckles.

"That's right. *Tekeli-li*, motherfucker.

"Now, mush."

The gutted remains of the violated moon lie heavy and fulgent in the blood-black night as we crest a final rise and look down / cast our eyes upward at the sickening crag formation / abyssal flood plain that lies at the centre / on the perimeter of R'lyeh. We have walked the Maze That is Not a Maze, come close to this point a thousand times, only to be shifted away by disobedient angles, monstrous lies of the light, chuckling spatial corridors, minutes that cross-dressed as millennia. But we are here, finally. R'lyeh. You tease.

This place can only be called a landscape with tongue firmly in cheek; there are shifting planes of agitated stone folding in and out of perception, vast blocks of masonry behaving like water, like plants, and a conniving horizon that refuses to separate ground from air from sea. The whole is awash in an emerald fog of peculiar and malevolent density that soaks our skins and armour, slides with intention down the back of the throat to raise bile and fear.

It is the Hour of the Southernmost Pinnacle, and we are on his doorstep, finally. There is the fabled door, near and far at the same time, slightly ajar in its twisting fractal frame set in the side of a mountainous slab of dripping stone, the bas reliefs leaping and foaming like a river on either side. I am thinking of the first dead hexentech and considering my next step.

"So, do we, I dunno, knock?" Sil growls.

"I thought it would be here," Tillich says. "I've corrected for every deviation we've been through. These are the coordinates. I thought we'd see it."

"It doesn't have to be here. It's probably below," I say. "Or between. Off-planet, even. It's free now. Has been for thousands of years. Would *you* stick around if you had to?"

Tillich's face is blank, a bloodless mask of indifference.

"You're making assumptions about a being you can't possibly understand," he says. "And so am I. But in answer to your question, no. No, I wouldn't stick around."

"Wherever it is doesn't matter. This place is its throne. Every insane ley line on the planet converges on this spot. The high priests agree: We detonate here, and R'lyeh collapses. The event horizon we crossed to get here contracts, taking everything inhuman with it back to where it all came from. Back to hell."

"What about us?" Sil whispers.

"We're human. Enough." She glares at me like I've whipped her. "We're human enough."

We pick our way across the migraine canyon / plain, every step threatening to become a fall into the sky, an orthogonal slide into a higher dimension, a stumble into a compressed lifetime of agony. The hexentechs prod the shoggoth with makeshift pikes and the perverse thing moans and whistles with delight at each assault. I get on the radio to Grantha.

"It's time."

My stomach drops as I say the words and my feet follow, rushing away beneath me in a single vertiginous plunge. A moment later and we are at the door, our vertebrae cracking and quaking with the effort to keep upright, our eyes bleeding. One of the three remaining hexentechs gives us a cheery thumbs up and proceeds to reduce the front of his skull to slurry on a bas relief.

"Dreams for the Dreaming Lord!" His laughter becomes a wet red gurgling as his head rockets back and forth into the stone. It's over in seconds. His fellows and Sil and Piotr stare at me in mute horror as I key the radio again.

"Send it through, Grantha. Full Oppenheimer. Repeat, we are at full Oppenheimer."

"Activating Hoffman-Price bubble now, Captain Strunk. Deployment of Little BoyGirl in ten, nine, eight . . . "

The anchor gasps once, twice. The Vantablack coating makes it difficult to see the contractions in the angles of the tetrahedron, so that when it happens, it seems to happen all at once. The anchor condenses, pops out of existence to leave an oily bubble of nothing hanging in the air. A sizable chunk of the young shoggoth goes with the anchor to wherever it went; the beast yowls with sick pleasure.

The void sizzles in anticipation, warbling shafts of light and scenery coming into view: the deck of the *Hassan-i Sabbah*, Grantha's misshapen mug in a silent anticipatory leer, another sky, a different time. Another moment of this and the bomb is here, shedding light and polymer plates like a lotus blossom sheds petals.

The shoggoth roars and changes state in an effort to escape, becoming steam and memory, leaving Little BoyGirl to hover in the air. Green mist recoils and pulses in a peripatetic rhythm at the periphery of the golden light that builds and builds. Tillich is passive in the glow, the hexentechs have tears in their eyes. Sil is on her knees, openly weeping, with her long hands palms up on the stone between her knees. Worshipful.

"So beautiful," I hear her say.

She's right. The footage of the early bomb tests did no justice to the experience of being here, at Ground Zero. The bomb is the most beautiful thing I've ever seen. Little BoyGirl shines like a beacon from heaven as zhe rises, the darkness sloughing away from hir like scales, like a bad dream after waking. Gravity, despair, madness, all the things that could pull hir down to the tormented earth; these have no hold on hir. Zhe shines like the sun; no, better than the sun. Pure in a way the sun could never be. Zhe shines like the Platonic ideal of the Sun, with a light that welcomes the eye instead of burning it away, a light that is Life and Hope. Zhe is clean-limbed and symmetrical, perfect in hir form, with a noble forehead and graceful hands, a golden mane of hair in a halo around hir head. Hir generative members are aroused and pleasing to the eye, thick and moist and swelling with the potential for life, human life, the real *human* lifewave that has been gone from the world for so long and I am weeping now, weeping with the others in this awful place, my hands outstretched to the floating being, this bodhisattva, this gorgeous creature who will sacrifice itself for us, for our future. I want to touch hir face, to tell hir *thank you*, to press my deformed mouth to hir perfect lips and know the grace of hir accepting smile for a single second, know the warmth of hir enlightenment on my wretched wintered skin before zhe saves us all with her glorious ignition. I cry out, once, an inarticulate sound of longing, a longing to be consumed, to be ended in hir light . . .

My cry is answered.

The emerald mist begins to howl. In the air, on the stones, streaming from our fingertips and filling our lungs: Each drop of it begins to vibrate and scream, and not with fear or anguish or rage. This scream is one of lust. Triumph. And worse, a species of gleeful indifference.

Little BoyGirl halts in the air for a moment, and casts hir shining eyes down to the monsters below, to us, hir worshippers, the monsters zhe is here to save. A fleeting cloud of concern passes across hir beatific features before it all comes to an end.

The mist condenses in a thunderclap. It was everywhere: here, across the impossible length and breadth of R'lyeh, and in our dreams and our history, in our genes and our philosophy and most especially in our hubris. It was everywhere, and it had always been. It had never died, only dreamed, and had awakened long ago, and would now, at the birth of stranger new aeons, conquer death. The mist condenses, becomes a mountain that walks, stumbles, screams to end the world.

We answer it, all of us. Sil, Tillich, the hexentechs, myself. Little BoyGirl screams too. The bomb screams most of all as the mountain plucks it from the air with limbs I know are not limbs, only the suggestion of limbs, only seeming to be long muscular feelers to my lower-order mammalian eyes. Little BoyGirl is plucked, and dissected, and raped across all levels of reality, hir perfect soul and hir weaponized enlightenment rendered into a mewling paste. It takes seconds.

There's not much left of hir, but what is left is extended to me, speared on the tip of a writhing pseudopod. A parting gift of awareness. I grasp the contorted remains—the head, part of the upper torso—with numb hands and pull hir to my chest. A golden eye looks up at me from a face made insectoid, reptilian. The perfect lips, smeared into a jackknife smile of derangement, crack and hiss into my ear. The mountain is already moving away, its vast bulk blacking out the moon and the reeling stars, but the words I hear surely belong to it, siphoned through a mouthpiece it has already forgotten it owns.

Captain, Little BoyGirl says. Captain, do not all the old texts state that this would come to pass? The time would be easy to know, for all men would be as we, shouting and killing and reveling in joy. This is the foretold holocaust of ecstasy and freedom. We shall teach you new ways to shout, kill, revel. Enjoy. Your friends are.

In the distance, Piotr is dropping the waxen mask of his humanity and assuming his ideal fungoid form. A hexentech lies convulsing at his feet, obscene mycelial cultures bursting from his mouth and soft tissue. Another is pinned to a slab while Piotr feeds the glowing growth from his ruined shoulder down the hexentech's throat. Piotr hums while he works.

There is a sound of tearing fabric and I feel a sudden searing pain in my core. I look down to see Sil between my knees, my secondary generative organs dangling from her crimson teeth. I drop the saviour's remains at my feet and cuff the ghoul-girl across the mouth. She laughs in derision as her cheek bounces off the slimy rocks with a crack.

"Don't be pissy, Deimos. I'm five by five, still, your Sil, your servant. Stay with us." She moans and twitches and dances like a dog cornering prey. "The dead should serve the living, and there was never anything as alive as the Lord of Dreams. Stay and serve him."

She's not wrong, says the head of Little BoyGirl. You're already here, after all. So many times. So often you visit. Look. Look and see.

I look, and I see the ghosts of every other attempt we've made on the Lord of R'lyeh flicker in and out of view. Bodies and bombs strewn and ruined and draped across the land in a carpet of gore and failed detonations and detonations that *were* successful but made no difference. We are legion, and nothing. The eternal dirt from which nightmares grow. Not even the dirt. Crawlers in the dirt. Mites on the crawlers.

Enjoy, enjoy, enjoy, Little BoyGirl coos. You must work at it, though. The best and highest thing you can be is me, and you've a long way to go. Shout. Kill. Revel. Repeat.

The Hoffman-Price bubble is contracting rapidly, but I throw myself through anyway, knowing I'm too late. As it closes, I can hear the mouthpiece speak to a laughing Sil . . .

Do you think it misunderstood me?

On the deck of the *Hassan-i Sabbah*, I spend a moment in contemplation at the loss of my lower legs, and take some small comfort in the thought that Sil is likely making a meal of them even now, prayers remembered from her cemetery catechism dropping from her mouth between red bites.

I drag myself past the spot where Grantha has propped himself against a bulkhead. He is delicately removing his own eyes with a graphite blade, slice by quivering slice.

"Homie don't do that," the gnome mumbles. "Homie can't see *shit*. Straight up the *wgah'nagl*, coming at ya right straight up."

"Carry on, High Priest," I say, giggling at his futile efforts. There's still the pineal to be seen to. "The stars are right."

"That you, Captain? Mission aborted? Heh. Stars. Son, they ain't never been *wrong*. Y'all be keepin' it R'lyeh, now." He returns to his self-butchery, a wiser man.

I go below, seeking my one true and singular, pure thing. Of course I don't find it, no matter how many corridors I careen down on the stumps of my ruined legs, no matter how many blubbering crew members I tear apart in absent glee. I don't find it.

Instead, I sit in my sleep chamber / confess my sins to the ship / strip naked in front of a mirror, those manifold tusks, that prehensile whatsit, I'm a thing of rare beauty even with the red ruin at my crotch, oh yes / paint myself in bloody sigils / execute a decent pirouette for the gathered ghosts, thank you thank you I'll be here all aeon / make my way to the engine room of stuttering blue light / paint myself again, this time in the weak chakra-glow of depleted abortions retrieved from the overflowing waste hopper in back of the Tindlosi Drives / begin penning this narrative / place one hand on the icy curve of a sphere while the fingers of my other hand drop to a command pad, keying in the sequence that will crack the seal on the sphere.

It is the Hour of the Virginal Appraisal, appropriately enough, and my mind is as clear as the air around me is clouded with the hiss of approaching death. I know what the mountain said at the last, but I respectfully disagree with its assessment. And I may have my one pure thing, now. The best and highest thing I can be.

"Here, puppy," I softly whistle. "Who's a good boy? Who's tired of kibble? Who wants a real meal."

THE CHRYSANTHEMUM

I **'LL TELL YOU** something that's always bugged me, doc. I mean, ever since I got here, it's bugged me. Your chair.

I can tell it's not comfortable, you're not enjoying your time in it. Your time with me. Who would, right? Just doing your job. Making your notes, sitting in a basic, I dunno, it's a thing to keep your educated ass off the floor of my cell. Chair. A *metal* chair, which means that even if I could somehow get out of the jacket, over to where you're sitting, and force you off the thing, I wouldn't be able to, let's say, maybe break it in half? Into pieces. I mean, I'd *try*, at least. They help those who help themselves. Get a splinter or a big sharp hunk out of it to open you up with, to *expose* you. Naw, I'd have to resort to beating you with it, like a wrestler, a fake. Just for show. And honestly, what would that accomplish? Nothing. Less than nothing.

No, to really show them what I can do, to really help *you*, I'd have to open you up, like the others. That's how they've structured this reality. I'd feel bad for a moment or two, believe me, I would. You seem like a nice guy, with a decent shell. Smart, clean. Compassionate. Ya got nice, warm eyes, doc, don't think I haven't noticed. I have.

It's only a seeming, though. I see you, I see what you *could* be. I see you, the light coming through your seams. That's all they *want*, that's all I've been trying to tell you. And it's all *I* want, what *they* want. To bathe in that light, breathe that true air, unburdened by falsehood. I'll tell ya one thing for free, I am sick to death of lies! Let's just be *honest* for once, right? Isn't that a kindness? To live outside the shell, to finally drop the armour?

Is it crazy to want that? I genuinely want to know your thoughts on the matter, doc. Because if it *is*, if it's crazy, then you can walk outta here with your clipboard and that chair and we can end this right now. If it's crazy, I don't wanna be sane, y'know? Do you? Maybe you do. Maybe you want what I want, but secretly. I wouldn't put it past you, honestly. I think most people want what I want, in their heart of hearts. Maybe especially now.

Because it's getting worse out there, isn't it. Brighter? Yeah. Well, that's apocalypse for ya. All shall be revealed, in the end.

But in the beginning, everything was hidden. I didn't know who I was. I knew what I could *do*, but I didn't know who I was, what that meant. Even as a kid, I could feel the falseness in things. School. Religion. Names. What's in a name, right, doc? Yours. Mine. Empty sounds. What are they *there* for?

I remember the man who fathered me, I remember him taking me to the beach, presenting shells to me in his rough palms. Telling me how the soft sea thing inside, whaddaya call em, *molluscs*, telling me how molluscs secrete their shells, build up their armour over time.

I was much more interested in the broken shells, picked over by gulls and cracked under rolling rocks thrown in with the tide. Inside, there'd be this wretched lump of tissue, scraps of flesh quivering. That was true, it seemed to me. It felt real and true, that shaking, that quiver. The shining and the shaking. I'd always laugh at it. The shell was pretty, durable, organized. You're a smart man, doc, you've gotta know about the Fibonacci sequence. It's like, this really gorgeous bit of mathematics. That's there, in the shells, in their spiral construction. In other things, too, a lot, actually. Math as shield, order as offense.

Behind that shield, though? That falseness? The real, raw stuff. That quiver. The colours, the forms that swam in the air around the truth as it tried to show itself, to grow into itself.

So I didn't know who I was. My names? Shell. Parents? Overprotective shells. Faith, shell of delusion. Patriotism, shell, education, shell, desires, shell. Love? Hate? Giant, bivalve barb of hell shell. Something that you secrete, easily or painfully, or gets added on to you, layer after calm, orderly layer, until you begin to look, act, think and feel like a person. A *seeming* person. *Persona*, that's Greek for mask. We are masks of our own facelessness! I've *learned* this, and passed that learning on to others. I didn't know who I was, and I don't think, now, that I ever particularly cared.

But I knew what I could do. In the beginning, I thought everyone could do it. I thought everyone could see the way I saw. How to explain it to you, doc, so that I don't sound insane? There's literally no way. Why I'm in here, I suppose. Well, that, and what happened to my garden.

I only wanted to help them. You need to understand that. I only wanted to prepare them for what's coming. They learned from me, but they couldn't get there on their own, they needed me to help them. To get them right, to cultivate them. Which is why you're here, isn't it? Isn't it.

I remember how it felt to learn that other people, other masks, couldn't see things as I did. That when their true nature looked out beyond their armour, they saw things as the armour saw them! Can you imagine it, doc? That level of disconnect? But of course you can't. You can't. There's a certain investment that needs to be maintained, to live in the world of shells.

Still, you're here, which is making me wonder. I've told you all this before, in our sessions. You in your chair, me in my jacket. You with your notes, and me with my rambling roses rising. What's changed, now? Yes? Something! Yeah. I sense it in you, y'know. I can sense that you sense that I've sensed it, too, seeing as we're sensible creatures. I'll tell you about my sight, then, sensibly, and what I see in you, and then I'll tell you how I can help, because you're going to need it, if you've any sense. Which you have. That's established. I like you, doc, you got the nice warm eyes.

Are they panicking yet, on the outside? Running out of options, of ways to apprehend what's coming, to *deal* with it? Funny, because you can't make deals with the inevitable. Swarms of busy doctors like you, I'm guessing, descending on mental hospitals and psych wards, to visit the special cases, the outliers, the black swans. The fragile fucking flowers like me. Like you.

That's what I see in you. Around you and through you. Petals of possibility, of energy, but it's not your aura, it's nothing so hokey as that, it's something more powerful. *Potential.* The nearest comparable thing to what I see around you is a flower. There's your shell, mask, persona, your shield, doc, and then there's what your true self longs to be, to become, and *that* self, that being? *That* pushes into the future. Strives to make an impression in the stuff of time, blossoms forward into the next seconds, hours, eras. Open and accepting of the change you'll need to make to survive, to become what you'll need to be in the new world. And you'd *make* it, too, if it wasn't for the shell.

I used to think I served some evolutionary purpose, being able to see the forms of the future. As a kid, in class, daydreaming in the thrumming Eden of my classmates, their spreading, eager heads inclined to the teacher towering at the chalkboard, luxuriating in her cloud of humming pollens. I could see what we were to be!

That was before I really understood evolution, though. Evolution is for the *species* and it's slow. Evolution takes time, and at some point I knew we'd be running out of it, and the species was doomed anyway, considering what was coming. What's almost here.

Naw, doc, it's about the *individual.* As a psychiatrist, you must love that. Self expression! *To thine own self be true.* To be wild, to shout and revel and enjoy ourselves, to *become*, to *blossom!* To *revel*, I love that word by the way, to reveal, it's a reveling revelation I experienced, that I could see unravelling in every blooming blown skull! The chrysanthemum! The star-headed ones, coming in sideways at godspeed from the trepanning trans-continuum! Those Who Shit Above in Shadow cleansed and empty and full of light, finally falling towards us from the future, backwards beautiful, a revel of reversal! The Forgotten made manifest, memorable, meaningful, moist and multiform!

Monsters? Moron! Sorry, but don't look at me like that, don't dare! You will strain your pineal, looking at me like that. Because you know! You *must* know! Have you been briefed on them? All those pages on your clipboard? They're thicker than usual. Thicker than the last time. Yes, of course you have, you can't hide from me. I'm guessing, let's see, some of Prinn's pages, and the elders of the Starry Wisdom group always had good insight. They were certainly a help to me when I was just starting out with my own plot, my little garden. I wonder if you've any material there I haven't seen, may I see, those seeds?

No? Well, fuck you, doc. Come in here for my help and then treat me like a crazy person? See how well you do when they return, we will. We're not equals, y'know. You might think otherwise, in fact I'm sure you do, but you're not the superior one here, in this relationship. I have seen the dark universe yawning! Black planets rolling! And what have you seen, doc? What have *you* seen, besides the inside of this cell, the insights on your clipboard, the interior of that insidious shell?

Did the photos there make you sick, I wonder? There's the price of ignorance for you, a little loss of lunch, a dig at your dignity. They called it a crime scene, my garden. A place of transcendence, of glory, and *hope,* doc, real hope for the future! A "mass murder" site, they said. Cult sacrifice.

They were never supposed to die, doc.

We'd planned it all out. There were doctors in my garden, doc. Not like you, *real* ones. Surgeons. Anesthesiologists. All kinds of people came to me, wanting to become more than they were. Doctors, scientists, artists, mothers, criminals, priests. All wanted to grow, to bloom. They'd seen it, in their dreams, what was coming. They'd heard from the star-headed ones, and they knew me. They *knew* me, they'd been *told* about me. And so I helped them. I couldn't *not* help them, see?

But they shouldn't have died. That was wrong. We'd missed something, in the planning. I mean, obviously. I'm still real tore up about it.

Oh, but to be as they are! I wasn't wrong about *that!* To be aligned with the ones coming, spiritually and physically, changes had to be made. The soft slippery thing inside the armour had to be revealed, to shine and shake and laugh in freedom. The shell cracked, the seed burst, and the flower allowed to seek the light of truth, to incline the head toward their radiant being in full knowledge and trust.

I worked with the doctors. Those were exciting days! It wasn't just surgery, not at all. It was art. Sculpture. We practiced a divine mimicry! The armour, the flesh, peeled away and repurposed, if you please. The purpose of petals: to attract, and to guide, to feed and fold. The chrysanthemum, forever flowering fractals of flesh, that was the golden goal. The pineal as pistil, the corneal stalks stamens, ready to receive the germinating transmissions. They should have lived. We worked so hard. *I* worked so hard, so hard. They should have all lived, free and true and trembling.

I was to be the last. I would by then have the knowledge, and the spiritual power, and the will to perform my own transition. The first of the deaths was a shock. Shock and trauma, they said, the coroners coarse and unfeeling. Shock and trauma. But not blood loss! No, we adjusted for that, had plenty on hand, all types, fridges full of it, and the Hemosep machines besides, and it should not have happened. They were supposed to wake into glory! All of them. Not pain. Not dementia. Not to what happened.

Anyway. Tore up, still. That's me. That's me all over, revealed. Therapy, huh? What a thing.

Doc, I'm tired. I am. Can we break? Can you come back later?

Right. Right, I forget. There probably won't be a later. How bad is it out there? Can't you tell me? I mean, does it make a difference at all, now? No. No, I get it. Professional standards, ethics, I get it, I get it.

Say, doc, just between you and me . . . if it *is* bad out there, if it gets worse, much worse, and you feel like maybe you'd like to keep living, you could always come and, I dunno, maybe visit me one last time? Because I'd like to help. I would. Whaddaya think? Because, and I mean this sincerely, doc, I feel like I'm close to a breakthrough, y'know? That maybe it just wasn't the right time, with my garden. Seasons change, after summer is winter, after winter summer, and all that like the Arab said.

Well. If I do see you again, doc, that'll be nice. You've got the nice warm eyes. Just, y'know, maybe bring me something to work with? Even a wooden chair would do.

I could work with a wooden chair.

THE DAMAGE

THE PLAN AT breakfast had been to do at least fifteen kilometers that day, then to finally camp at Hecate's Crib, where the famous blowhole put on its show at high tide, but by mid-afternoon they were both bone-tired from a hard slog across steep-angled beds of moisture-slick shale, and a persistent marine layer of chill fog that sapped their reserves. They had turned off the beach for a while, then, and into the forest to make another attempt at the actual trail; within an hour she had turned her ankle slightly, stepping off a crumbling chunk of cedar. A minor injury that hardly made a difference to their pace, but it was enough to make them stop and reconsider when they reached the little cove.

Kel sets up the camp stove in a clear space between two ancient spans of driftwood and uses the last of their drinking water to brew tea, then heats seawater to cook their boil-in-a-bag meals. "Not that *con carne* stuff again?" Dev says. "I don't know what that is, but it isn't chicken."

"We're saving the paella for the last night, Dev. You know this."

"With the goat cheese? Yeah. This is good tea." He shields his eyes from the glare of sun through fog and scans the klick or two of beach, then collects their water bottles and two Camelbaks into a marine bag. "So I guess we're low on the potable stuff, now."

"Yeah, that was the last of it."

"There's a stream up a ways, I'll fill these up."

"Good."

"It's nice here. There's a decent spot to tent over there. Little rise above the stream and some old campfire leavings. Blackberries. Tide's up so I can't be sure, but I think I saw some sea caves over at the point."

"So. What? You want to stay?" There is sand on her tongue from the lip of her cup. She sticks out the tip and flicks at it with a forefinger, then stops when she notices the black grit already beneath her fingernail. "I thought we wanted to get to the Crib."

"Well. Yeah. I mean, yeah, we do. And we will, tomorrow. It's just, y'know, we're both . . . " He clasps the back of his head with both hands and grimaces for a moment, baring his teeth at the glare though the fog. "Christ, that's bright. I mean, look, I'm pretty tired. And there's your ankle."

"Yeah." She nods. "No. You're right. We should rest."

"It's not like the blowhole is going anywhere."

The fog clears by late afternoon, the glare replaced by a searing blue sky and sharp-edged discs of white sliding over each other atop the waves. They spend a curious hour wading through the chill tidal pools, their legs tangled in the thick, cold rubber of seaweed. The strands feel good wrapped around her ankle, but she is nervous about surges, and lingers near the smooth entrances of newly revealed sea caves while he plunges deeper, hollering at times when he spots anemones clinging to the rocks in the dimness.

"Kel! You should come in here! Thing's fucking huge!" His voice is weirdly hollow and resonant from within.

"No thanks!"

"C'mon. Genuine sea monsters in here!"

She leaves him to it and thinks about the night ahead, casting her gaze back along the beach to their campsite. The tent pops from the black and green of the forest like a faceted ruby jewel, glowing in the sunlight.

She calls in to him. "It's going to be clear later."

"Yeah?"

"I mean it's clear *now*. I was just thinking that we haven't done any stargazing yet . . . "

"Yeah. Yeah!" He's out of her sight, but she can hear him sloshing roughly towards her. In a moment he rounds a bend to appear at another cave mouth, ahead of where he'd entered. He's panting with the effort of wading, his t-shirt soaked to the chest.

"Man, it got tight in there for a second. Hey, baby."

"Hey. I wish you'd be more careful."

Devon waves that away. "Nah. I'm good. Say, if you want, we could eat those mushrooms. Watch the cosmos wheel. Whaddaya think?"

"I just wanted to watch the stars, really. Unenhanced? I thought we were saving those for the . . . "

"Oh man. Don't. Just . . . " He pulls a hand through salty hair. "We've got, like, two *ounces*. Plenty for tonight *and* later."

"I don't know." She feels suddenly exhausted, pushed in a single moment to a grey place beyond the physical ache of her limbs and bones. He could take her there instantly, with his stubbornness. Other things. There is a pressure behind her eyes, and she finds herself unable to look into the churning, fragrant dark of the caves, so she turns to begin the slow walk back to the campsite. He follows after, and she has to fight against the impression that his figure is looming larger, unspooling in coils from the water to press into the air at her back.

"It's going to be cold." She crosses her arms and clasps them to her chest. "I don't want to be cold."

"Baby. I'll make us a viewing platform. In the sand. We'll lay out the thermal pads and sleeping bags." He catches up with her, drapes a heavy arm over her shoulders. "You've only ever tripped with me in the city. It'll be fun."

"It's going to be different." In the city, he would tease her by reminding her of a throwaway statement she'd made the first time they'd gotten high together, on MDMA. *This is good stuff,* she'd said after an hour had passed. *I mean, if I had to drive someone to the hospital, I could!* It was stupid drug-talk, and she'd known it for what it was the moment it left her lips, but he'd held it over her ever since.

"You mean it's going to be dangerous." He laughs, and the sound of it grates. She can hear the drive to the hospital waiting behind it. "It's not. It's really not."

"How much do you want to take?"

They reach the campsite. Devon starts to clear a space with the edge of his foot, etching out a large circle in the sand below the rise. "Enough. We'll take enough. Take what you like, Kel."

"I'll make us some food first."

"Hey." He shoots out an arm as she passes by him, catches her elbow. "It's not like you haven't zoomed before, kiddo. You *do* know you'd have to eat, like, a pound of the stuff to be in any real trouble, right?"

"Sure." She tries not to pull against his grip, but does, even so. He doesn't seem to notice, but lets go anyway, goes back to his kicking at the sand.

"There's just no way to O.D. on shrooms. The LD-50 is through the roof and even then, the worst part would be the psychological presentation. Anyway." He shrugs, reaches down to dislodge a burnt piece of driftwood, throws it at the tideline. "I'm going to make it a nautilus. Nautiloid."

"What?"

"The viewing platform. Sand sculpture. We'll cozy up in a nautilus shell." She can see it now, as he gets down on his knees to describe sweeping arcs from the centre with his hands. "Gonna Fibonacci this thing! I'll ring it with stones. Hella sacred. It'll be cool. You'll see."

"I'll make something."

"Yeah, we should eat a little. Not too much, though."

She isn't cold. Or if she is, she doesn't notice, or chooses not to notice. The Milky Way pulses and throbs in the moonless night like a titanic ophidian river above them. Each pinprick of light sheds spectral petals into the black on a continuous loop, linked with other pinpricks in delicate traceries of shuddering light. It is almost too much; her breath comes hot and ragged into the air, weighted with wonder, fear, nameless anxieties and joys. She pulses with the stars, she is thick with heat behind her eyes, her spine a column of molten gold. She isn't cold.

"Are you cold?" Devon asks.

Yes, she thinks. "No. No, the bag's enough. And I have my hoodie. I'm okay." She pauses. "Are *you* okay? Are you cold?"

"Baby, I'm fan*tas*tic. Did I tell you? Didn't I?"

"Yes."

He tries to quote McKenna. "It's like, y'know, we're so alienated from our own being. The soul, right? And Terrence, he said, that because of that . . . Wow. Okay. So we'd meet ourselves and only recognize the alien. Right? Like we came from up there. Only not?" She feels the insecurity that drives him flaring up, chopping his ability to speak to pieces. "Anyway. We're not, is what he meant. Alien. I'm sorry. That's . . . that was weird. The shrooms talking."

"What was weird?" She pulls her arm from the warmth of the sleeping bag, reaches out to find his hot hand in the sand.

"What I said. I shouldn't talk. Least not until after the peak."

"No. I like it."

The rush and churn of the rising tide moves up the beach, from their left to their right, the sound of it buffeting the salal and cedar of the forest, echoing behind the source like a following shadow. Two tidal surges close on each other, the brush of water on pebbled beach and brush of wind and sound waves on leaves and needles and furrowed black bark. The same breeze pressed to her left temple; she feels urged to turn her head to the right, to look at him. The whites of his eyes reflect starlight in the dark.

"Really. Keep talking."

"It's not weird? Kel."

"What *isn't?*" she laughs. Encouraged, he launches into what is, for him, a kind of standard trip narrative, the kind that had attracted her to him in the first place, during the early days with his shamanic outreach work. Manning the chill tents at music festivals, sitting in compassion with the paranoid and the broken as they rode out bad nights on bad drugs and worse demons. Psychedelic triage, mostly: distraction, reframing, changing the set and setting. The usual.

"That movement, that flow. You know what I mean. Look. The stars don't move like this, normally. That filigree between them, and the black gulfs they cross. Focus on the black, and that lacework just . . . it's intense. It pops. *Moves.* Know what causes that?"

"It's just the hallucination."

"Sure. Rapid eye movement, probably. Shaky eye. I'll tell you my theory, though. I think the psilocybin . . . it's breaking down, right? In our brains. Neuroreceptors. And the shroomy energy it releases is enough to disengage the psychic governor on, I dunno, our temporal sense. So what we're seeing, these stars, or the grain in wood, or the pattern of the linoleum in the bathroom as it flows like water, and then reforms, and then flows again. That's the thing itself moving forward in time, and we see it moving, just enough to create the visuals."

He sighs, and violently shifts his bulk in the sand. The movement, so sudden and convulsive, alarms her. She sucks in an anxious breath, her hand flying from his like a bird. He does not seem to notice.

For a moment she wonders about his competency. How many ravers had freaked out under his care back in the day? Before she had drawn him away from that life? She can't recall clearly, but in that moment it seems to her that there had been more than a few. He draws a deep breath, lets it all out into the air in a ghost of steam.

"But the governor kicks back in, always. Which is, y'know, that's *why*. That's why the hallucination resets. The star stops wheeling about and goes back to its place in the sky. The wood stills."

She shakes herself, tries to focus on his words again. "The linoleum stays ugly."

"Fuck, that floor! Right, kiddo? I'm gonna ask the landlord to pull it up. Put down some tile, maybe. Or laminate."

"Shh." She doesn't want to talk about the apartment and its run-down ambience. She much prefers the ceiling here, and says so.

"Glorious," he says after a while. "Did I tell you? Fucking glorious."

She doesn't notice when sleep comes. Her dreams are strangely coloured and full of sound, movement. Murmured conversations in unknown languages become the sound of zippers, opening and closing. His weight, so slight, pressing against her, insistent. She feels his finger running along the band of her basketball shorts and, suddenly eager and half awake, she pulls them down and off, then turns in to him to grasp at the crest of his bare hips. Still half in the dream, she pulls her underwear aside and guides him. The heat from his hands where he buries them in the sand next to her ears has a sound, like engines in the earth, churning. The trees roar at the sea, drip light into the void from their shaking tips, push salt-caked limbs and insistent needles to the stars.

She cries out, once, before sleep claims her again.

She wakes to the dim grey of a pre-dawn hour, with pressure in her bladder and a depression, already filling with moisture, in the sand to her right. His shapeless tracks in the sand moving away into the day's fog just beginning to rise from the warming water. Near the caves, she spots him: bulky and shuffling, the suggestion of a head balanced on shoulders bunched and obscured by the gathered folds of a sleeping bag.

"Dev? You all right?" she calls. The head turns and inclines toward her voice, and a pale arm appears from the bulk and chops at the fog, once, twice. He says something in reply that she can't catch.

Pulling her cold limbs from her own bag, she stands, brushing sand from her hands and the front of her legs. "I gotta pee!" she calls, and points to the brush near their tent. She doesn't *need* privacy, but the prospect of squatting right there in the sand unsettles her. His arm moves in acknowledgement, but he doesn't turn to look, too busy examining something in the water.

A kingfisher, thrumming emerald and black, speeds past her out of the fog as she picks her way into the bush. She shakes, then sighs and tugs at the waist of her sweatpants. Her underwear is swampy and damp from the sex, and she wrinkles her nose as she squats.

A minute later, she stands, and sees the other tent for the first time.

It is deeper into the forest, maybe fifty meters or so. Deep enough that she wouldn't have seen it at all, had not a wash of dawn light caught at a patch of its fabric, causing the faded artificial yellow of the thing to flare into gold. Through rents in the clustered salal and deadfalls, the other tent shines. Steam rises from its sides as it warms. A moment passes, and another; it is not until the light has moved aside, allowing the other tent to fade into dimness, that she remembers to breathe.

She gasps, puts a hand to a tree to steady herself, and hurries to pull up her sweatpants. The pressure of yesterday returns to the space behind her eyes, and the muscles in her neck grow stiff and hot, her mouth immediately dry.

"Hello? Hello, the tent?"

There is no movement, no sound. If she hadn't known it was there, her eye would have passed over it without registering anything.

"Hello!" A terrible species of anxiety colonizes her voice. Had they been listening in on all their drug talk? On the sex? Who camped back in the woods, surrounded by brush, secreted away between slabs of rotting wood and weeping stones? Not reasonable people.

For a moment she considers returning to the beach to get Devon, force him to investigate. Anger overcomes her nervousness, suddenly, and she decides against it.

"Fuck this," she whispers.

She crashes towards the tent, her forearms lifted and bent at the elbow before her to part the thick, dripping foliage. "Hey! Wake up, you!" The yellow fabric steams as she approaches. A breath of wind causes the whole construction to ripple like a sail. And then she is through, her hoodie soaked and stuck through with burrs and twigs. She's through, and the other tent stands before her, open to the elements and unoccupied. It's a dome tent, and a similar model to their own, if a few years older. The rainfly is rolled up, folded back over the right side of the tent, the loops that tie it off neatly slipped over small plastic tabs. The mesh entrance is unzipped, and also neatly rolled and folded away, fastened by similar loops on the interior wall. Kneeling, she peers within. In the exact centre of the space, a single insulated pad keeps a red mummy-style sleeping bag from the chill of the ground; the bag has been laid out flat and smooth on the pad, half zipped up and folded open as if awaiting a sleeper, the head of the bag closest to the entrance.

On either side of the pad, arranged carefully, as if on display at a sporting goods store, a small assortment of objects and tools. On the right, two plastic bottles half filled with amber water, a Maglite, a single unopened packet of saltine crackers. On the left, a pair of wool socks, rolled into a ball, and a spiral notebook with the stub of a pencil trapped in one end of the coil. Dust and the smells of long disuse, mold and stale air and damp fabric, waft from the entrance, make her nostrils flare in irritation.

She stands, and examines the ground around the tent. Aside from the trampled lichen and forest mulch beneath her feet, there's no indication that anyone has moved or stepped here. She isn't a tracker by any stretch, but it seems obvious; bright white miniature shoots of some fragile plant she has no name for peek from the thick moss at the tent entrance. The only broken branches around are the ones that snapped under her feet.

She turns to look back the way she came. The red of their own tent, perched on that rise above the beach, is just visible from here.

She reaches a hand into the other tent, surprising herself with the clear thought that she shouldn't put her head inside. It is awkward; she has to shuffle her feet and position her hips in parallel with the entrance to reach inside, but she does, and brings the notebook out into the growing light, hopping to her feet instantly and stumbling away from the entrance, almost overbalancing. She pulls the covers of the notebook apart in a single impatient, violent movement.

Blank. Each page a void.

She bites her lower lip. There is a low hiss in the air that she barely registers as sound. She only realizes that it comes from her when she tastes blood on her tongue.

"Jesus. Jesus Christ."

She throws the notebook into the mouth of the tent, and it slides across the nylon floor to rest against the back wall. She half-considers reaching in again, maybe with a stick instead of her arm, to nudge the notebook back to its original resting place, but finds herself already tearing back through the brush instead. Her hissing becomes great gulps of air, gulps that fuel a series of ragged shouts as she leaves the woods and stumbles onto the black sand. She casts her eyes about in frantic passes. Where is he?

"There's a . . . there's something back there!" She can't bring herself to say *tent*. "Dev! Where are you?"

The chill morning fog has rolled in seriously now, obscuring every visible detail of the cove. The rocky headlands that enclose the bay appear as lumpen ghosts that fade in and out of sight. The sea caves to her right slosh and foam in the vagueness. She bends over, resting her hands on her shaking knees, feeling the warm wetness of her soaked sweatpants press into her palms.

"Where the fuck have you gone?" she whispers.

"Over here!" His voice rings from the unseen shoreline, somewhere to her left. "Get over here or you'll miss it!"

She runs forward, toward the water, and when the dark plane of it resolves from the fog she banks to the left, until his shape grows from the black sand like a graphite smudge, or a column of smoke becoming solid. He's lost the sleeping bag somewhere, and is naked from the waist up, pistoning his arms. A referee calling a foul, signaling her to look out to the water.

"There! There! Do you see it?"

She turns, looks, instantly recoils. Very close to shore, a black, humped shape breaks the surface.

"Kel, do you see it? Oh my God!"

It is large, too large. It pulses and shifts, and she feels her sense of space, of the relative sizes of things, struggling to tell her a truth. It shines with a wet slickness that resists the hold of her vision; her eyes slide all over the thing, searching for some feature to lock onto, a part, however small, that could explain the whole. The shape continues to rise from the chill water, and now it begins to heave and tremble and turn, birthing uneven, quivering waves from the line where its bulk breaks the water.

"What a whale!" he screams. He hoots and pumps his fists and points. "Look at you! Magnificent!"

Nausea blooms in her guts, and she closes her eyes to the shape in the water. She stumbles forward blindly, her hands finding the twitching flesh between his shoulder blades. "Come away. Oh, come away, don't get too close." She hisses into his neck. "Please, Dev. *Please,* come away, come away from it."

He turns quickly and grips her still upheld wrists, a wild, lopsided smile on his face. "Hey, what's wrong? Don't miss this, look at it! You never see humpbacks this close to..." and he half-turns back to the water. The shape is gone.

" . . . shore. You never . . . "

He lets go of her to kick at the sand, sends a great spray of glistening silicate into the air to lose itself in the fog. "Goddamnit. It was right *there.* What were you yelling about?"

The water where the shape had been is still, black. Like glass, like a mirror in a steamy bathroom.

"There's someone in the woods. I think."

"What?"

"Someone is in the woods."

"Show me," he says.

She stands away from him as he circles the tent.

He goes round the structure again and again, peering inside, kneeling down to tug at a tent peg before plunging it back into the soft loam, playing a guide wire like a guitar string.

"It's weird. I'll give you that."

She shakes her head again, tugs at her lower lip with nervous fingers. She can still taste her blood.

"It's more than weird. Look at it. *Look at it.*"

He throws his hands up. "I am. I'm looking. It's a tent. And I'll tell you what else, it's nothing more. Someone's abandoned it here, is all." At the tent mouth, he crouches again, and begins to reach inside. "I don't know why they'd arrange it like this, but . . . "

"I want to leave." The words come from her sharp-edged and hard and she covers her mouth instantly, surprised at herself. He rocks back on his heels and stands up.

"What?"

"I want to go." She comes forward, out of the brush, to grab at his wrist. "Now. Come away. Let's go."

"Okay, okay. Sure." She pulls, but he resists. "I wonder who left it, though. Whaddaya think?"

"I don't care." She tugs again, and manages to shift him away from the tent. "Let's go."

They break camp in the fog. She hurries, randomly stuffing clothing, food and gear into their two packs while he methodically takes down the tent. That done, he lopes off towards the sea caves, returns a few moments later with his dripping sleeping bag, holding it aloft like a fresh catch, a stupid smile on his face. She catches him looking toward the trees several times.

"I mean, weird. Right?" he says.

"What. What's weird?"

"I wish we had some coverage out here, I'd look up this part of the trail on my phone."

"It wouldn't tell you anything," she snaps. "It's not a feature."

"Maybe it's a memorial. Y'know? Like the markers you see by the side of the highway, with the flowers and crosses. At the dangerous spots."

"Are you done? Can you just . . . can you be done?"

"Yeah, yeah." He rolls up the tent and slides it into its carrying bag, straps it to the top of his backpack. "This whole trail was basically a rescue line for people shipwrecked along the coast. Ships went down around here all the time back in the day, before they changed the shipping lanes. I'm just saying." He stands back, surveys her packing job. "That is lumpy as shit, kiddo."

"Whatever. Can we just go?"

"Two seconds." He scouts around for some minutes, finds the remains of their sleeping area, kicks the border of stones away and blurs the scalloped sand with the edges of his feet. She says nothing, already moving north towards the headland, but feels satisfied with his action. He catches up with her at the sea caves.

"Thanks for doing that," she says, but doesn't know why.

He shrugs. "Leave only footprints."

They keep to the shoreline for most of the day, the sibilant metronome of waves infiltrating pebbled stone always to their left. The sight of the waves themselves is lost to the now impenetrable fog; they sometimes find themselves ankle deep in a sudden surge of foaming water, but at least they know where they are in relation to the sea.

"This is stupid," she says. "I can just about see my own feet. We'll be lost if we keep this up."

He walks ahead, wrestling with salal and clutching, snapping ivy, devil's club. He can only grunt in response, and it sounds to her like a reproof.

Several times, they think they have the trail beneath them, only to have the firm ground fall away like a bad guess. Hazard after hazard, barely seen until almost too late, looms out of the blinding grey, triggering a near-constant stream of curses from them. He gasps with amazement and relief whenever the flat blank wall of fog that indicates a new beach or cove rises up to meet them.

"We could just stop." His feet keep moving.

"So stop."

"We could. Right here. One place is as good as . . . " He stops. "Okay.

Okay. Look." He turns, and she catches up to him. They stand chest to chest, weary, their faces limned in sweat and salt water.

"Let's just . . . can we, I dunno. Can we re-frame here, hun?"

"There's nothing to frame."

His hands fly up to her shoulders, clamp too tightly. She bares her teeth. "I just feel like we're panicking here and I'd like to know why," he says. "We need to stop. Talk."

"So talk, Dev. Go on, like you do."

"That's unfair. You know that's unfair. Look, we didn't have breakfast. Do you want to eat something? Let's at least eat something," he says.

They sit in the damp sand, uncaring of the moisture wicking into their clothes. She pulls food randomly from the top section of her pack: rye crackers, a zip-locked bag of nuts and dried fruit. "There's chocolate in here," she says.

"Give it."

"How far have we come already?"

"Fuck." The word comes out soft and ugly around a mouthful of crumbled cracker and sweets. "Dunno. I mean, what, we've seen three, maybe four coves so far? I think."

"So a couple of kilometers?"

"Oh, easily."

"Check the map?"

"Sure. Okay."

As he digs for the map, she says, "It can't be far. The Crib. I just wanna get there today."

"Right." He pulls the paper from its waterproof bag, unfolds it over his knees. The topographic lines seem to spill from his ribs, remind her of flattened viscera, the fjords and coves and headlands stony villi combing the water for nutrients. His fingers are unsettled across the paper, jabbing, stroking.

"Here," he says. "And here. We passed this surge channel, right? Two coves back?"

"I guess?"

"Yeah. Yeah, I'm sure we did. I heard it, at least."

"So we're close . . . "

He begins to fold the map again, but tears suddenly at the paper, one shaking hand pulling away ahead of the other. He swears again and hurries to finish, making a bad job of it. He stuffs the abused sheaf of loose material back into the bag.

"Yeah, we're close. We have to be. Damn this fog, though. It's ridiculous." He kicks at sand, then buries a fist in it. Sand fleas leap in all directions, brine wells up around his knuckles. "Tell me something."

"What."

"What got you so upset back there?"

She rises from the sand and slips on her pack.

"Come on. It was a goddamn whale. A humpback," he snaps. "It was beautiful, it was awesome, it was *there*, and you missed it."

I didn't miss it, she thinks, but says nothing.

"I'm not leaving this spot until you tell me what's going on with you, Kel."

"I don't know what to tell you. Isn't it obvious? That tent." Just saying the word causes her heart to skip. "And if you think that was a whale, I . . . " She presses her palms to her face.

"You were tripping still. The whale . . . "

"Don't you do that." Her hands fly from her cheeks, clench into fists as she steps toward him. He scrambles to his feet, arms pinwheeling. "Don't you blame the drugs. Bastard."

"I'm not! Look! I know it's been strange since last night, but c'mon! You gotta admit that—"

"Well, you're up now, so let's go. Let's go! I want to make camp before dark and I want to do it at the Crib!" She starts pressing her fists into his chest, pushing him off balance, pushing hard.

"Fuck! Jesus. Okay, lay off!" He hauls his pack on, glares at her, as she jams the snack foods back into their place with pale fists. They move off, and she takes the lead, keeping well ahead of him. It's a longer stretch of beach, and before too long he speaks again.

"I swear, some people are just, y'know, not cut out for psychedelics."

"Fuck you. I asked you not to blame the drugs, man."

"I'm just saying, kiddo."

"What, like you've never pushed too far into it before? Not that I *did.* I ate maybe a quarter-ounce. You had way more. A lot. I watched you."

"I have pushed it. Too far, like you said, but in the past." She doesn't say anything to that. "So I'd *know* if I had last night. If *we* had. And we haven't.

"This was a couple of years before I met you. Up at Shambala, when it was still really spiritual. Like, some true light-working happened there before they sold out. Shambles, right? What a joke it is now.

"I had a night off from the chill tent. This was maybe the third night in. And I'd seen some truly heinous stuff while working. People flailing their way through some pretty bad shit. Lotta dense energies coursing through the woods and the DJs weren't helping, or maybe they were just picking up on what the people were feeling, but yeah."

"Yeah," she says under her breath.

"So I decided, y'know, let's get to the bottom of it. Right? Do my job. Find out what was hurting our collective consciousness, or feeding on it, and just do the shaman thing. Heal.

"I dosed high. I didn't *measure* or anything, but I know I had something like three ounces of shrooms when the festival started, and I'd only had a couple of grams on the first two nights, but yeah, next morning there was just crumbs and dust in the baggie.

"And a point came where I knew. Full-on black gnosis. I'd unpicked the thread of the world, and it was all coming apart around me. I knew, *knew,* that I'd broken myself. Passed through a membrane, an energetic barrier between states. Speaking in tongues and pissing myself. I knew that they would find me in the morning with my mind gone. Not *drooling* or anything, but with that essential thing missing that keeps you among sane people. I guess.

"I was done. I'd broken myself, and broken Time, and all that would ever be for me from that moment on would be this mad paddling around in my own damage. That sense of the eternal now, right. Time locking down around me with each tumblered second. It was like I'd entered eternity, and it would always be *this.* This busted up, insane thing. So I just lay there, my head hanging out of the front of the tent, bugging out. I must have fallen asleep eventually. Morning came and I was fine."

She snorted.

"Well," he said, "I still feel like there's a part of me back there, sometimes. In that space."

"So go back," she says. She wishes she could send him there, in that instant. "Go crawl up your own ass and check. Jesus."

He's puffing now, and doesn't bother responding. "I just want out of here," she whispers to herself. "The highway. The linoleum in the kitchen. I don't care which."

"You know I would," he said finally. "I would if I could. Shambles."

An hour later and the grey grows more dense.

"Sun's going down," he groans.

"How can you tell?"

They stop again, unfolding the map. The fog has slipped into the bag and soaked the paper. Parts of the torn sections press into others, forming new place names, phantom headlands. Before long the map starts to come apart in their hands.

"Nice job, genius," she says.

"We don't really need it, do we? On a coastal trail."

"Still."

"Look. Water to the left. Trees to the right. Sand in the middle, always. What's to wonder about?"

"Where to sleep, for one thing." She is looking at the sand when she sees it. "Hey. People."

He follows her gaze. There are tracks in the sand, huge and deformed by the seepage of water from below and the scuttling of beach creatures across them. The fog collects in the depressions, curling around as if to rest.

"Okay. Well, that's good, right?"

Not much farther on he half-trips over the first of the scattered stones, then pauses, grunts.

"What?" she says. "What is it?"

He kneels down, turns over the stone. "I dunno, it's weird. This is . . ." He runs his fingers over the damp surface of the rock, then digs in the sand next to it. Another stone surfaces. He rises, takes a few steps, drops again.

"Look. Another one."

"Rocks on a beach," she sighs. "Well, it's official. You've lost it."

"No. No, I haven't." He glares at her. "I spent, like, two hours building that platform last night. I selected each stone."

"So . . . what?"

He shrugs off his pack, and it lands with a sick thump she can feel in the soles of her feet. He's down in the sand again, on his hands and knees. "These are them. Fuck. I *recognize* these."

"Fuck you."

"I do! I'm serious!" He runs off to their right, toward where the treeline would be. The fog swallows him. She unshoulders her own pack and goes down on her knees, picks up a stone. Black, igneous rock. Glacial litter, streaked with dark green and speckled with quartz, maybe. She doesn't know from rocks, or care, but his manic reaction does something to her. She finds herself unable to look towards the forest.

There is an inarticulate moan of anguish coming from the trees. He follows it with the hollow thunk of a stone bouncing from bark, and then another. Devon is throwing things in the gloom. Finally, speech. A long, harsh string of negation, then a "Jesus!" and a choking sound. "Fucking hell!"

Kel covers her ears against his distress and steps toward the water. Her eyes close against the perpetual grey and glare, and she sees stars moving against her lids, describing slow, palpitating arcs in the red night. Stars, or particles in the benthic seeps; plankton, bits of shell, calcified shit, molecules of ancient plastic. The walk takes an age, and at the end of it she notes the water circling her ankles, feels the agitated wavelets, a thousand at once, lifting the fine hairs of her legs.

When she opens her eyes, finally, the thing is there, waiting in the water offshore. A too-symmetrical sphere of darkness, humming low. A mountain, or a beast that believes it's a mountain, or something else. Something that floats and crushes. It occupies the space the way a black hole wouldn't. She thinks of rape.

"You're worse than before," she whispers to it. "You were never a whale."

She drops to her knees and the splash causes the thing to shimmy and retreat a foot, maybe two. She laughs once, and then a high keening noise is suddenly in the air. For a moment, she wonders how the shape can make that sound, before she realizes that she is the source. She grinds her fists into her eye sockets, heedless of the grains of sand that immediately find their way under her eyelids, burning.

"They changed the shipping lanes," she says, and the blackness inclines to her slightly. "The blowhole wasn't going anywhere. We were gonna celebrate with paella, later." She chokes on the last word, shocked at its sudden lack of meaning, then begins again. A clumsy mantra, so stupid that she begins to grin.

"They changed the shipping lanes . . . "

He cries out again, from further into the forest. She feels her grin sliding away to the right, away and off her face, to slither away into the tide, though she doesn't dare to look and confirm the sensation.

She follows the grin down, kneeling in the freezing water before lying down on her back. The ocean grips at her shoulder blades and neck, firm and unyielding, presses eager fingers between her legs. When the arc of the darkness comes into view over her, she is not ready, but it advances anyway.

THE TRANSITION OF TOBY THE TWITCH

YOU WANT TO know what happened to him, sure. I get it. Every few months or so, someone like you shows up, hoping to get the real story on Deckard. You look the conspiracy type, so I'll bet you've seen the footage. Uh-huh. Convinced yourself it's legit, too, despite what they said about it, about me.

Well, alright. Fair warning, though: you're not going to hear anything different. I'm going to tell you *exactly* what I told the cops, the scientists. The stream of journalists, now mercifully down to a trickle. And the other people like you. Anyway. Let's just say you won't be walking away with fresh revelations tonight, alright?

Want a drink? I've got wine and . . . well, *more* wine, I guess. What? Coffee? *Coffee?* Christ, *no!* Don't think you can rile me up with a request like that, either.

It *started* with coffee. Or rather, it started with the poem about coffee.

If you're an addict, which is to say a *serious* coffee drinker, then you've read the poem. Written in 1587 by Sheik Ansari Abd-al-Kadir, about a month after he replaced the previous Sheik. *That* Sheik, not coincidentally, had railed against coffee as a dangerous and addictive stimulant, and found himself, well, let's just say *removed* from the position by a baying horde of caffeine addicts. Abd-al-Kadir, however, clearly knew which way the beans bounced when he wrote "In Praise of Coffee."

Now, Deckard was *serious* about his coffee. Serious enough to have collected a bunch of nicknames at the agency: Twelve Cup Tobias, Demitasse Deckard. And the perennial favourite, Toby the Twitch, of which he always seemed proud. He refused to drink drip and plainly loathed anyone who would. He used a hand-turned burr-mill to grind his own beans: "A uniform grind, less friction, more flavour," he explained to me once. I'd never seen it, but the man kept a La Marzocco GS3 at home for perfect espresso. There was a French press in the agency staff lounge for his exclusive use. He kept a moka pot in a little case always on or near his person. "My works," he'd call it, only half-joking. Deckard was an addict and knew it.

And Deckard knew the poem. He loved the poem, lived by the poem, had burned the poem into his memory. "Let's hear the poem," I'd say when I found him labouring in the lounge over the monkish production of yet another cup of aromatic black gold. I'd say, "Praise that coffee, Twitch. Go!" and he would. It quickly became a kind of tradition. He'd breathe deep from the cup and launch right into it. Reverently. A man in love.

Oh Coffee, you dispel the worries of the Great
You point the way to those who have wandered
from the path of knowledge.
Coffee is the drink of the friends of God
and of His servants who seek wisdom . . .

At which point, I would interrupt him (again, tradition), reminding him that what coffee *actually* did was keep God's friends and assorted servants so buzzed they wouldn't have any other choice than to stay up all night studying the Koran. As a Muslim and a coffee booster, Abd-al-Kadir's motives were suspect. That was my interpretation, anyway. Deckard would smile, call me a cynic, take a sip, his eyes rolling back in his head only a little, and continue . . .

No one can understand the truth
until he drinks of its frothy goodness.

Sure, that's not the whole poem, but how could I not interrupt again to tease him after a line like that? I'd ask him if it really translated as *frothy goodness*. Seriously? Who wrote this guy's copy: Folgers?-

"Abd-al-Kadir was a holy man, Morgan. The Saint of Coffee," he said. "A Sufi mystic of the first water, with access to a higher order of reality."

What? Yeah, this was on the day in question. My recall for that day is really clear: conversations, smells, the quality of the light in that breakfast nook. The humming. Perfect recall is a side-effect, I'm sure of it. I mean, I didn't have a lot of coffee in my system when it happened, but I was . . . y'know what? I'm getting ahead of myself.

"It's a low-grade stimulant, Deckard, not a strip of blotter acid. There's no truth in it," I said. I really believed this at the time, understand. "As sacred drinks go, it's not even cheap communion wine . . . "

"Ah! But what are sacred drinks but liquid pathways into a divine experience! Rivers to the spirit!" He could be a poet himself, I always thought. It's what made him a halfway decent ad man, after all.

"The Hindus have their milk, a thoroughly nutritious and nurturing liquid in which their universe floats. Pagans, or at least the Irish, have their whiskey, which burns them in a fire of intoxication and insight. And the Christians have their wine! But wine dulls the mind, weakens the body, clouds the senses! The perfect drink for the little deluded lambs of God. As the Sheik said: *Whoever tastes coffee will forever forswear the liquor of the grape.*"

"Hey now. A modicum of respect, please. Lapsed Catholic over here. Besides, that's only true of wine if you drink a gallon of it."

"And if you drink a gallon of coffee?" His look was sly.

"Other than visiting utter ruination on your bladder? I dunno. It's gotta be toxic at some level, right?"

"Oh yes. Absolutely. You'd need levels of at least 200 milligrams per kilogram of body mass. That's 80 cups of coffee for an average adult, roughly. Say 100 cups, just to be safe. And by safe, I mean almost lethal."

"Huh. You've done your research. Symptoms?"

Deckard grinned. "About what you'd expect. Restlessness, fidgeting, extreme irritability. You become a walking muscle twitch, basically. Rhabdomyolysis. That's a breakdown at the cellular lev— well, it's brittle bones. Plus mania, psychosis, hallucinations."

"Jesus!"

"Of course, it's rare, those levels of toxicity, and it almost never happens with anything other than a caffeine pill overdose. I mean, who could *drink* that much coffee in the first place?" He laughed, took another reverent sip.

If anyone could, I thought, it would be Deckard. And there was something about that laughter, coupled with the expression on his face and the bizarre revelation of just how deep his knowledge went. It didn't sit well with me. Sufi mystics and lethal doses of caffeine and the thought of that gleaming La Marzocco GS3 espresso maker in his kitchen swirled in my mind for a dizzy minute and yeah, I'll admit it: in behind a nearly overwhelming feeling of curiosity, I shuddered a little.

"But you wouldn't ever . . . "

"Caffeine pills? No. No, Morgan, that's not the way for me."

"The way? I'm sorry, but . . . *the way?* What are we talking about here, Deckard? The way to what?"

It was maybe three in the afternoon, and I knew that already he was on more good coffee that day alone than most people consume in a week. His face was completely serene, though. Calm. Composed. It's funny, because until that moment, I hadn't realized how much his behaviour had changed in the last month. He *used* to be as jangly and fried as anyone would be on the amounts he normally drank.

But at that moment? Toby the Twitch looked at me, then, from above the rim of his cup, and he looked like a man who could hold his brew. He wasn't twitching at all.

"Why, the way to God, of course."

I was concerned, obviously. *Alarmed.* We weren't close friends, but we'd worked together at the agency for three years, and my worry that Deckard's coffee habit had damaged him was very real. Had he finally burnt out some essential wiring, resulting in this weird repose? I convinced him that he had to prove to me that he wasn't insane, that he wasn't planning some jumped-up, java-fuelled suicide attempt or killing himself by accident trying to get into the record books.

"To do that, I'll have to explain some things," he said, a statement that didn't exactly make my concerns evaporate. "There's an experiment I want to do. Well. That's a lie. I've been *doing* the experiment, and tonight I'm . . . " His eyes brightened at a sudden thought. "Actually, that's perfect. You can be my witness! Meet me tonight at my apartment. You'll come?"

I said I would, and I did, arriving at his building a little after eight. Deckard buzzed me in and met me at his door with a steaming demitasse.

"This is for you," he said and passed the porcelain cup to me. "Come in, come in."

"I usually don't caffeinate this late, but okay. Thanks." I took a sip. Goddamn if it wasn't the best espresso that had ever passed my lips. Words like *rich* and *complex* and *nuanced* came to the tip of my tongue and then failed in their descriptive power. Deckard watched my face carefully as I drank again. And again.

"That's damn near divine," I finally said. "This from the famous Italian machine?"

"Yes, the La Marzocco. I call it my Engine."

"Delicious. You're an alchemist or something, Deckard."

He grinned like a satyr. "You're not far off there. And thank you for the comparison; I like it very much. This way, I've set up in the breakfast nook." He led me inside his sparsely furnished apartment.

Deckard didn't have a lot of things, but what he did have was quality stuff: the sofa was fine soft leather, the bookshelves and side tables teak and rosewoods, the few pieces of art on the walls originals as far as I could tell. In the small kitchen, the Engine dominated the counter space, all gleaming chrome and matte black knobs and handles.

It would have been a clean, modern space, too, had there not been books, magazines and journals piled high on every flat surface and up against the walls, making the place look more like a sorcerer's den. Most of it was coffee-related: trade journals like *Fresh Cup* and *Barista* and *Roast*, and coffee history books, memoirs. I noted a slim volume of the collected writings of Sheik Abd-al-Kadir on the sofa. I say *most* because there were also engineering and chemistry books visible here and there, splayed wide and bristling with Post-Its, their margins crammed with notes.

You don't want to hear about his library, though, do you? You want to know about the breakfast nook.

Well, it was exactly what you see in the video, which is to say nothing all that impressive. I thought they were speaker towers set up in the corners. Damn ugly ones, too. Really industrial looking, bare wiring hanging off the back of dull metal cubes stacked in dull metal frames. I was about to ask Deckard what they were for, but he'd already sat himself down at the little table with his own steaming demitasse cup and that little black box with the dial on it. He motioned for me to take the chair across from him.

I heard the humming, sure. It was so faint, though, I thought it was the building making the sound, like the older places do sometimes. A generator in the basement, maybe.

Now, this is where it starts. This is the part that's covered in the video footage. I didn't know he'd set up a camera: it was sandwiched between books on a shelf on the far wall, opposite the nook. I don't need my ridiculously sharp recall of the evening for this bit. I've watched that video hundreds of times, just . . . just trying to *understand*, y'know?

"I may be an alchemist," he said, "but I'm not interested in the gold anymore. *That* I've found already. Coffee is the common man's gold, and like gold it brings to every man a feeling of luxury and nobility . . . "

"The poem again?"

He nodded. "Gold is easy. Gold is merely the first step. The real goal of alchemy, the completion of that great Work, is the creation of the Philosopher's Stone."

"I'm sorry, Deckard. I don't actually know all that much about alchemy. Don't know why I used the term, even. What's the Philosopher's Stone?"

His eyes gleamed. "You used the term because you're a good ad man and you sensed its rightness! Entirely appropriate for my endeavours here. Look, you know me well enough. I'm a thoroughly caffeinated man. I think I might be unique. Genetically, I mean. My tolerance for it is off the scale. Coffee's my drug of choice, it's in my blood."

"Deckard, it *is* your blood," I laughed. "But you still haven't told me what this Stone is . . . "

"In a moment, in a moment. When I'm caffeinated, which is, yes, pretty much all the time, I feel a kind of transcendent clarity. My mind, my thoughts . . . everything is sharper, better, faster. I'm more efficient, ideas come smooth and clean and there's a lightness in my chest . . . "

"Pretty sure that's arrhythmia, Deckard. You should see a doctor for that."

"Ha. Yes, probably. But recently? Say the last six months or so? That clarity has refined itself even further and . . . well, I don't quite know how to say it, but I feel I'm on the edge of something. Something vast and perfect, just beyond the reach of my awareness, my caffeinated consciousness . . ."

He paused, made a little tent of his thin fingers, and closed his eyes.

"Have you ever heard of the Experiment at La Chorrera?"

I hadn't, and said so.

"Legendary story in the drug literature. The underground, I mean. Happened in 1971. Two brothers, the McKennas. Dennis and Terrence. Genius-level guys, but children of the Sixties, too. Ethnobotanists, both of them, working in the Amazon, which is to say regularly ingesting truly heroic quantities of psilocybin mushrooms and God knows what else."

"Like you do."

"Like you do, yes. When in the Amazon, right? Anyway, what with one thing and another, the brothers came to believe that sound waves—their voices, basically—carefully modulated, could be used to tweak the electron spin resonance of the drug molecules in their brains. They wanted to bond permanently, at the level of DNA, with their mushroom allies and then, using their voices and certain alchemical techniques, somehow exteriorize their souls! Manifest them as a physical object!"

"And that's the Philosopher's Stone? A human soul?"

"Out of the box, yes! Made solid. The moment of enlightenment, crystallized."

It's clear, in the video, how much my ears were blown back by this. Tobias Deckard, relatively stable caffeine addict, was revealing himself, in the privacy of his own rooms, to be as thoroughly far-out as the Brothers McKenna in their Amazonian be-in. I didn't know what to think, and felt on the edge of something myself.

"Well, shit!" I said, followed by possibly the most embarrassing thing I could ask. "Did it work?"

Christ. Right there is where I lose any sympathy the viewer may have had for me. Deckard looked at me with amusement.

"Umm. No? They were stoned hippie scientists from Berkeley, man. Singing at each other in the jungle. Of course it didn't work. But the principle is interesting. Bonding with a compound! Imagine it! They would have entered into a new state of awareness and *remained there!* High all the time."

I was nonplussed. "Even if that's possible, you're not an engineer. Or a chemist."

"Alchemist!"

"See, I'm not sure they're even in the same room there, Deckard. What do you actually *know* about any of this stuff?"

He swung an arm around in a loose arc, taking in the towers of magazines and books and journals.

"I've been doing my research. We can addict to just about anything, but it's the simplest compounds that have the most profound affects: the tryptamine hallucinogens, alcohol. Caffeine. Even as the drug alters your consciousness, the body is busy breaking it down, flushing it out of your system. If it could be made to stay, though . . . it's called *intercalation*. Slipping molecules in between other molecules. As long as the molecule you're jimmying in there is relatively flat, the DNA won't deform along its length and then . . . well, I won't bother you with technicalities, but *think*! I mean, what if they were on to something? The McKennas?"

"And I suppose the caffeine molecule is flat?"

"Flat enough for my purposes."

"Your *purposes*? But . . . okay, look, you just said it didn't work! The experiment failed."

"The way they were doing it, sure. The human voice wouldn't be enough on its own. You'd need something that could resonate your molecules at the right frequency. Something with a bit more oomph at the low end." Deckard spread his arms wide and pointed to the columns in the corners of the nook.

"Something like these babies here. Sub-sonic drivers. Russian surplus gear, from a decommissioned weapons lab in the Caucasus. Morgan, you wouldn't believe some of the stuff they got up to on the other side of the Iron Curtain. You wouldn't believe the trouble I had getting them, either."

It was then that I paid more attention to the nagging hum that filled the air. You can tell because that's the moment in the video where I execute a comical half-jump, half-fall out of my chair and back away from the nook.

"I take Abd-al-Kadir at his word, Morgan. A truly caffeinated consciousness exists, at a higher frequency than what we live in now. Coffee is a river that flows to God, to pure awareness and *wisdom*! But our bodies betray us, sluice it all away before it can complete its divine work! I love the stuff, but it's not enough to drink it anymore . . . "

"You are scaring me beyond all sense," I stammered. "Deckard, this is like . . . shit, this is the opposite of wisdom! Are those things actually on? What am I hearing?"

"Of course they're *on*, Morgan. They've been on for a month. I spend entire nights in this nook, bathing my cells in coffee and sound waves. At the current frequency, the bond is nearly complete now, almost stabilized. I can feel it. Tonight is the night, though. Tonight I take things to the next level. Thanks for being here, Morgan, it sure does mean a lot to me."

He reached for the little black box on the table and gently turned the dial to the right. The hum, barely perceptible before, now filled the room. I could feel my teeth shake in their sockets and my guts turn to water. Deckard only chuckled, shook his head a little, as if even he couldn't believe what he was about to do.

"I've had *so much coffee* today. Really surpassed myself. Nothing like the lethal levels I mentioned this afternoon, but, y'know, quite a lot." Then he smiled and folded his hands as if in prayer.

"Quite a lot indeed."

This is the moment where they say I, or Deckard, tampered with the footage. That the black light that begins to shine from the edges of his eyes is poor CGI. That the distortions and bursts of blinding static that come soon after were deliberately introduced, meant to cover up the moment when he simply stood up and stepped out of the frame. They say he didn't vanish, that his so-called *transition* is a fake, that Deckard and I were the authors of a rather badly constructed hoax.

They even say that my reaction to Deckard's disappearance is over-acted. The way I goggle at his vacated loafers on the floor as I'm picking up his empty shirt and pants from the chair, and the weird high-pitched wailing I made. It's unfair. A man doesn't know how he'll react to the inexplicable until it happens to him. Turns out I gibber like a frightened chimp and paw at cloth before fleeing the scene. Honestly? I think a lot of people would.

So I'll repeat to you what I've told everyone: I didn't even know about the camera until after the cops turned the place upside down. This was during the initial investigation, while they were thinking I'd killed him. They don't think that anymore. I was cleared, though it's done me a fat lot of good. Cost me my career, my friends. Now all I've got for company is conspiracy nuts like you coming round every few months.

No, they don't think I killed him, not anymore. He's still missing, though, isn't he?

What do I think happened? I was there and I still don't know. But I've been doing my research, too. It's all I've got time for. He kept a blog through the whole experiment. Did you know that? Sure you did. It's public record. That last post, entered an hour before I arrived that night, it haunts me.

The Philosopher's Stone isn't a stone at all. Or at least, not in my case. It's a bean.

A goddamn *bean*. Toby the Twitch wanted a purely caffeinated consciousness, desired a coffee-fueled enlightenment and he got it. *He got it.* What I think, and what keeps me away from coffee entirely now, is this: it goes both ways, this alchemical thing. The alchemist creates the Philosopher's Stone, but he's got to use his soul to do it, right? People have asked me, well, where's the Stone? There should have been something left behind after he transitioned. His soul made material, some shining, impossible thing, just sitting there in the breakfast nook.

But see, I think there was. And it's so obvious, so common, that we've all missed it. *He's the Bean.* Deckard *is* coffee now. He's in there, in every cup, every hit of frothy goodness. He's in the leaves of every coffee plant everywhere, from Colombia to Cameroon. He's surpassed his honoured Sufi saint in ways I don't think he ever imagined. I mean, there's a weird new coffee cult popping up every other week now, isn't there? They're benign, sure. So far. But knowing what I know, I'll tell you: I'm scared.

Toby the Twitch is the Spirit of the Coffee Break. He's the Ghost in the Caffeine. I'm worried for the species. Not as lapsed in my Catholicism these days, either.

And I drink a *lot* of wine.

TURBULENCE

THEY'RE SEALING THE silo today, and the cavern below it. One hundred fifty thousand tonnes of concrete poured down the wet black throat of the thing. I hope it's enough.

The facility is down to a skeleton staff now. Topside security and just enough eyes on the monitors to hit the red button if things change down there. I'm not really needed; my MSc is in Avionics Engineering, after all. I don't even work here anymore, but I felt like paying my respects. I'm not alone in this. Declan made friends easily and there's a lot of project folks here that don't need to be.

His official funeral was just so goddamned *unsatisfying*, for one thing. That eulogy! "Oh, I have slipped the surly bonds of Earth . . . " They ran that Magee poem into the ground, which was about as tasteless as you could get, considering the circumstances. Considering his resting place.

That's just it though, isn't it? Declan isn't at rest. Declan will *never* be at rest. I know what they told everyone. That he died testing the DreadMoth. That's only technically true. I know he's not dead. Ask anyone who ever saw him down there, in the cavern. They'll tell you.

They talked about Icarus at the funeral, too, which is all mytho-poetic and sells the American hero line, sure, but it's a flawed comparison. Icarus *fell*. That kid kissed the dirt.

Declan may be half a mile underground, but he hasn't touched down yet.

The tech wasn't new, exactly. Tillinghast Resonators had been around since the 1930s, but no one besides cranky pseudo-scientists and soft-headed ghost hunters paid them any attention. Hell, until a few years back, you could order the plans and parts for a simple device off the internet. Slap it together in your garage over a weekend. Entertain your friends with some low-resolution trippy visuals for an evening and, once the novelty of vague blobs and vibrating eels wore off, forget about the thing.

Then a couple of physics students at MIT did just that. Only the novelty didn't wear off; they got their professors interested in it. Turns out, once you got beneath the clunky psychedelic effects, the Tillinghast tech had some revelatory things to say about M-theory, dark energy, *gravity*. Name your flavour of physics, that machine had surprises for you. Pretty soon, the military got involved. There were *applications*, of course. The project was born.

Well, projects. It was a big tent: clean energy, faster-than-light communications, weapons. The important stuff that takes time to research and develop. The flight-suit was fast-tracked, though. It was the first and easiest application. They moved my team to Edwards AFB and before we'd even settled in they started pushing, and pushing hard, because let's face it, a flying man? A man in a *real* flight-suit, not a jet pack or mini-copter, soaring the way every kid ever imagined himself doing? That was some straight-up superheroics that would sell any application to follow.

With the T-Resonator technology, a kind of differential pressure could be generated *between* our dimension and an oscillating cascade of other dimensions. I don't pretend to know the higher-order physics of it; that's for the big brains at MIT. I'm in avionics. I understand things like lift, drag coefficients, Bernoulli's principle. And this differential pressure? This tug-of-war between our reality and the infinite layers of every other reality as they flowed across and against each other in the incomprehensible depths of the resonator? Well, spread that out across a physical membrane, a wing, and you could create a kind of lift. The spookiest lift I'd ever seen.

It was barely flight. More like levitation. Not even that: It was as if the wing, and anything attached to it, like the suit and the pilot wearing it, stayed absolutely still and the world moved around it instead. They called this effect "the Pinch," and maybe that's what it was, but as far as my team was concerned, it acted like lift.

The wing wasn't even a wing in the traditional sense. It was a super-light reinforced graphite armature, six stubby rectangular panels, three to each side, extending out from the hub at angles. Between the panels, a mesh of miniature hexagonal graphite plates, pliant and smooth. The hub held the T-Resonator unit and a prototype FTL communicator, developed elsewhere in the project. The whole thing slotted and locked into the back of the suit, nestled between the air supply and the chute. Like every other application of the tech, the thing powered itself, something the clean-energy people loved. Wherever it was pulling the power from, it wasn't *here*.

It looked completely fragile, like a brittle grey moth. We expected it to fall to pieces in the wind tunnel the moment we turned it on. We dreaded that moment. So, the *DreadMoth,* a name that stuck, despite our immediate successes with it. Because when the mesh began to glow with that impossible light, the wing became rigid, as unyielding as stone, and no matter what we threw at the suit in simulation, it would maintain its position in the air.

All we had to do was figure out a control system, in-suit avionics for moving "the Pinch" between, around, underneath and on top of the panels. We were in the initial stages of that when they brought in Declan to observe. He's a lieutenant-commander now, a posthumous promotion, for what that's worth, but he was a major then. Major Declan Reese, USAF. Our test pilot. We were introduced: he knew he didn't have to salute me, but he did anyway, out of respect for what I did. I liked that. Then I showed him the DreadMoth.

"I've been up in almost everything that can go up. And that has gotta be the most goddamned ridiculous thing I've seen. That's supposed to lift a man? C'mon."

So I had my team put on a bit of a show, run it through some high-speed maneuvers. I watched his face as he watched the DreadMoth perform, floating in the serene way that things like that shouldn't float, not at those speeds. Not in those conditions. Hell, not at all. Declan's expression moved swiftly from credulity through to wonder, then a childlike excitement. It was charming. Pure pilot.

"What kind of gees could a guy pull in that?"

I told him what I'd been told. That, as far as the real brains could tell, the field generated by the resonator cancelled that out. Acceleration, banking, deceleration: G-force did not apply. So much did not apply. But it could fly. It flew.

Declan let out a long whistle.

"Christ! How soon can you get me up in it?"

A week before the incident, there was a party on the base. Nothing too crazy, just one of those things to help bleed off tension. I got a little drunk and I cornered Declan, who may have been in the same tipsy boat, which we ended up steering into a bed. Just the one time. It wasn't serious; we'd been working together for months and we were friends. He was attractive, and a pilot, and I've always liked pilots in bed, if not in my life. And I was curious about him.

Afterwards, I asked him why he flew. Other than the obvious alpha-male reasons.

"Terror. I like to piss myself with fear," he said, grinning, and when I punched him in the shoulder he laughed.

"Nah. It's the view. You can't beat the view up there."

I may have asked him not to be a cowboy. To power down and pull his chute if anything seemed even a little off. Declan laughed again.

"It's going to be great," he said. "The suit's been tested to death. Your avionics? Easy as breathing. It's ready. I'm ready."

He wasn't wrong. Only that morning Declan had taken the DreadMoth for a spin around the inside of a hangar; a test of the controls keyed to the gloves and forearm plates, and the HUD in the helmet. Tethered to guide wires for safety, he'd stayed in the air for fifty-three minutes. I recalled the light in his eyes when he landed and removed the faceplate. That was probably the moment I decided to get him into bed. I asked him what it had been like.

"Oh, now, you *saw*. I never wanted to come down."

The incident.

After the initial howl of pure joy as he launched into the cloudless Mojave blue, Declan had composed himself. Mostly. He'd been sticking to the flight plan: keeping within visual range of the two HH-60 Pave Hawks accompanying him, staying above the hard deck, never accelerating above 300 knots, announcing each maneuver before attempting it, relaying his impressions after. A steady stream of radio chatter, and through it all, beneath the professionalism of Major Declan Reese, seasoned test pilot, you could hear the glee of a little boy flying, finally, on his own.

The first indication that something was wrong came exactly twenty-three minutes nine seconds into the flight. Declan had just completed a textbook hammerhead at 200 knots, a move that drew appreciative whistles from the pilots in the Hawks. We expected to hear similar from Declan, but instead he went silent, and stayed silent for another fifty-one seconds. Then he spoke, panic rising in his voice with each syllable.

"That . . . what? No, that can't be right. No. No no no. Ah! Mother of Christ! Ground, are you seeing this? Are you guys seeing this?"

All there was to see was clear blue desert sky and the floating figure of a man with a grey moth pinned to his back. A figure which immediately began to execute a tortured series of acrobatics: dives, multiple rolls, instantly steep climbs, moves a lesser flyer in a machine susceptible to G-forces would never think of trying. Avoidance maneuvers.

"Ground! I can't . . . Jesus! How are you not seeing this? There's too many of them! Everywhere! Shit! I'm going to—"

Then, at twenty-five minutes thirty seconds, the DreadMoth vanished. The shocked chopper pilots immediately reported the loss of visual. Declan was gone from radar and GPS, too.

Nine seconds later, he popped back up. Fifty-three miles SSW from the point where he had vanished, and 8300 feet up. Two seconds later, the same again: gone, then back, only now he was ten miles due east from the base and a jaw-clenching 210 feet from the ground. Again: thirty-two miles NNE and a mile and change up. And again. And again. The silent gaps between his appearances were awful, but not as awful as the screams that came over the radio when he did.

He was being shaken to death in the sky.

Then, by some miracle, one of the Hawk pilots got a visual on him, managed to train their cameras on his last moments. He'd warped in again, practically in their laps. The eggheads were already babbling

203

about "dimensional shear" and "super-positional turbulence." He'd deployed his chute, like I asked him to, but it couldn't save him, not at the speed he was going. The useless tissue tore away, streaming above him like a spider's nest.

The earth rose up to meet him, but that fatal kiss never happened. The video shows one final vanishing act, a half-second before impact.

Declan Reese was gone.

Eight hours later, in the middle of the kind of insane scramble you'd expect after a disaster of this magnitude, the prototype communicator in the DreadMoth pinged its location. We never would have found him otherwise. The T-Resonator, humming the very faintest of signals from deep within the earth, directly below the spot where the DreadMoth had disappeared. The cavern. It seemed unlikely that Declan had survived, went the general consensus. The suit needed retrieval, though, if we were to understand what had happened. As one of the suit's designers, I was put on the team.

And so the shaft was sunk and, after we found him, widened into a silo. The space was narrow, maybe thirty metres across. You couldn't see the bottom, so the catwalks and gantries had to be bolted to the roof. Difficult, nerve-wracking work. I admire those engineers. They had to work *around* the DreadMoth and its pilot, and that's a sight no one should ever get used to.

Declan hovered there, nine metres below the ceiling of that lightless void, the crackling glow of the DreadMoth's wings encasing him in a lambent sheen of violet light. A lot of him was missing: the left leg to just above the knee, most of the torso on the left side, and chunks out of both arms, as if they'd been lifted out with an ice-cream scoop. There was also a large section of the left side of the head, just above the ear. Gone.

That was bad, but there was worse. He was missing so much, but what was gone had not been torn away. Declan was not *wounded.* The outlines of his body, and of the suit that held it, had changed: they just *stopped.* He'd become a cut-away anatomical model. Blood and organs and bone on the other side of his new edges, all clearly visible, all clearly *working.* Veins and arteries still pumping blood from a heart that was only half there. At first they thought he'd been rendered invisible, but no: you could pass your hand through the space his left lung should have been. A lung that was clearly still breathing, wherever it was.

Declan was alive, sunk in a deep coma. And there was worse, still.

It became apparent that the T-Resonator in the DreadMoth was experiencing power surges. The graphite mesh of the wing would flare with light and, if at that moment you were watching the man and the machine from the right angle, from the right spot on the catwalk, then you could catch a glimpse of the outlines of the thing.

So of course we brought in *more* T-Resonator units, repurposed as trans-dimensional floodlights. We wanted to see it clearly.

It was a fractured crystalline structure, but organic at the same time. The entity was largely still, though it exhibited an arrhythmic pulse along its shining length, a length that stretched down into the black depths of the cavern. Fine hairs or tubes would sprout from its surface and then burrow below again. Small, obscene fissures would appear, gape, then seal themselves.

The tip of this perfectly still, impossible, monstrous thing passed right through Declan's body. Where Declan was missing pieces of himself, there was the thing, except it wasn't really *there*. It was and it wasn't, like Declan himself. The eggheads went out of their goddamn minds with excitement.

Moving him was out of the question. They didn't dare risk disturbing the entity, this now-sleeping beast that had roused itself only long enough to pluck a man out of the air and fling him across hundreds of miles and how many realities before bringing him to rest in this black pit. They couldn't move Declan, so they declared him dead, though we all knew better. They called him a hero. That funeral. That goddamn poem, with its "high, untrespassed sanctity of space" and its "touching the face of God."

What do you do when a moth brushes *your* cheek while you sleep?

All this was very bad, but it wasn't the worst part. That came when Declan woke up, three weeks ago, in the middle of the night. He wasn't awake long; there's only thirteen minutes of footage. His vitals barely shifted and he didn't move at all. How could he, with that thing in him? He spoke, though. Whispered, down there in the darkness. No one topside noticed while it was happening; the audio monitors were turned low and some idiot had *Coast to Coast AM* turned up high. We only learned he'd awakened the next day, when someone noticed the larger-than-usual size of the audio files.

He was terrified but lucid. He remembered everything. He knew where he was and what gripped him. "I know all the places I am, at this moment. So many places. I'm spread so thin. And I know its name. It's bigger than the world. I know its name," he said. He spoke the name, then, and the ears of everyone in the room began to bleed, though none of us noticed at the time. He asked that his parents be looked after and he wept, quietly, for everything he'd lost.

Declan Reese warned us, then, of the things he had seen on his short flight. He warned us of what was out there and what was to come. In that soft, small voice, he prophesied and raged. He begged for the cavern to be destroyed, even as he laughed at the idea that it would make any difference.

Then, moments before he fell back into unconsciousness, he sighed. He sighed and spoke my name. He wanted to thank me. In spite of the horror of it, he wanted to thank me for putting him up there, in the DreadMoth.

"It's the view," he said. "I can see forever. *Everything*. Goddamnit, but you can't *beat* this view."

He *thanked* me. I heard his sanity crack open as he did, heard that joyful flying boy inside him wail and plummet into the dark. I couldn't stand it. I quit that day. I'm only here to pay my respects.

They'll watch the thing on their cameras, waiting for movement, their palms hovering over the red button set to trigger whatever tiny stinging weapon they've put down there, collapsing the cavern. The focus of the project has shifted, I've been told, but they won't shut it down. So much still to learn, right?

Fools. It knows we're here. We can be seen now: moths, flapping blindly around a light we can't understand.

They're sealing the silo today. One hundred fifty thousand tonnes of concrete.

It won't be enough.

WONDER AND GLORY FOREVER

THIS IS NOT a confession.

The old man wanted this. Wanted me to throw him overboard, and so I did. With these shaking hands that I can barely write with, I choked him half to death in a red rage and put him over the side. I can still see his face when I close my eyes. Like the moon underwater. And his hands that did so much violence, like chunks of anemic coral, I see them too, grasping at nothing. At the memory of a girl, which is as good as nothing.

This is not a confession. He wanted this.

God help me. It's what I want, too.

We were living in Monterey, at the beach house. Mom got home from her job at the New Age bookshop, grabbed her board, kissed me goodbye, and went out for a ride. They found the board, or pieces of it, washed up hours later. *Distinctive bite pattern,* the coroner said. The waters around Monterey are lousy with the men in grey suits. Dad never recovered, and I lost him to a bottle and pills not long after. I was eight.

You'd think a thing like that would put a kid off of surfing, keep him out of the water permanently, but the opposite happened. Kicked around between foster homes, miserable and failing everything at school, the ocean was the only place I felt at home. Safe.

Surfing is about living in the moment. When you're sliding through the perfect bliss of the green room, or counting up a set, or hell, even getting maytagged by some bomber you weren't ready for, there's no past, no future. No dead mothers. Only the Now of Ocean.

I grew up there, *lived* there, in that space between the water and the wave. From a little grommet to a grown-ass waterman, I had saltwater in my blood, and I got good. Good enough to compete on the pro circuit, and that Now turned into a lot of years of fame and women and drugs before I realized the ride was over.

Deep down I knew I was done, sure. I'd won some prizes. Got paid. Made the cover of *Surfer* a couple of times. I was getting old, though. Not *old* old, but old enough to start feeling restless, bored with the Endless Summer of constant touring, the egos and attitudes, the competition. I was losing my focus, losing my sense of the Now, but it wasn't until I got axed by a mushburger of a wave during a hung-over dawn patrol at Trestles that I really knew: I wasn't *surfing* anymore. I was just going through the motions like a goddamn kook. Getting clumsy. Tore up my left rotator cuff, broke my jaw, and opened up my cheek on the rocks.

Lying there in the sand, bleeding out into the foam as the tide pulled at my legs, I heard the Bell again. I'd been hearing it for years, this persistent audio hallucination. Doctors told me it was nothing to worry about. Tinnitus, maybe. Too much seawater between my ears. It came and it went. It had been gone for a long time, but now it was back: a bell tolling, deep and far away, in time with the pounding of my heart, a barely-there vibration that only registered as sound because I had no other sensation to compare it to. Stronger now, though.

Just like that, I knew I was done. Maybe it was the Bell, or maybe the twin blazing suns of pain in my shoulder and jaw, or the sweet iron taste of the blood pooling under my tongue, or all of those things, but I knew it. It was time to leave. Time to move. Away from pro surfing and shallow SoCal.

North, maybe. When I was a kid, hearing the Bell, I'd feel drawn to it, like you do when you hear something beautiful and strange and far away. *What's that sound?* I'd imagine that it was calling for me. I was small, you think things like that. *Where's it coming from?* North was always the answer.

North.

Now north seemed as good a direction as any.

So the minute I'd completed enough physio to enjoy a working shoulder again, I quit. Fired my agent, blew off my sponsors. I had money, time. Why not? Strapped my favorite gun and two shortboards onto the roof of the Bronco, threw a bag of clothes and my passport in the back, and lit out for the 101, the swell of the Pacific always to my left. Surfed every break I could find, camped on the beach most nights. Trying to get my focus back. Connect with my inner grommet, that kid who felt safe and at home in the water.

But always north, up the coast. Always towards the Bell.

I knew it was stupid, following a ringing in my ears. So what? People did worse things for worse reasons. It was stupid, but I'd talk to the Bell. In the water, I'd ask it things. *This wave? Or the next one?* On the road, pulling into another coastal town, I'd whisper to it. *How about here?* Not really thinking about what I was saying. *Is this it? Is this the place?*

I only imagined an answer: the Bell getting deeper or softer or changing in resonance. I only imagined it got stronger the further north I went: Oregon, Washington, then across the phantom border in the waters between the US and Canada, to Vancouver Island. And north again, north along the coastline, through boreal forests of yellow cedar and beneath grey, lowering skies of endless rain, always north.

Hallucinations hold no wisdom. I only imagined the Bell had answers. It was only an excuse to move.

So when the Bell went silent, finally, and I stopped moving, shocked into stillness, why did I feel so abandoned?

At least I'd been abandoned in paradise, in a piece of country called Clayoquot Sound. Miles of beaches coated in black glacial till. Pirate coves and migrating humpback. Crusty teen hermits and ancient hippies in their driftwood shacks and moss-choked geodesic domes, while squeaky young professionals from the cities classed it up in luxury boutique hotels and rent-by-the-week condos.

And the surfing was world-class. I soon found that there were gonzo breaks all up and down the coast: the Twins, Lando's, Henry's, Solwood. Beach and reef breaks, wicked double overheads most days. Great locals, too. Relaxed and mellow, with none of the aggro territoriality I was so used to. They knew who I was, and it didn't matter. I was welcomed. Most ran their own surf schools, making money hand over fist off the squeaky yuppies who wanted a taste of the life.

The Sound was, literally, the end of the road: the #4 ended at a dock in the town of Tofino. Next stop, Japan. But I wasn't going to Japan. I had money enough to rent a cabin and keep myself in food and beer and a little local herb. I wasn't going anywhere. The Clayoquot was my last stop. A wave-rider's Eden.

So of course it had a serpent.

This is where I met him. The old man.

Zero.

There'd been a minor hurricane off Japan a week before, and we were reaping the rewards. It was good everywhere on the Sound, but it was going off at Lando's: triple-overhead waves incoming for hours, set after set, peeling off to the right on the regular. Rain coming down hard and a sky like slate, but everyone with a board and decent skills was suited up and in the water.

You don't notice a lot when you're in the Now, so when the old man snaked me just as I was powering into a truly righteous wave, it was a shock. Bastard came out of nowhere, like he dropped down out of the sky. I hadn't even seen him enter the water, which was surprising, since he had what I'll call a unique presentation: built like an orangutan, with nasty thick dreads down to the middle of his ridged spine and the grin of a depraved squirrel. Those of us with sense were steamered up in full wetsuits, but he was in a ridiculous and obviously worse-for-wear springer, the skin of his arms and legs gleaming a dead white in the chill black water. Against that ivory shine there was the glint of gold at his wrists and ankles, and around his neck in loose coils of chains that held hunks of metal, bone, shells. Aggro elder was sporting mad jewelry.

He was screaming like a demon, too, as he rode my stolen wave into shore. It wasn't words, exactly, but his voice made me shiver in my suit. A cracked ode to brokenness, the sound of madness, and it had no place here, on this clean ocean with these good people. Geezer could carve, though. That's what I thought as he barreled away.

"The fuck is with that guy?" is what I said. Yelled, really, and to no one in particular, but then a kid I'd met maybe once or twice in the lineup (Grendel, I think he called himself) paddled up and gave me an answer with wide eyes.

"Dude. That's Zero. Zero just dropped in on your wave."

The way he said it, I figured it wasn't a blessing.

"And that's . . . what? Bad luck? Who is this asshole?"

"He's been here for, shit, decades, man. O-G colonist, yo, from back inna day. Came in on the Four when it was a dirt track. I've only ever heard about him. Never thought I'd *see* the dude."

Zero had by this time finished his run and was paddling back out, now silent. The old man saw us watching him, paused, and sat up on his board. I could see his eyes, bright white against the white of his skin. He raised the backs of both hands to me, fingers splayed in a strange hieratic gesture, like some figure out of a Greek myth. It was nothing. Weird behaviour from a weird old grey with too much saline in the brain.

Grendel nearly rolled his board when he saw it, though. "Aww, fuck," he groaned, and pointed his nose to shore. "Fuck it. Not up for *this*, man. I'm going in."

A few moments more and Zero took his place beside me. He lifted his gnarled old hands again in that same gesture and I nodded back at him. Up close, he was really something to see: built of ropes and hair and deep hairline cracks packed with salt. Geezer wasn't even the right term. Dude was *ancient*.

"Old man, they don't seem to like you much," I said. "Can't say as I'm overly fond of you either."

Zero grinned, spread his arms wide in mock humility. "My reputation precedes me, always."

"You hopped me like some kook sponger! I've been watching your technique, you're good, so I *know* you know better. But fuck your rep, I'm talkin' first impressions here."

The grin got wider, displaying bad gums, worse teeth. He cocked his head to the side and his eyes bugged out. "Where'd you learn respect for your elders? I hopped ya, sure, but only so's you'd notice. I *wanted* you to see me. Now, watch closely, boy."

The old man seemed to explode with energy then, and I soon saw why Grendel had fled. Furious strokes of those long arms took him out to the break, where he proceeded to drop in on every last goddamn wave he could. He missed a few here and there, but if Zero was at the break, then someone was going to have their ride stolen from under them.

"You're *nothing!*" he'd scream.

"Stupid monkeys!" He'd spike a bro as soon as look at him.

"Zero! Zero! Zero!" A complete menace, dropping from the lip into the bowl like an anvil. No one could stay on their board, let alone catch anything with him around, though he did seem to avoid repeating his performance with me. I got a few good rides in, but otherwise it was total chaos and bad vibes. Screams of outrage over the crash of the waves and the hiss of slashing rain on the water.

After a half hour of this, the ocean emptied. Mass exodus. It was still going off, bomber after bomber, but no one stood up to him. Three dozen or so prime surfers abandoned perfect waves, slinking off into the forest with sullen faces, their leashes dragging.

I'd never seen anything like it. I sat there beyond the break, rolling in the swell, stunned. Zero paddled up.

"That oughta do it. We got some privacy, boy. You wanna ride a few more, or start our chat now?"

"You are unbelievable, old man," I said. "I don't have anything to say to you. That was fucking appalling."

"Ahh. What are they? To you and me, I mean? In the fullness of Time, what are they? Monkeys. Nothing. Momentary dust. Dust in the wind." He narrowed his eyes against the spray. "You look like her, you know. Well, not *physically.* Not yet. But you've got her aura." He traced patterns in the air around me with crooked fingers. "All around you. She taught me how to see. I can *see!*"

"Look like who?"

"Little leaper. Who do you *think?*"

There are dreams, sometimes. Repeating ones that I don't know I've had before until I find myself in them again. Dreams I've never been able to remember upon waking. They all came back in that moment when Zero spoke, steaming islands rising from cold depths.

I'm clinging to a piece of broken longboard, tossed in a raging sea of blood and filth and surging bodies. Or there is no board, and I'm sinking, blood and salt filling my mouth and lungs, my legs and arms churning uselessly. Or I'm at the door of the beach house at sunset, with the salty wetness of my mother's last kiss on my cheek.

She's in the water, in the middle of a feeding frenzy, a blissful look on her face as she's delicately taken apart by the men in grey suits. She's riding a massive wave with complete grace, enters the green room, doesn't come back out. She's at the door, and the salt tang of her mouth is from the blood that drips from her rows and rows of serrated teeth.

"Little leaper," she says as she's devoured. By sharks, by the water, by the closing door, by Time. "Little leaper, come. Wonder and glory, my son. Wonder and glory. Come."

The Bell tolls once, and the dream ends. I wake up and forget.

Only there, in the empty swell and the black rain, sitting on my board in the company of a madman, I didn't forget. I didn't forget and the Bell didn't fade. It was back, louder than ever, so loud I clapped my hands to my ears, felt my teeth shaking in their sockets, fell back onto my board and howled into the sky. Zero was smiling, his eyes on me while his hands pawed instinctively through the mass of gold chains around his neck. He found what he was looking for, reached across to me and held it above my face.

A trinket, a fetish. I don't know what it was. I'm looking at it now, as I write this, and I still don't know. I tore it from his neck before I put him overboard. It's gold, and it has a shape. A twisting, asymmetric coil that I can't hold in my mind, that refuses to stay still, like something alive.

I saw it, and Zero's grinning mouth beyond it, forming words. I couldn't hear them over the Bell, but I read them all the same.

"Let's go," he said. "Momma's waiting."

The golden thing before my eyes flexed and bulged strangely as the Bell tolled a fresh peal, deafening, world-ending. I was swallowed up in black.

I awoke to black light, and the sensation of being softly rolled in gentle waves. Back and forth, back and forth, the eternal rhythm of the tide. I was still in my wetsuit, strapped tight to a cot, and that cot was in a room. A cabin in the bow of Zero's boat. The *Deep Dendo*, he called it.

I'm writing this in that cabin. Looked around on deck, in the wheelhouse, for better bulbs to write by, white bulbs, but there are none. Zero was a hippie to the end. Black light it is, then, illuminating these last pages in his logbook. Black light for his driftwood and bone idols, his black velvet paintings, his bong collection and moldy von Däniken paperbacks. Black light turning the dust in the air to glowing protozoa dancing a slow benthic waltz. Black light for his sick shrine to violence and horror and old magic, to his lost generation of Endless Summers and Making Love Not War, and the blackest of lights for my mother, for her giant gilt-framed portrait in the bow, at the center of the shrine.

I can't look at it. It's her and it's not her. It was covered when I woke here, and I'd cover it again, but it makes me sick to look at it and I can't get close enough to do that.

I woke here, and shards of memory returned to slice into my awareness, moments my brain had managed to register between the obliteration of the Bell . . .

Zero leading me off the beach like a puppy, my board dragging behind me on its leash . . . the patchwork rust on the roof of his decrepit Volvo station wagon as he bundled me into the back . . . the bark of a seal somewhere near the docks . . . rank tang of creosote, brine, and rotting fish . . . starlight in a clearing sky, black water below . . .

"Now is the time of testing, little leaper."

Zero's rough hand on my scalp as he guided me, almost gently, below deck.

I remember everything after waking, though. I thought I was going to die, so I missed nothing. My breathing came ragged and harsh; I couldn't seem to get enough air and my muscles burned with exhaustion. The Bell was there too, and the sound of it hammered every detail of that room into my mind, all Zero's gestures and tics, his crumpled posture on the stool he drew up next to my cot. His every fucked-up word . . .

"You won't scream. Or call for help. This makes sure you won't." He pointed to the golden fetish round his neck, where it nested with the others. "And even if you did, no one would hear you, or come for you. We're at sea. In her waters." He fingered a different twist of gold and emeralds, and another of something that shone wetly, like obsidian.

"These make me a ghost in this town. A ghost, living on a ghost ship. Eating ghost food. I'm local legend. Those monkeys I frightened off earlier? Right now they're wondering why they left the water. They've forgotten the old hippie was ever in the water. They're hitting their pipes and shaking their monkey heads and talkin' about *getting zero'd* out there. I'm a *thing* that *happens*, not a person. Zero, the Nowhere Man.

"It was your mom made me this way, to better serve her. She was a goddess, and I loved her from the moment I saw her. That was, what, '67? '68? Man! Cruel bitch, Time. How is she these days?"

"Time?" I said. Zero laughed, reached over and actually tousled my goddamn hair. Awful, but I was strapped tight and couldn't move away. I couldn't move and I couldn't not listen.

"Aww. Little leaper's confused. That's normal. It'll pass." He settled back on his stool, produced a lighter and a joint from somewhere, lit it. "Naw, I meant your mom. How's your mom?"

"She's dead," I whispered, the tissues of my throat raw and unyielding. He asked how, and as he smoked I told him. Zero nodded.

"No body, though?"

I shook my head. In the black light, with the Bell, and the strange energy of that cabin, and Zero so close to me, right in my face, it all felt so fresh. Like I'd just closed the door to the beach house a minute ago.

"Yeah. Yeah, that sounds like Glory." Hearing her name was like a punch to my gut. He knew her. Zero clapped his hands to his knees. "Well. That is not dead which can eternal lie and so on and so forth."

"Old man, you're insane." He barked with glee at that. "Mom died in 1990. She was 27. She would have been a toddler at the time you . . . "

"No! No! A goddess, newborn and fully formed from the foam, a primeval Venus! Aphrodite! I was here! I bore witness to her wonders. I and the others. I am the last. Her loyal one. Most loyal. It was fate.

"See, I came here to escape the draft. Dad was an army chaplain at Oakland, my older brother a Marine. I went hippie early, because how could I not, growing up where I did? They hated me for it, but even they knew Vietnam was gonna be a shit-show. You wanna talk about insanity? One-year tours, little leaper. Nobody learned anything. We didn't fight a ten-year war, we fought the same war every year for ten years! And slipping daisies into rifles State-side was not going to stop it, man. Civil disobedience only goes so far. Sure, I burned my draft card, but they'd only issue another. Who wouldn't flee that?

"So I dodged LBJ's little round-up and came here. Just found my way, like you, like the others. Migrated to a socialist paradise, right? Nothing like America. You could just *be* here, and no one would bother you about it. And out here, on the edge of things? Total freedom. Smoked a lot of good green, got in with some Canadian suppliers. It was early days in that business, nothing like how it is now. Fucking ferocious now, y'know? But I made a fortune arranging a shipment of Thai stick for them. Over from Bangkok in the hold of a long-haul trawler. Bought the *Deep Dendo* here with the proceeds.

"Surf all day. Party on the beach all night. Sweet leaf and sweeter chicks. Man, the life. You know what I mean. We thought we had it. Enlightenment. Pack of hippies with our half-assed Zen and daddy issues. Bucking authority, like that *meant* something. I mean, it's *human* authority, dig? *The Man.* He's nothing. Monkey-man authority. *Ooooh-ooh-ack!* What's freedom when your flesh is a cage? What use is a high if it ends? What's love, when that love dies with the flesh? Free Love. That's what we called it, but c'mon. We were as free as we *could* be, I guess.

"And then Glory walked out of the waves that night, exactly like that Andress chick in the Bond movie, only without the knife and bikini. Exactly like Aphrodite. She walked out of the waves and right up to our beach fire and she made each of us, one after the other. I was half outta my mind on some really decent windowpane, but I knew I wasn't tripping. I mean, I was *tripping,* but I *saw.* I saw what she *was.* Little glimpses. Tears in the light around her, where her cherubs were, like, still draping her in seaweed and ribbons, y'know? After that night she was more careful, stronger, but then, fresh outta the sea? I saw what she was and I knew and I didn't care. I let her fuck me because she was a goddess. We all did. You just . . . how do you say *no* to that?

"And she changed us. We changed. Everything changed, with her around. Little leaper, it got *better*. She made us *better*.

"The *things* she knew. Magic. A couple of us were into Crowley, but the stuff she could do put the Great Beast to shame. And I'm not talking about the kinda hoodoo jive we'd get up to while high, little leaper. Convincing ourselves we could feel our chakras spinnin', that we could expand our consciousness with enough weed and good lovin'. I mean the *authentic* shit! Next-level practice, Castaneda-style, but way beyond him, even. She had us finding our hands in dreams and walking the *nagual* before any of *his* followers. *Authentic!*

"She'd take me on the sand and open up whole worlds to my eyes, other dimensions and planes of being. I got *expanded!* I saw things with her you'd never believe. The secret history of Earth. Cavern kingdoms and lizard men. Realms of fire, realms of water. Her people were gods, but they had gods above them. Her gods reached down out of the humming skies and blessed our union, ya dig? Her gods rose from the sea."

Zero was insane. It was all I could think, then. I watched as a tear formed at the corner of his eye, shining like a jewel in the black light.

"Why leave me?" he whispered. "Why'd she leave me? Can you tell me that?"

"No. I don't know. She left me, too," I heard myself say. My voice sounded dark and liquid. *I* sounded insane. "She left me."

Zero looked at me, eyes wet and burning. "That's part of it! That! Right there! Little leaper, that's their *way*. Their test. I never saw it happen, but I know she just walked back into the water one night. *I know it.*" The old man wiped at his eyes with a gnarled forearm.

"Our little band drifted apart after that. I stayed. She wanted me to stay. I knew *that*, too. So I did, and she protected me." He wiped his eyes again, finished off the joint in one long drag and then lit another. Zero snorted.

"Sharks. Fuck, man. She could ride a shark like a pony, if she wanted. She was a goddamn queen of the surf, man, didja ever watch her ride a wave? Hell! All her kind could.

"Her caste were wanderers, nomadic sorcerers and scientists, on a long migration across the earth to places of power and knowledge. Atlantis. Cities of pillars. Athens. Leng. Cities of coral, onyx. Once in a very long while they would visit a place she called the Real, where their high priest slept and dreamed. The only real place on the planet, she said. The oldest. The first city, built of alien stone. The most *true* place. Dead, but real.

"There were other castes, too. Decayed and decadent people. In visions, she showed me their cities and settlements, their failures. Their migration was all about *breeding,* see? Gloria's caste, I mean. Spawning. Finding the *right* people, the true children of the Real. Bloodlines. The *sangreal,* right? The ancient truth behind the Merovingians! Hey hey, we're the monkeys, and people say we monkey around, but see, we're not all monkeys to *them!* That's what she taught me. We *came* from them. There's a little god in all of us, some of us are *sea monkeys,* and their task was to bring it out, help it return. Except, y'know, we had to wait longer than six to eight weeks for delivery, right?

"And when it went wrong? Man. Crazy shit, little leaper. Regression. Mutants. Insanity. War, little leaper. War with other castes, with the monkeys who caught on. War. What's it good for? Right? Absolutely nothin'. Ha! Good God, y'all.

"And it always went wrong when they settled, when they tried to just *be* in a place and do their holy work with the local stock. They'd get indiscriminate in their selections over time. There's a look that shows up when it goes wrong, a *mark.* It happened at Ponape and it happened in the Yucatan and it happened in Massachusetts back in the 30s and, shit, so many other places, over so many centuries.

"But Tolkien had it right: Not all who wander are lost, dig? Wandering was best, for their purposes. Migration. They could stay hidden, fluid, and spread their love where it would do the most good.

"This place was on her route. These waters were special to her."

Zero got up from his stool, stepped over to the place in the bow where my mother's portrait lay concealed behind a tangled drape of crusty purple velvet. He pulled at the fabric until it fell away and I saw the terrible picture for the first time.

Like the trinkets Zero wore, the painting pulsed and writhed in its frame. It was my mother, her dark hair and grey liquid eyes, her high forehead and cheekbones like gentle curving blades under her pale skin. It was Gloria and it wasn't Gloria, but something else that shimmered behind the pigment, something that gasped and clawed and watched, as if behind glass. A mirror. Something impossibly black and green and slick that would show itself, then vanish, like those lenticular stickers we had as kids.

I couldn't look at it then. I can't look at it now.

"She painted this herself. For me. Special pigments. The magic she used keeps me strong between the tests, *for* the tests. It's been so long between tests, since the last one came. But look at her! So beautiful. That's a face to keep a body strong. I'd wait forever for her."

Zero stepped back to the cot and dropped to his knees beside me, the muscles of his ancient face twitching wildly.

"But it's not all magic! There's a science to it! We only just dropped down outta the trees, but they've had *millennia* to perfect their arts! She told me, taught me. The deep science! Down there in the tissues, in the code, at the core of Life. About the Change, and how it happens. In the cells, slowly. About the Call and the Bell . . . " His hands dropped below the cot, where I couldn't see them. I heard a scraping sound underneath me, metal on metal.

"Little leaper, did you know? There are species of fish that can store sperm for months at a time. It's true. They can store it, select the best code out of a mix of happy fish-daddy milk. It's called *cryptic female choice*. And that's just mindless little fish mommies. Imagine what you could do with conscious intention and that skill! Far out, huh?

"And, little leaper, did you know? There are amphibians who can regenerate missing limbs . . . "

He was swift about it. Fire blazed in a white ring at my left wrist. Zero leaped up, threw a leg over the cot, straddling me, a black dripping blur of something shining in his hand, and seconds later my right wrist caught fire. I pissed myself with the pain and shock of it, and I screamed, but it didn't sound like me. Zero brought his face to mine. It was like the moon coming down to earth, all craters and dust and doom.

"I'd answer that ringing if I were you, son." His empty hand came up, patted me on the cheek. "You're gonna do fine."

I left the black light and entered the black again.

This isn't a confession, but I should say that Zero was right. Not about everything, but the things that mattered. He knew her. My mother. He could even pronounce her name the way she pronounced it, with the funny soft click between the *G* and the *l*, and the gasping sort of *yah* at the tail of it. She only ever said her name like that around me, when I was small, and there was *more* to it, which I forget, but I remember the first part, at least.

I remember her stories, too. About the Real, which she also pronounced in a funny way, like her name, just as Zero spoke it, and the minds that dreamed there still, and her travels. She had so many stories, more than anyone could have collected in a lifetime, and all told as if they were hers alone. She had been there, she would tell me, which is how she knew. She would write them down for me someday, she had said. They were my bedtime stories. That, and the verses from "Octopus's Garden" she'd sing me to sleep with, verses which would change, becoming stranger as I fell away into the dark.

And then she took her songs and her stories away. She left me. She took herself away into the sea.

I don't know how I'm able to write these words. Zero the Nowhere Man took my hands with his blade. He took them, and I blacked out, and I only woke up when the water closed over my head.

I woke up, but I didn't kick for the surface. I sank, the black gout from the stumps of my wrists barely visible before me in the water, and after that I don't remember much. I remember the feeling of seawater filling my lungs, and how it felt good. The clean, solid pressure of it in my chest, better than the harsh, thin air I'd been struggling to breathe above. And the Bell tolling, as ever, each peal bringing visions.

My mother, further below, a shadow in the depths, present in the embrace of the water, present in the Now. My mother, not as I remembered her or as she painted herself in the sickening portrait, but as she is. As I know she is. What is Time, after all? What is Time to the ocean? To her? To me?

She spoke to me down there. "Come, little leaper. Wonder and glory forever. Glory forever. Glory," and when she said her name it was so much more. I held up the bloody fountains of my ruined arms to her and she mirrored me with the same ceremonial gesture I'd seen Zero use, the backs of her hands to me. There was something like a fine gauze or lace of light covering them, flowing between her fingers.

"Find your hands, my son," she said. "Find them and come to me."

So I did. I knew what she meant. The *how* of it was in the sound of the Bell, had been all the years of my life, and the *why* of it was all around and above me, below me, for countless leagues. Surging in my lungs. Humming in the nautiloid chambers of my heart.

So I found my hands. The pain of that finding was worse than losing them to the old man's blade, and brought the rage that sent me to the surface, to the deck of the *Deep Dendo*, to Zero's throat.

I found him hunkered down behind the wheelhouse, eating my old hands. Stripping the cold flesh from the fingers of my left with flat yellow teeth. He saw me and moaned with fear, then laughed, his eyes wide and white.

"Glory said I could." He grinned and held up what was left of his meal. "That it would help keep me strong, make me ready for this moment. Maybe help me change, too, I don't know. See if I'm more sea-monkey than monkey. Worth a shot." He dropped the stringy mess to the planks. "You came back, little leaper." I stood there, on the deck, shaking with rage, huffing damp sea air as he shuffled over to me on his knees. Zero wrapped his arms around my legs, looked up at me in wonder.

"They never come back. All the tadpoles I've tested. So many dozens of them. Her leapers between the worlds. They come, and I test them, and I never see them again. I never know whether they pass or not. They never come back."

He was weeping now, burrowing his dreadlocked old head between my knees and shaking.

"But *you* came back. She said it would happen. Your mom. Glory said that one would come back. The last one, the one she'd save to the end. And I know why now. It's her cycle. I know. *I know why you're here, son.* To send me to her . . . "

So I did.

This is not a confession. Confessions are for monkeys, and men, and creatures that feel guilt. Creatures locked in Time, pinched between their sad pasts and their hopeless futures.

If I'm confessing anything, it's that I don't know what I am. A child of the Sixties, maybe. A true child of the sea. These hands are mine, and they're not. They're new, and as old as ocean. I hold them up before my face and watch the light of my aura dance around the fingers, wash over the stiff webbing between them in shuddering waves of green and black and quicksilver.

I can see auras now. I can see so much.

The Bell still calls me. *North,* it says. But it also says *deeper.* And it says *wonder.* It says *glory.* It's her voice. It was always her voice. Calling me home. Calling me to her. I'm sure his reward won't be the same as mine, but it's what Zero wanted.

This is not a confession, and it's not a suicide note, either. A testament? A will? No. It's just what I want. To follow him down there. To enter the green room and not come back out. To meet her there, if she's still there and knows me, though perhaps that won't matter to such as us. To visit that old octopus in his garden, someday, and see if I remember her songs well enough. To go home, as soon as I'm finished here. Today. Now. To truly enter the Now of Ocean.

Where I'll be safe.

.

ACKNOWLEDGEMENTS

Gratitude stretches away from my feet, a vast, benthic plateau, thrumming with ethereal lights. It's taken a while to get here, but the place is brightening up. My thanks go out to my editors, Scarlett R. Algee of Trepidatio, who took a chance on a relative unknown; proofreader Sean Leonard and publisher Christopher Payne; Mikio Murakami for the amazing cover art and design; Ross E. Lockhart, who has been a mentor, a listening ear, a savvy adviser, and an early booster; Silvia Moreno-Garcia and Paula Guran, who were the first to buy a story I wrote if you want to point the finger of blame; Brian Sammons and Glynn Owen Barrass, Ranylt Richildis, and Nick Mamatas, each skilled with the red pen, to my writing's great benefit. Deep gratitude to Ramsey Campbell, Helen Marshall, Cody Goodfellow, Gemma Files, Jordan Stratford, Matthew M. Bartlett, Jeffrey Thomas, Mike Griffin, Orrin Grey, Molly Tanzer, Nathan Ballingrud, s. j. bagley, Anya Martin, and Scott Nicolay for their inspiration, encouragement and unfailing support of the weird horror communities. Thanks, too, to beta readers over the years: Maya Madsen, Ken Vaughan, Leeman Kessler, Lucas Corte, Jeff Hendren, Kat Eschner, and Amy Walker, among others. Finally, thanks to my wife, Sasha, for pretty much everything else.

ABOUT THE AUTHOR

Scott R. Jones is a Canadian writer living in Victoria, BC, with his wife and two frighteningly intelligent spawn. His stories have appeared in many anthologies in the past decade, as well as *Innsmouth Magazine, Pseudopod, Andromeda Spaceways Inflight Magazine*, among others. He's also the author of the non-fiction work *When The Stars Are Right: Towards An Authentic R'lyehian Spirituality* (Martian Migraine Press) and the editor of the anthologies *RESONATOR: New Lovecraftian Tales From Beyond; Cthulhusattva: Tales of the Black Gnosis; A Breath from the Sky: Unusual Stories of Possession*; and *Chthonic: Weird Tales of Inner Earth*. He was once kicked out of England for some very good reasons.

CPSIA information can be obtained
at www.ICGtesting.com
Printed in the USA
FSHW012235030520
69879FS